RESURRECTION

Pearce Cadwell

www.resurrection-the-book.com

This novel is entirely a work of fiction. The names, characters and incidents portrayed in it are the product of the author's imagination. Any resemblance to actual persons, living or dead, or events or localities is entirely coincidental.

www.resurrection-the-book.com

ISBN-13: 978-1-974-04350-7

Copyright © Pearce Cadwell 2017

PEARCE CADWELL asserts the moral right to be identified as the author of this work. All rights reserved in all media. No part of this publication may be reproduced, stored in a retrieval system, or transmitted, in any form, or by any means, electronic, mechanical, photocopying, recording or otherwise, without the prior written permission of the author.

For Dante and Sofia

Chapter One

Thwock! Thwock! Thwock!

It was as if the inner sanctity of the village Regency house had been violated. They had been rather proud of the ostentatious period door knocker when they had first moved in, but on the rare occasions like this that it actually performed its sole intended use, the magnitude of it was visceral and frightening, like casually inflicted violence.

Thwock! Thwock! Thwock!

'Go away,' she mumbled hammily into her pillow.

But it was no good.

She reluctantly instigated that embarrassingly self-conscious and, she supposed, English peculiarity of attempting to effect the ruse to the outside world that the house was naturally unoccupied. Why, she wondered, should she be made to feel like a naughty schoolgirl at her age and in her own house?

The morally correct tack you see was to take all reasonable steps to prepare to open the door and greet the visitor, by which time they had probably gone away and then, ah well - if only they had been a little more persistent.

By the time that Anne arrived at the top of the first-floor stairs, her modesty engulfed in an array of hastily and randomly acquired clothing, she thought she was close to the sneaky win of not having to descend them at all.

Thwock! Thwock!

'The Fu—' she could not believe the doggedness of the caller. This had better be good. This had better be at the very least something off eBay. She was always placing orders for one of her latest artistic projects. A set of pretty glass drops for the hallway's optimistically titled *chandelier* perhaps. Or some book on the smaller Georgian house, to add to the gradually expanding collection that she never quite got around to reading.

The seduction of her new line of thought induced a slight sense of desperation. It still wasn't quite enough to propel her headlong to the hallway and the front door beyond but her latent furtiveness would have to be blended with at least the possibility of immediate online asset acquisition, realisation, *gratification*.

Smart moves were required here. Two stairs at a time whilst hugging her back to the curving staircase wall, as if the presentation of her side relief to the gawking outside world would create the affectation of minimal, breezy, undefined mass - witches you never quite see, even though they are there.

She felt she had one last chance to ride the waves of probability that seemed to emanate from what must surely now be the final throw of the dice by the *thwocking* pretender outside. She crept to the front window and pushed her cheek up against the wall to its left, straining to determine if there was some semblance of officialdom that might herald something coveted if long forgotten. Clipboards (insinuating needy intrusion), handheld meter reading devices can all fuck off, she thought. Black shorts, red jacket, trolley wheels - come right on in.

But hold on, here were bicycle wheels. Does the postman ride a bike rather than push a trolley these days? she frantically tried to recall. The bike wheels were turning in on themselves - the visitor had had enough. Deeply afraid now of missing out on the excitement of indeterminate goods, Anne threw caution to the wind and pressed her face directly against the hung sheet of muslin cloth that adorned the window, a concession to privacy which she thought extremely tasteful, *avant-garde* even, and a far cry from the awful net curtains, dirty and dull, which strangulated the old woman's house next door.

But it was too late.

The bird-like face of a late middle-aged woman suddenly appeared. Such a hawkish intrusiveness could never be the bearer of official goods. This was the face of imperious community interference, of unsolicited neighbourly meddling, the face of a day about to go horribly wrong. A face that had not just seen hers, obliquely and dispassionately, but with all the lurid intensity of a venomous stalker cornering its prey. Despite all of Anne's guile, procrastination, god forbid the divine right to privacy, it had all been for nothing.

She was undone.

And yet Anne felt that she would not go down without a fight - her humiliating reverse was metamorphosing into a brooding vengeance and, with all her earlier contrivances stripped bare, she tore through the hallway and found herself pulling at the front door with all her strength, before she had even completely turned the latch, such was her tangible indignation at the sheer effrontery of the stranger. 'Fut the, can I help you, you there, you there?' the words tumbling all ugly and incomprehensible from her spitting mouth.

Oh the shame. The shame of her hideously discourteous tirade was immediate and all-encompassing and, transfixed by the equanimity of the stranger's measured, smiling face, she balked then softened, and, if it were not now too late she thought, self-edited her spasms of hatefulness into a sort of malevolent grin.

'I am terribly. Sorry. To bother. You,' the stranger said, each word staccato but heavy as if she were fully aware of the listener's maelstrom of mind and sought to diffuse, to disarm Anne, evidently prone to holding a dripping knife, fulsome with the blood of butchered innocents passing by her rustic lair.

Her words must have had the desired influence upon Anne's inertia, for the stranger picked up her rhythm, staccato turning to clipped, 'Only I used to live here in your house many years ago and there is so very much I could tell you about it…' a seemingly meaningful pause for effect as if probing Anne's aptitude to fight or flight, '…that is, if…you were ever…one day…interested?'

Whether still encumbered by the awfulness of her reaction to the unsolicited intrusion or seduced by the possibility, surely the *probability* of greedily and hastily acquired domestic provenance, Anne almost catatonic now in her demeanour, simply smiled a smile of care-free abandon and said, she thought most curiously as she said it, 'How nice of you to come. Do step inside.'

Even as she said the words, Anne sensed that she was initiating something quite surreal. 'Please do feel you can leave your bike…ahh yes…in the hallway,' she quickly revised her sentence, seeking to avoid yet further embarrassing conflict: the outside wall is what she had meant, but it was too late.

The lady and her bicycle now firmly *intra muros*, it seemed to Ann that she should stop acting quite so neurotically and try (was it really so hard?) to enjoy what might well prove to be the most interesting visitor she had yet to receive to the house.

'Hi, it's Bernie,' the lady said offering her hand, 'as in Bernadette. Ha ha, that is actually me. I don't much look like a Bernie do I? But that is what they all call me. I am very pleased to make your acquaintance my dear.' Anne waited for more to come but Bernie had clearly thought it enough, so it was to be her turn.

'Anne. How do you do?' The affectation deliberate, nauseatingly so, she thought; it always was, so why did she do it? Her desire to ingratiate herself with those of a perceived higher social standing was endemic to her core and yet, she instinctively knew, utterly pointless. According to the book she was reading, a biography of a famous British painter, he only ever hung out with the aristocracy and the working classes. Those in between, the inescapably gauche, the bourgeois, anathema to him.

'Anna, how delightful.'

What is in a name? thought Anne, but it was no good - she would have to explain. You cannot have someone coming into your house not knowing your *name*. Bumping into someone in the street - *don't I know you?* - fine, just fine. But in your house, it seemed a hollow sort of compromise. 'Well no, it's Anne with an *e* on the end but like with the Dutch pronunciation, almost sort of *Anna* but not quite. And the *A* is more like *Ahn*, So basically *Ah-nn-e*.'

And the contrivance of it all seemed to her at that moment positively desperate. The truth is that she had been christened simple, boring *Anne* as she saw it and whilst a complete name-change to fashionable, romantic, exotic *Anna* would have been identifiably, demonstrably pretentious, it had seemed to her as she entered her mid-teens that she could vaingloriously invoke the very slightest grunt of a vowel at the end of her name to persuade any listening lotharios that she was independent and exotic, someone to intrigue, be perplexed and mesmerised by. It all seemed like a distant self-indulgence as she stood in the company of the impertinently confident Bernie.

'Seems like I have found my match with the name explanations,' beamed Bernie. 'But I know you Anne don't I? I don't recognise the name. Did you move from Brenham? You look terribly familiar.'

Anne wondered if there were some truth in it herself as it was conceivable that she had seen Bernie before, but try as she might she could not recall the event either. Lounsley was but a satellite village to Brenham – anything was possible. 'Well no actually,' said Anne, 'we're quite new to the area in a way. We sort of stumbled on it as we were driving though this part of Kent. We, we're from Hampshire originally.' Anne had absolutely no intention of elaborating on this fatuous simplification of her hitherto, to some extent, complicated life. 'We can laugh about it now, but I saw the *For Sale* sign and I ordered Paul to stop the car immediately. Something about the house just…just spoke to me.'

'Oh how charming I must say,' Bernie replied but somehow annoyingly, thought Anne, making very little eye contact as she seemed furtively to dart her eyes, like a little nervous hatchling around the open plan living room - kitchen - diner. 'It was a similar story for us in the late sixties really - a hunch - a sort of madness took over.'

Anne felt herself warm ever so marginally to her guest and began to relax. A resonance hovered somewhere in the air between them, the cadence of Anne's voice, the canter of the story of how she had arrived there in perfect harmony with the bemused curiosity of Bernie's eyes flitting around the hallway, landing on some long-lost point of reference perhaps. This is absurd, thought Anne; why am I opening up to this perfect stranger? Is it the spirit of the house? How ridiculous. 'And so here we are,' finished Anne as if by way of confirmation.

The introduction of the *play* to the audience complete, Bernie now took centre-stage and room-by-room, here fussed, now purred, there educated; remnants of discoloured wallpaper explained, even stretches of skirting board analysed, window sills perfunctorily referenced to a particular era. By the end of the tour of the ground floor Anne resigned herself to discarding *The Small Georgian Townhouse* completely; she'd found the hardback in a secondhand bookshop. Might the previous owner have yet encountered the dulcet educational tones of Bernie on some lost occasion and thus discreetly, within a carrier bag, placed it by the shop's steps one dark, quiet evening?

'You have to remember,' continued Bernie, as she swept further into the open-plan ground-floor, 'back in the late 1960s, yes we young designers were pioneering the new look, the clean lines and moulded foam and polypropylene, the Psychedelic India of David Hicks and the dull whites and shiny blacks of Dorothy Draper - but we never lost our reverence of the *being* of the house. To Patrick and me, sorry that's my husband, it was the fusion, the adaptation of the new look to the *essence* of the Regency town house.'

Anne nodded avidly, her pretensions to being a period interior designer herself momentarily flummoxed by this visionary, sage professional who had *been* there. She had done it - not by endlessly peering through monthly glossies, albeit tasteful ones, but probably by smoking weed and pulling up her top for Jimi Hendrix at the Isle Of Wight festival, inspiration for a radical pioneering of what was to become the Modern Look. Bernie's mellifluous and unfettered telling of her great story of creation breezed among the edifices of the stone-flag floors and arching remnants of brickwork, whose scattered and uneven purpose were but a mystery to Anne and which were almost all explained in the annals of her little special bookcase in the tiny study.

The bookcase which, through her innate indolence, remained but a visual distraction, a bemused and self-conscious *Objet d'Art*, ready to thrill the hordes of visitors that never seemed ever to come.

'And this, you see this wood panelling that partitions the hallway from living room?' said Bernie. 'Why it was taken from the walls of the corridor itself. Oh yes my dear, the hallway was just part of one long corridor that led all the way to the garden.'

The history really was a story, thought Anne. No wonder the Romans held the same word for both she wanted to say to Bernie, to show off like a truculent, erudite teenager to her mother.

And now Bernie and she sped up the staircase, which just a quarter of an hour ago had been the covert conduit to Anne's fruitless stealth, yet now it seemed, the corridor between two very separate worlds, joined in a common spirit of history. 'Ah yes you've kept it all the same, very good, very good,' glowed Bernie as she surveyed the layout of rooms on the first floor.

But Bernie was already away to the next room and Anne was beginning to feel overwhelmed. Actually she began to feel very much annoyed - she experienced a fleeting moment of wanting to slap this charming, discerning, knowledgeable imposter, slap her really hard across her face - just to see the look of shock on it, a spontaneous and murderous urge: 'My house, get out!' But instead she allowed her placidity to ooze oafishly, idiotically onto the boards of the unfolding theatre, Bernie always slightly ahead of her as, like a trainee management consultant, she blundered her way behind an imperious company director, striding through the corridors of corporate power, into…

The Master bedroom, as she connivingly called it, in a nod to the TV property make-over programmes that she adored, knowing full-well that it was simply the largest bedroom of three. It was about to present its own challenges, this time in the form of her knickers that she must have thrown towards the laundry basket at some point yesterday and characteristically missed. She wouldn't have minded if they had been Agent Provocateur, or something retro and ostentatious, something you would find in a Georgian Terrace gone all seventies. But they looked like what they were, cheap supermarket items, scrunched gormlessly on the parquet floor, next to a desperate pile of Country Living magazines. The pile that could never be in a *pile*, the bourgeois pretender to Country Life; belying who they were, what they had underwhelmingly brought to the history, inadequately to the provenance of the house.

And then the rage was all done, vanished so quickly that Anne wondered if this was the way of the schizophrenic. Or the man who, she recently read in the papers, quietly chatted with a woman police officer in his living room, whilst the bludgeoned cadaver of his stepson lay feet away in an adjacent room, the murderer's fingers trembling not a jot as he poured them tea for two.

But if Anne's withering self-analysis, let alone her momentary thoughts of barbarism, were a source of embarrassment to her, Bernie hardly seemed to notice.

'Ah you see, we had the bed here...' began Bernie, before trailing off, as if she had finally herself discerned the impertinence of her wanton invasion of this, the innermost sanctum of the house; had struck herself as all needy, clawing away at time now removed. She seemed lost in herself, eyes askance, and within a silence that for the first time Anne felt pounding, pounding her sensibilities.

Thus it was a relief when Bernie was Bernie again: now into the study, the loo, the bathroom (*yes, yes you've kept the storage cupboard at the end of the bath - Patrick built that*). She was in charge once more of The Grand Tour and bounced up the final flight of curving stairs to the top floor: two rooms, the ones the Georgians so cleverly, Anne mused, crammed right up beneath the slightly sloping roof. She considered this aspect of the Georgian town house so functional and yet so beautiful. Oh how hateful are roofs she wondered - even converted ones. Were the Victorians so pious and ashamed that they sought to create a barrier between unspeakable acts of fornication and God above?

At the front of the house, facing the road, was the slightly larger of the two bedrooms, the current *Guest*, as Anne relished calling it, with its Victorian antique reclining chair in the corner and French-style dressing table gracing one of the walls, intended as marvels and points of discussion for those very guests that never seemed to materialise.

'This was our art-room you see,' said Bernie, seemingly unimpressed with the *fin de siècle* affectations before her. The late morning sun poured soft braids of tentacled light through the ceiling dormer window, surely a 1970s addition thought Anne, and inviting Bernie to weave her anecdotal magic: but nothing.

Instead she stood impassively as if meditating and casting her half-open eyes to the eaves above, and searching for something lost, something precious. 'I suppose you have wondered why there is a perfectly rectangular gap in the carpet?' she said as if in a reverie. Anne thought it a rhetorical question and remained silent, as did Bernie – and the answer never came.

And finally the girl's room. Ellie's that is. When they had first viewed the house they felt it curious that a clearly girl's pink-themed set of curtains filled the long expanse of window that framed beautifully the back garden and surrounding trees and shrubs. Grazing ponies had graced the gently rising fields to the south and they all hummed

'Perfect, isn't it perfect Ellie?' And she confessed that it was, and so it was that it became her room.

Bernie stood there at the girl's window. Hands wide-apart upon the glistening white gloss windowsill, face tilted, not melancholic, but majestically and slightly upwards, the late morning sun bursting forth, all dappled to her left between the thinning branches of the tall elder to the south-west. 'New windows,' she whispered, 'Beautiful, beautiful new windows. But they still fit perfectly...'

And Bernie appeared to Anne as a prism, strands of differing colours of light pervading the room. Bernie was she again, she of the house. And it seemed to Anne that she was sensing her old life below in the garden once more. Their friends. Hippies perhaps? Yes probably, possibly, with their shimmering robes of white in that unaffected time, hope and innocence but something dark perhaps too; yes. Light and Dark. Like her own life. Her wanting to slap Bernie around the face not so very long ago but Bernie all Earth-Motherly now. Light and dark and hidden stuff within corners of rooms never before explored, perhaps never before known or imagined.

'The Sexual Aetiology of the Psychoneuroses,' the psychoanalyst had said to her in her early twenties. Even as a first-year psychology student at London University she had no idea what it signified, nor was she meant to, as the ageing practitioner let slip his guard and revealed unintentionally the dark arts of his profession. Do they even have psychoanalysts anymore? thought Anne. Isn't it all psychotherapy, of the dutifully cognitive-behavioural variety, the choice of the busy modern person requiring odd little tweaks to their existence? But back then she had just escaped her old life in Ireland where she had grown up in what she now realised was something of a strange world because of the singular and unique circumstances of it. She could compartmentalise it now but in her early twenties she was frightened and vulnerable and unable to form meaningful friendships, moreover relationships with men. Then there was her dead older brother and more recently her ageing and now dead parents; her gentle ostracisation from her peer groups there in the West of Ireland. For being the daughter of a Dean of the Church of Ireland was an incongruence in a sea of green and the crossing of the heart and the hailing of the Virgin Mary, and yet High Church all the same. With its billowing scented smoke from swinging canisters of mystery and chanting voices from the chancel, such that she never felt at all at odds in God's other houses of the other kind, and for some reason that she had never fully understood, neither did her father.

And as the strands of light all split and bore into her from the heart of the old house, from the heart of the old lady of the house, she felt a momentary pulse of long-forgotten happiness. Something that transcended Paul and even her lovely step-daughter in whose room she now stood: she bathed in it all. This mellifluous life force that cast its frequencies from sun to tree to Bernie to the inner heart of herself.

And with that Bernie seemed simply to vanish, gliding down the two flights of stairs. By the time Anne arrived back on the ground floor, this other-being was the imperious and autocratic Bernie in charge once more, the tour-guide, thanking her visitors as they left. But it was Bernie who was leaving and Anne was startled to realise that she didn't want her to. It was a maddeningly confused feeling, for had she not ten minutes ago felt annoyance, a tendency to violence even towards this stranger?

'Well you simply must come over to ours quite soon. We can show you all the old photos, the *before and after* stuff -so perfectly interesting,' chirped Bernie. 'We don't have emails or the Internet or any of that sort of thing; let me write down our details.' She offered a final 'thank you so much Anne' before trundling her bike to the front door, smiling briefly over her shoulder and disappearing into the remainder of the morning.

Anne felt a curious compulsion to wave her off, before she corrected herself, embarrassed. She returned to the living room and picked up the piece of paper.

Bernie and Patrick Palmer
The Old Vicarage
Brenham

Anne was thrilled. Was this a new friendship in the making? A pretence, indeed a fast-tracking, of their social mobility? Now the day, so long savoured as a respite from the mundane, could not go quickly enough.

And she could not wait to tell Paul everything.

Chapter Two

Paul bounded up the stone stairway of Brenham Station to the leafy alleyway that bordered its southern exit. 'Ha, first off the train again,' he congratulated himself. What a sad man he had become, he thought, but somehow as he approached his fiftieth year, he no longer seemed to care. The truth be told, he was in a fairly chipper mood this evening. Anne had had the day off from work and this usually meant that her latest arty project would have been given a lot of attention and that really was all that mattered. She would be buzzing with enthusiasm and he was a good listener.

This was the dark art of the Sales Manager - he was a natural at it. He no longer resented never having made it into acting at school - it was too late for all that now, but he often wondered if his line of work might not be considered a close second-best. All you had to do was to talk to potential clients so that they liked you and you did that by liking them, or affecting to do so. He didn't know how he had picked up these skills and often wondered if it was because of his slight loss of hearing in his right ear many years ago. When he first noticed it in his late twenties he had panicked, especially when the doctors told him that there was no cure outside of pervasive, investigative surgery and there were risks involved with that. He found that he had to ask people to repeat themselves in crowded, noisy environments. A bit of a pain socially but potentially career-threatening for a young man trying to sell creative design solutions to small media businesses.

He'd soon found that he had an innate talent for presenting the perfectly nuanced and correct body language, reflexive gestures and reassuring sounds to any explanation of some situation or other, whether he understood what was actually being said or not. He'd thought it only a matter of time before he was found out, but the moment never came. The trick was to impart sufficient affectations of interest and then, after the meeting, ask the potential client to confirm whatever requirements they had by email. 'I never take notes in meetings,' he would boast to them. 'I need to feel the *zeitgeist*, get a real feel for what you want.' He would then go on to say something about 'the devil is in the detail' which they seemed to like though he still today had no idea what it meant.

The technique seemed to work really very well in relationships too he found. People just wanted sympathy, their partners to take an interest in them, understand them and share in their dreams. True, he did have a vague idea of Anne's dreams; certainly they were very creative - it's after all how they had met in the first place. Her psychology degree had led to, or was a symptom of, he was never quite sure, a fierce and vitriolic interest in various global injustices, which invariably meant wackily designed T-shirts; and, perhaps when the rage began in time to wilt a little, a rather more commercial focus on how she could justifiably sustain her contribution to the emancipation of certain peoples and animals around the world. She had taken out a bank loan on a next-generation Apple Mac computer when words like Intel and Core seemed both esoteric and enigmatic - a bejewelled corridor to design solutions of the future. And that's what had brought them together. Anne in her little factory-cum-office, piles of T-shirts everywhere, Paul's CD-ROM whirring away in its drive, he not realising that the technology was already moribund: *The World Hurts T-shirts* he had optimistically ventured as a brand, unsolicited within his remit, and she had liked that and she had liked him. He in turn thought that she was unorthodoxly pretty, with a beautifully cadenced voice that swam in a perfectly English channel with undercurrents of flowing Celtic mystique.

In time either the maelstrom of global movements died out as everyone started thinking of themselves, or else the fire within was replaced by the fear of the fire outside, the one that made you realise it was a dangerous world after all and you had better start thinking about building a bunker of some sort. For that you needed a proper job and that is how it happened and really, if he thought about it, why it had all worked rather well, had done so now for some eleven years. Possibly it was why they had never had children - how did people afford them? She was gracious and lovely in accepting her inevitable role of part-time stepmother to his then two-year-old daughter, now a precocious thirteen-year-old who stayed with them at weekends before Paul drove her home to her mother in London each Sunday evening.

But her employment in marketing in London never quite afforded her an outlet for her nascent creativity. She was good at her job, not least because her directors thought that a psychology degree plus a proven, if short-lived, track record in 'global environmental design' as she had rather convincingly pitched it at her interview, was the perfect profile for the edgy tenders that they generally contrived. But this was all shit and she knew it. Her perfect dream was to build her own successful interior design company, a bastion of word-of-mouth bijou exclusivity. 'Oh you need

Anne de Meja for that.' For her name would speak of some sort of Flemish heritage, a long line perhaps that she traced hundreds of years back to the early painters and dye-manufacturers that successfully immigrated to England. Her Irish family were all dead now and for reasons she had never quite understood, despite her gratis therapy sessions at the university, she had never felt particularly galvanised to maintain the kudos of her Celtic roots. Being raised as an Anglican made that route a little tricky anyway if she were honest. Previous dinner party conversations with strangers had rather wilted when, as she discerned it, they felt cheated by what they perceived to be this rather perverse take on Irishness before them, with her English received pronunciation and decidedly un-Hibernian warm and olive skin.

No, thought Paul, evenings like this were those sort of win-win situations or whatever ghastly cliché he religiously avoided at work these days. *Low-hanging fruit*.

Lounsley, just over an hour's train commute from London was another world. And though there was a further twenty minute walk from the station to go, on a mid-April evening like this, seven o'clock seemed practically balmy beneath the setting sun. He could almost smell the sharpness of the lemon rind in the aperitif that would dutifully be handed to him as he walked through the door. The gin hitting his veins as the ice clinked in the glass would be the perfect backdrop to his own dutiful fascination with whichever project Anne had been working on all day. Sometimes, if he was lucky, and his zeitgeist sufficiently resonant with hers, he would be rewarded with a mid-week shag.

The trick was not to expect it, but the deception of the unconscious mind is, by definition, impossible and as he entered the village his body was involuntarily preparing itself for something unashamedly lurid. But the timing was all wrong. You had to have conversation, show interest in the things that are said between humans, before you became lovers.

As he approached his front door, he urgently tried to recall the bridges of the Thames running from east to west across London, but nothing gave and with great reluctance he resorted, successfully he began to sense, to naming the players of Chelsea's FA Cup-winning side of the 1970/71 season, the replay naturally.

'Yay! Good day darling?' asked Anne, as she smiled, shined, all gorgeous and lovely, effortlessly, thought Paul, as he rapidly tried to discern some art project or other upon the kitchen table where she perched.

'Not so bad darling - what have you been up to, my delicious little *gelato*?'

And so the customary, absurdly formulaic and yet reassuring exchange of pleasantries began - lines repeated over countless working days of endless years, with sufficient minor variations to keep everything fresh and alive and to divert the sorts of hideous feelings of self-consciousness that they both deeply suspected were the harbingers of relationship-decline. And, as always, it worked.

Tonight Anne seemed ecstatic as she began almost at once to make excuses for not having anything to show him, not even the semblance of a business plan. She proceeded to tell him the tale of the strange visitor in all its manifestations, though she elected not to go into quite so much detail regarding her original opening gambit of defiance, denial even. But the Grand Tour itself and all its implications, culminating with her denouement of presenting to Paul the piece of paper containing the words *Old Vicarage* reintoxicated her twice-over as she gulped the remainder of her glass of wine. For his part, Paul was genuinely entranced by the story and fast-realised that his usual affectations of interest were hardly demanded at all on this occasion.

'Ha, can you imagine?' fantasised Anne, 'OK it's like this: can you imagine that they secretly, desperately, wanted their old house back. They are now too old for The Old Vicarage, get it? They want to swap with our house. Ooh I cannot wait to see where they live, honestly Paul, I can almost dream it up in my head.'

'How could you *say* such a thing? Slut, harlot. Home-breaker. Bed-hopper!'

She slapped her hand over her mouth in mock penance. 'Ooh sorry house, we love you, didn't mean it.'

Thus began an evening within which they both animatedly constructed all manner of variations of social mobility, centred upon the Palmers and their access to new-found echelons of Brenham society.

'You have no idea Paul. Some of these houses, with successful people of their age - they will of course be in with all the arty designer types. They will most likely love my stuff. I could give up my day job.'

There was a chink of an opportunity here for Paul and he took it. 'You know I will always support you, my very beautiful lady,' he grinned. 'I never stopped believing in you. Tell you what - send her a brief letter and tell her how delighted we would be to come over to theirs soon. Mention Ellie? Do they have children themselves?'

'Ooh, don't know, never really came up. Hold on, yes it did. I am sure she referenced Ellie's room to one of their own. But hey, Ellie, that could work. A sulking, brooding thirteen-year-old girl, yes that could work!'

And suddenly Anne was his, all his, in every way that he wanted that evening. He led her to the bottom of the stairs and then let her go before him. Her gasping giggles were all he needed to hear: he grabbed her from behind and pushed her forward.

For Anne, she could not avoid the suspicion that the unusually rapidly escalating undulations within her were somehow not just a result of their accustomed grubby, puerile fantasies, in the style of the Regency Master of the House with underling servant. But also its being undertaken within the very recent conduit of an earlier tour of her home by a perfect stranger; herself the former Lady Of The House.

Chapter Three

The five-minute drive to The Old Vicarage was completely unnecessary but social mobility has to start somewhere, thought Anne, as they turned the final bend of their short journey into the narrow lane that led to their final destination. They had recently upgraded the family car from the customary ten-year-old vehicle to a ground-breaking five-year-old one and the few dents they had managed to acquire in the short set of months that they owned it, failed to dampen her pride at having something far less embarrassing from which to disembark. The invitation to visit The Old Vicarage had taken a few weeks to arrive but the fact that it had been delivered so formally by post, virtually requesting their attendance on this particular Saturday, *for late Tea,* seemed to add to the sense of decadence of the occasion. Not even the ominous thirteen-year-old silence upon the back seat could detract from her anticipation. This particular silence it seemed was predicated, if it needed any encouragement at all, on Anne's thoughtless remark as they prepared to leave the house, that Ellie looked absolutely lovely. The worst thing you can say apparently to someone who has just entered her teens and wants you to know that she despises the world and resents accompanying adults anywhere, is the intimation that they might actually have made an effort to present themselves positively to the greater world outside.

'Crikers,' said Paul as they swept through the spacious vintage iron gates and onto a deceptively large and seductive semi-circle of gravel, 'It's not even a driveway is it really? More of a, just an enormous piece of land with small stones on it.'

'Oh. My. God.' Ellie blurted out from the back, separating her words for dramatic effect as is the wont of girls her age, mused Anne. 'The gates are closing behind us automatically. We are actually never going to leave this place alive...I have to text Mum; she may never...like...see me again...ever.'

Paul inexplicably circumnavigated the car around the gigantic cedar tree that dominated the grandly spacious gravelled area to arrive back to where he started his flamboyant manoeuvre, to shrieks of further protestation from Ellie. 'What is *wrong* with you Dad?'

'Oh Paul. Just *look* at it,' began Anne as they all stepped out from the car. The quadruple-fronted house set over two main storeys with windows set into the roof in addition, presented itself supremely and majestically to them.

'There'll be a cellar too,' said Paul, 'So that's four floors altogether I don't doubt.'

'But look, look,' said Anne, pointing to a large additional wing that jutted out to the left rear of the house, 'it goes on and on round the back, it's enormous. I mean that would do, I'm not greedy.' The creeping ivy of the wing seemed more out of control than the neater affectations upon that of the main house, affording it a sense almost, of dereliction.

'Could be later, it's difficult to say,' ventured Paul. Both he and Anne knew that he had absolutely no authority in the matter but he possessed that peculiar tendency of men of his age, she thought, in stating matters of historical opinion with such fortitude that it was rarely challenged.

'Yes we think so too,' came a voice aside, unannounced. A man stepped forward and it was clear from his deportment and age that he must be Bernie's husband.

'Patrick?' said Anne. A brief pause ensued. 'You must be Patrick.' Anne's first thought was that the tall gentlemanly figure before her seemed slightly younger than Bernie which is why she hesitated very slightly. True, he had grey hair but it was full and swirled almost dramatically back from his forehead, perched all silky, to collar-length wisps and curls of silver. His tweed jacket of the country gentleman type with its *de rigueur* elbow pads was adorned above, purposefully but casually with a gold and silver-striped neckerchief and his olive-fawn skin spoke of an English gentleman retired to the Old Town of Corfu. He wore moleskin trousers which rested against a pair of slightly scuffed tan brogues and, if she were honest, was all decked up in the sort of clothes that she tried in vain to persuade Paul to wear. 'I'm not an old man,' Paul would complain, 'and I'm certainly not Lucian bloody Freud.' But Patrick presented himself, she felt guiltily, in the way into which she secretly hoped that Paul would one day mature.

Anne administered the remainder of the introductions as if Patrick were long-lost family, Ellie thought, chuckling in contempt to herself but privately increasingly impressed by the emerging turn of events. She was coming to the end of her second year at one of the finest girls' state schools in south-west London, which courted an environment of excellence and, though it never admitted it officially in its prospectus, a barely-hidden encouragement to the girls to aspire to ever-greater social status. She may not have the poshest parents at the school but she thought that *Ellie* could hold its own among the Imogens, Tabithas and Beatrices; in fact she could always promote she wondered, if ever the occasion demanded it, the unchallengeable fallacy that it was short for Eleanor or something. She would probably have to run some Google searches first, for today's Henrietta could soon become tomorrow's Haley with frightening viral rapidity. Already the possibility of a surreptitiously opportunistic *selfie*, to be shown around the school playground next week, was beginning to form in her mind.

Her thoughts were interrupted by the appearance of the lady whom she supposed to be Bernie. The woman stepped out of the house and onto the driveway muttering, 'Oh welcome, welcome to you all,' with such majesty and enthusiasm that Ellie really was beginning to wonder if there were some hitherto unmentioned family connection, or more sinisterly - some blasphemous unravelling curse of which this was the ghastly denouement.

At last they entered the house and were immediately ushered from within the hallway to their right into an overwhelmingly fussy side annexe, a sort of artisan workshop of some kind. *Tradesman entrance at the front*, thought Paul cynically. *Hardly a Reception Room*, thought Anne disappointingly. *Hilarious*, thought Ellie.

Reservations were soon forgotten as Bernie and Patrick regaled them with old photographs of the house in Lounsley, all set out purposefully and geometrically upon a huge old bench-table beside the enormous south-facing window. The perfectly natural light illuminated a fascinating array of images of the house that the Palmers had first acquired at the end of the 1960s.

The visitors were shocked to realise that it had once been an absolute hovel.

This voyeuristically impudent insight into a dormant squalor that time had surely forgotten was in stark contrast to Anne's optimistically placed thoughts of Georgian grandeur. This was a forgotten England. A sixties kitchen sink England. *Cathy Come Home in the Georgian Town House England.*

'There was an old fellow living here, I mean there,' explained Bernie as she ran her finger along the monochrome photograph before them. 'You see that sink in the old kitchen? That would have been his place of ablution as much as where he peeled his potatoes and washed his ham; he was of Irish extraction we were told by the landlord. And when we visited for the first time with water dripping from the floor above, we were shocked to be told that he was still actually living there, can you believe it?'

The photographs proved to be a hugely thought-provoking insight for all the Fewings, Anne in particular. For Paul it was better than The Second World War In Colour TV series, but in reverse, as the battered walls and underlying morphology of impoverished existence, set within his own lifetime, seemed utterly incongruous with the grandeur to which their middle-class pretensions currently aspired.

As the guided tour moved further along the museum-like display table, Ellie wondered if this was any different to one of those annoyingly contrived school trips, the most recent of which, in some huge vaulted old building in central London, had tried to explain the evolution of the complexity of the pyramids from one Egyptian dynasty to another. For before her was nothing less, she thought, than one of Anne's favourite TV programmes, the ones where you start off with a mouldy old barn from the middle ages and some smug architect couple (which she was fast-determining the residents of The Old Vicarage to be), probably called Simon and Samantha, pile-drove carefully sourced pine wood from Norway into the crumbling walls and coated the whole thing in glass to keep it all together.

We kept the original first floor husbandry dung-heap, dried for a thousand years in the middle of the kitchen, because it's like really important that we preserve the integrity of the conversion.

Whatevs - and yet she could not help but be fascinated by the appearance of photos now in colour. Photos that looked, OK, ancient to her, but rather similar to photos of Dad, when he was little, in a living room with weird bendy chrome furniture besides straight lines and everything all clean and plasticky and, if she were honest, a bit like one of the other museums that she had visited with the school earlier this year. The one that showed life in a typical house just after the war, yes, that was it, *the Evolving Living Room of the 20th Century,* because it was followed by the one in which she and her classmates had giggled as they posed all lady-like and yet downtrodden in a 1950s lounge with its lovely cosy furniture that reminded her of her great grandma.

They eventually entered the room of the next decade, the one in which the women wore mini-skirts and no longer cared if their husbands wanted their dinner or not. Ellie and her class mates had luxuriated with fictitious cigarette holders in their mouths within an altogether *risqué* environment. They were now women in a sort of metaphorical sky beside their baffled but grateful husbands, mitigating their spendthrift martini-sipping indolences with the rewards to the men of glamour and haphazardly exposed thighs.

Ellie's meandering flashback was halted as a mischievously beaming Patrick leant over Anne's shoulder right next to her and, clicking his teeth playfully, asked her, 'How much do you think we paid for it?' The room fell silent. Anne recognised the neediness of the questioner immediately, as one is wont to do when faced with any such supplication of an older generation. The *I fed the whole table of us for a shilling with potatoes to spare* generation. And she coolly calculated the figure which teasingly sat reasonably above that which she supposed it should be.

'Twenty thousand pounds.'

Paul thought he was the first to notice the clichéd flicker of his eyebrow but Anne was already there. Patrick's eyes trail-blazed the unexpected quorum within his house. 'No!'

'Then what? Higher I suspect,' cavorted Anne.

'Two thousand pounds.'

Paul felt the need to say something, anything.

'Gosh Patrick old fellow. That is wow - certainly puts it all into perspective. Golly. Wish we could swap generations,' he laughed nervously.

But abruptly, all English awkwardness was swept aside as Bernie stepped forward. 'Scones and tea in the conservatory everybody?'

As they ventured back to the hallway Paul was momentarily amused to see Patrick put his arm gently but flirtatiously, he thought, around Anne's waist and guide her towards the right of the back corridor of the house, whilst he and Ellie were piloted to the left by Bernie. They soon found themselves in a medium-sized conservatory, also facing south, within which was a coffee table displaying an array of scones, small sandwiches and a pot of tea.

'Oh what is he like?' muttered Bernie, causing Paul to reflect on the obviously implied habitual and formulaic mischief of Patrick, guiding younger women around the house. At that point Paul made the mistake of glancing at Ellie who, utterly in her element as Bernie turned away momentarily to rifle the drawers for some cutlery, effected a *faux*, and Paul hoped, completely uneducated take on a passionate kiss between a woman and a man. They both welled up in mutual hilarity and disbelief at the implied scenario of Anne and Patrick becoming transitory lovers and were forced to look away from each other as Bernie handed them a plate each. Towards the end of his cup of tea, Paul's nuanced delight at the thought of Patrick coveting Anne soon gave way to a creeping sense of unquiet at the very thought of her enjoying the machinations of his interest. He felt a palpable relief when she soon returned to the conservatory with Patrick in tow.

Small-talk followed and Ellie was glad to be left to herself for a moment. She needed some space - to be herself even just for a couple of minutes. Bernie, initially chatting to her avidly, had left her side and was now ardently in conversation with Anne, leaving Patrick and Paul to pour over another album of old photos. Were these *before* or *after* photos she wondered, no longer caring to understand the distinction; to her they were just old photos.

She glanced outside and was surprised to notice how much the light had faded. They had only been there just over an hour after all. There were some birds flapping around the old tree and cars driving up the adjacent hill had their side lights on, seemingly in a rush to get somewhere before…and then she saw it: a huge dark cloud bulging menacingly across the whole sky, feigning premature evenfall. She tried to make out the large lumbering shadowy form that leant against the outside entrance to her left and imagined for a moment that it was the silent and foreboding presence of an old resident gardener staring in at her. She dared to stare back defiantly, to show that she was unafraid, before realising, she could just make it out, that it was instead a large old tree root of some kind, recently plundered from the earth no doubt and purposefully placed against the wall, stark in its self-conscious nakedness and lack of purpose. She looked back over at the large tree and started suddenly at two eyes looking at her through the glass. At first she wondered if it could be an owl, a bit early for the night ahead, but no, they were definitely human eyes, watching her, then moving to one side momentarily before peering back at her.

Then there were clearer forms before her and she jolted at the realisation that these were in fact reflections from the inside of the room, as if the gloaming formed the silver of the mirror that was the window. Now the eyes upon her were Bernie's and her momentary glances away were to engage occasionally with Anne. Ellie slowly swivelled around on the sofa so as not to draw further attention to herself, but all she succeeded in achieving was to come face-to-face with Bernie. It was an uncanny experience. Clearly Bernie was talking to, and engaging with, Anne, successfully it would appear from the latter's body language, but Ellie had the uncomfortable sense that Bernie was looking into her, into her soul, somewhere just behind the back of her eyes. She felt mesmerised and rather dreamy as she gave in to the sensation, relaxing despite herself. There were other presences in the room now and she could see, as in a perfect line, the image of a young woman connecting with her via Bernie. She wondered if this is what happens in those séances they sometimes had on Britain's Most Haunted, the programme that Anne would watch on TV some evenings.

'It's OK Ellie,' she would say, 'I have a good feeling about this house. Not the one on the telly, *this* one. I think good people lived and probably died here,' she would sometimes repeat by way of reassurance.

Ellie wondered sometimes if this tactic actually worked, stuck up on the second floor all on her own at night, with Dad and Anne sleeping below. If a good-girl-ghost had attempted to play with her she would be petrified, make her excuses and ask to be relocated to a damp put-me-up in the cellar and take her chances with the dead servants.

The dreamy notion of an unfolding séance was however soon replaced by the realisation that the young woman, real though she seemed, was in fact a photo on the wall. At that moment the trance broke as Bernie followed Ellie's gaze and interrupted the hypnotic arrangement they had dubiously and mutually enjoyed. She stopped talking to Anne so that the voices of the two men gently filled the void behind them. Then they too stopped talking and the void became a black hole. It was Anne that spoke first. 'Oh who is that, if you don't mind me asking?'

There was a hesitation Ellie thought, very briefly, for Bernie quickly reverted seamlessly to form. 'Ah Katie, our daughter. I love that photo.' She and Patrick beamed joyfully, if a little wistfully at the image of the slightly demure woman in the photo, who must have been in her late thirties or thereabouts and it was now Paul who cleared the momentary silence once more.

'Photogenic isn't she,' he chortled nervously, 'Does she live in Brenham?'

'No. But Katie isn't that far,' replied Bernie, 'Castlebury - do you know it? About twenty miles away. Good for the occasional visit if she can, but she is frightfully busy with work right now. She's in PR.'

And then that sort of roomy silence again thought Ellie. A silence of unanswered questions and histories and even lives unfulfilled, though she found it hard to imagine being unfulfilled growing up in this house. She wondered if Katie had been born here or in their house in Lounsley.

Almost as a relief thought Ellie, all attentions in the room switched to two separate piles of photo albums at either end of the coffee table. The first pile, the one that Bernie and Anne busied themselves perusing, consisted of 'project photos', showing the gradual transformation of their Lounsley house from its initial parlous condition to the cutting-edge glamour of its renovated state; this was the pictorial journey that fascinated Anne the most.

The set of albums that Patrick, Paul and a mildly indifferent Ellie set about viewing, detailed the more human, chronological story. The house was immediately more recognisable in almost all the pictures. The girl Katie was in most of them, as a very young child, no more than about three years of age, and Ellie had to admit that the hope and innocence that seemed to exude from the old colour photos brought a cheeriness to the house that all the more banished the thoughts of Georgian ghosts from her demonised imagination. One in particular made her smile: Katie sitting on her potty in the bathroom beaming up at the camera, the current fittings still there all those years ago. 'Well,' piped in Paul, 'maybe I was right about thinking of adding the second loo to the bathroom proper!' And they all laughed, including Ellie, despite herself.

Patrick turned to Paul and asked in a serious tone, 'And that cupboard that you see, the one at the end of the bath, with the lid that looks like a continued surface but actually opens up? We built it as a laundry basket. Do you still have it?'

Paul, always eager to please, quickly replied, 'Oh yes absolutely - great bit of kit. Yeah, nice feature that.' He didn't have the heart to reveal that it was no longer used as a dump for dirty laundry, their preference instead to throw it into one of Anne's ethnic-style baskets in the corner of the bedroom, the one that continually overflowed. It had become nothing more than the subterranean fulcrum of a sea of unwashed clothing, towels and bed linen that seemed to define that corner of the room, much to the delight of the cats which had made it their unofficial holiday residence. No, the cupboard in question was now home to all manner of cleaning products, scrubbing brushes and bulk-bought loo rolls, occasionally sluiced with soapy water by whichever of the family that tried to exit a too-full bath.

Behind the large rectangular plastic box that kept all these products from flying around each other, there seemed to Paul to be dead space and it was one of his *when I get around to it* projects, to investigate it further. His theory was that there would be a closed-in box of pipes and that sort of thing. He had to confess that he had begun to become mildly energised in his approaching-middle-age at the idea of pipes, pumping water around a large old house, the arteries of its functioning existence; the idea that he could create side-projects from its visceral life blood. A cheeky bidet perhaps, a second loo or simply yet another set of isolating valves to segregate the plasma of the beast into its constituent parts.

'Sorry, may I use your loo?' asked Anne rhetorically to the room as she rose from the sofa.

Loo.

Paul was embarrassed to admit to himself that he had even been enthralled once by the fact that the *gite* in which they recently stayed in the North of France was plumbed with 14mm cold water pipes, a millimetre less than those in England. '*Vive la différence.*' he had noisily declared as he micturated away the previous night's *Cote du Rhone.*

But by now the photos, noted Ellie, had somehow quite naturally, as if they were taking a tour of the house, shifted to the garden. It seemed almost impossible at first to reconcile her own very real garden with the images before her. For the interconnecting rear gardens contained hardly any trees and they were more akin to privately owned patches of grass and vegetation bordered by low hedgerows. 'Where are all the trees Dad?' she asked, to which Paul had no ready answer.

'Erm, Patrick?'

'You mean it's now very different to this?' he seemed to ask rhetorically as he continued, 'Well yes of course it must be. Whenever I've recently driven along the main road, there are clearly quite tall trees all around, but I never really thought about the context.'

Ellie seized the moment. 'Well Dad, you know you told me that even up to the Victorians, households didn't really use the gardens like they do now - there were no rubbish collections so they used to throw it all in the garden. Perhaps they weren't bothered about trees and stuff like that. Perhaps our trees aren't that old after all?' They all nodded and she could not have been more pleased with herself.

'But look, look,' said Paul as he took in the next photo. It must have been taken during a summer's evening because the shadows were long but a clearly thoughtful young Katie was barefoot with shorts and vest, her legs covered in sand in the middle of the picture, with Patrick pulling faces at her from an adjacent deckchair. 'That tree behind you: well it's not even a tree really, more a shrub. You see that's still there; it sort of sits astride next door's and our wall but its roots are definitely on the other side. It's still there, absolutely.'

'So who is that?' asked Ellie, 'Whose face is that peering out of the tree?' By now Bernie had sidled to the other end of the table and they all looked at it closer, puzzled, not seeming to know what she was talking about. The ensuing lull in conversation at first amused her but was soon replaced by an overarching exasperation she occasionally experienced with...adults. They seemed so knowledgeable about so many things of which she either cared little or simply did not understand. But here was a *person they could not see*.

Paul was the first to break the silence, a result of his habitual and chronic nervousness. 'I see it! I say, it's not one of those tree-trunk simulacra is it? Or a photographic version of the same?' The others looked at him blankly, which only spurred him on, his new-found authority on any subject that, through the implied ignorance of his audience, could only result in intellectual plaudits unforeseen. 'A simulacrum you see is any object of nature which seems to mimic convincingly a human form. In this case the boy that Ellie *thinks* she sees is in fact probably a part of the tree or rather a manifestation of its underlying morphology by the peculiar angle of light and the way that it has impacted the photographic emulsion.'

Daddy, Clever bastard Daddy. Wrong, thought Ellie.

'No, no, it's a boy alright,' chimed in Patrick, seemingly destroying Paul's intellectual narcissism in an instant. He suddenly looked sad and continued to stare mournfully at the photograph. 'Oh Bernie, do you know something, I do believe it's that boy from next door, the one that used to visit Mrs Carmichael now and again. What was his name? We always assumed he was one of the Irish relatives. A strange boy, we thought that perhaps...' He trailed off and Bernie looked deflated too and Ellie was really beginning to regret the whole thing: why had she said anything at all? Why was life so *complicated*? Something in the room, something she didn't understand, had changed for them all and she just wanted to go home.

Anne returned to the room and sensed an awkward silence. 'Well it's been so fascinating really it has. You've been so very kind in showing us all this. It feels like a bit of a dream, seeing our house and the garden and all these memories. So privileged indeed, what more can I say?'

'Yes absolutely,' affirmed Paul. 'How many families could ever expect such *provenance*, really. I mean I don't think we'll ever quite see the house in the same light ever again, it's extraordinary, thank you *so* much.'

It was Bernie's turn to return to full-on English normality. 'Gosh, is that the time? I must put the dinner on.'

For one awful moment Ellie wondered if it was an invitation to extend their visit and she prayed that it was not, the idea of complete strangers making *more* small-talk around an ornate dining table excruciating. But her fears were short-lived as Anne jumped in almost straight away with that quintessentially most meaningless and prevaricatory of English comments: 'You simply *have* to come over to the house again, both of you this time, so you can see everything properly - talk us through everything. Tea, dinner, just evening drinks, whatever you prefer.'

'Sounds splendid my dear,' replied Bernie. 'We'll send you some monochrome and colour photocopies of some of the old photos for your records. Actually, if you didn't mind covering the costs of those that would be very welcome indeed.'

Paul flinched at the parsimony of the suggestion but by this stage he was quite happy to exit the stage and ponder what he thought was a strange condition at a later time.

The end game was all very sudden, quick and jolly, thought Ellie, as they filtered *en masse* back to the huge hallway in procession with a last minute 'Ooh I do like that.' from Anne and a 'Think it's going to be a bit chilly outside.' from Paul, with suitably reassuring murmurs from their hosts. Bernie opened the front door and they shuffled outside. There was then, not just for the habitually embarrassed Ellie, but it seemed for all the adults, the invariable dilemma of how formally to acknowledge their departure. Anne may have been raised a Protestant but she was Irish after all and Ellie knew she could count on her to save the day; and she did. An extended hand from her to Bernie was but momentary and she quickly enveloped her in her arms and kissed her on both cheeks. Paul followed suit, grateful for this guidance in convention as Patrick looked on amused and seemed to relish Anne's embrace in turn. And then with a firm handshake between the men it was all over, well nearly, as Ellie did that sheepish, cute girl look and a silly half-hand wave, something she had perfected over the years in adult company so as to avoid the anathema of disgusting physical contact of any kind.

Climbing into the car, they all gave one final wave to their dutifully smiling hosts and, as her dad swung the car around and towards the gates, Ellie felt the need to throw a final glance over her shoulder.

But Bernie and Patrick Palmer were no longer there.

Chapter Four

Ellie was awoken by raised voices. She glanced at her phone. Eight o'clock. It was another Saturday morning.

Although it had been a good three months since their visit to the Palmers, she really could do without any dramas this weekend. Occasionally she was awoken at around this time on such days, long before her required lie-in was scheduled to end, on account of some sort of disgusting routine perpetrated by the adults. Their bedroom door would be self-consciously and quietly closed. It was left open during the night on Dad's insistence that he would be more likely to hear her cries of distress during a nightmare or 'something else', whatever that meant. She snorted at the thought that what was probably a good idea when she was five-years-old should be so ridiculously extended to her teens.

But these were raised voices subsumed below that ridiculously contrived veneer, attempted by adults, to promote the sense that there was anything but raised voices: a sort of shouty whispering that fooled no-one. A part of her feigned nonchalance and passing contempt for the exchanges below her, but the truth was that whenever they argued, it depressed her. Despite her message to the world of surliness, she secretly courted cheerfulness and certainty in her life, and therefore by association, within the house. They were her weekends too, after all, she often reflected.

She found herself pressing her ear to the gap between her door and the landing by the stairs, the ones that curved down to the landing outside *their* room. 'But you *promised* to set the alarm this time,' hissed Anne, 'You know how important this car boot sale is to me, there's so much stuff. Oh yes I remember now. Saturday mornings are all about what *you* want, aren't they. Can't you just once in a blue moon, *forego* some routines in our life?'

'Well it wouldn't be an issue if you occasionally thought to challenge some of those routines yourself, I don't know, wander down to the end of the garden with me one Friday night, god forbid, and lie back against the crab apple tree; wow that would be insanely adventurous: apologies for even mentioning the idea.'

Silence. Hmmm, thought Ellie; this could go either way.

'Look darling, I am genuinely sorry that I forgot to set the alarm. There is so much stuff I want to get rid of too. All those old sets of sherry glasses and cutlery; did you know I even put them into job lots. A pound for a bunch! Wine glass lucky dip! I am sorry darling, truly. Let's not let it spoil the weekend eh?'

Another silence, or was there a hint of a brief attempt at something else?

'Anne, sweetheart, I'm going to make it up to you. We'll still keep all the good books and, no, even better. We'll *keep* all the really good books, you know like the Kate Atkinson and Sophie Hannah stuff. And then we'll keep separate boxes for slightly not-so-good books that people will actually buy, like *Delicious Thai meals on a budget* and that sort of thing and then the third set of boxes will be all the shit stuff that we can take to the recycle centre today. You know, the one in the farm shop car park: it's not recycling just paper and cardboard: you put whole books into one of the containers, one at a time. And they actually go to charity shops, I guess, or maybe they send them to the other side of the world where books are hard to come by. It will be fun and cathartic. Just think how good it will feel to put *More Atkins Recipes For Life* in the bin, knowing full well that some fat bugger in Newcastle will buy it, take it home, shed a stone, get laid and then put it all back on again and thus the great cycle of life will repeat itself. People will have *sex* because of our generosity…'

A giggle, now that was a giggle and there was no mistaking it, thought Ellie. And she definitely heard the word *promise* being whispered back and forth a few times. And then silence and the door quietly closing, her customary disgust at the implication turning almost to contentment. Not even the thought of a trip to that most *exciting* of places, the farm shop car park, could prevent her from gently smiling, pulling the spare pillow over her head and allowing the soft sniffly purring of Graham the cat by her legs to lull her back to strange morning dreams of giant cats and cheese and people falling down in the street when a large flapping Arakuth (as it was called) swept over their heads to announce Ellie's impending world dominion.

Ellie loved Saturdays because they were always *going* somewhere, and that meant the car. And going somewhere *else* in the car was exponentially more wonderful than going home to London in the car on Sunday evenings. Even Dad's inevitable 'Saturday drivers…' joke, worn thin over the years, was reassuring in its way and she knew that after they had dumped all the *shit books* they would treat themselves to wandering the aisles of the farm shop itself. Anne would buy exotic cheeses from the deli counter whilst she would join Dad in the Italian dry foods annexe, where he would invariably turn to her and ask if she fancied a 'proper risotto tonight,' with the finest Arborio packed in a very expensive looking cloth sack. Or else pasta shapes so large and curiously coloured that they could make a creamy sauce with exotic mixed seafood. By the time that they came to the checkout and *treated* themselves to a bottle of local award-winning Kent wine, a string of organic garlic, a bunch *of real carrots* and large tub of *real* ice cream (basically just pieces of ice flavoured with locally-sourced stinging nettles or something), the bill seemed to Ellie to be as enormous as their usual weekly shop.

But first the books. Dad backed the car up to the *Used Book Booth* with a slightly optimistic *Undamaged books only* sticker attached to the side. She was certainly not convinced that some of their books didn't have bits of pages sticking out at funny angles. Earlier she had helped Anne with the *lifestyle* books. A single page with the header *Day One: Clear out the Nasties from the fridge!* she had thought to wedge just inside the front cover of *Flat Stomach in Fifty Days*. Though upon reflection that could have been less about fridges and more to do with dancing manically in front of the TV to the withering inculcations of an American military man, possibly still famous in second-hand shops. Dad had howled when Anne said a set of books had to go; she'd helped him sellotape the front cover back on to *Why Don't You All Just Bugger Off!*, astride a picture of a miffed looking tall man with curly hair and those funny old-fashioned jeans that Dad sometimes wore.

Dad began stacking the boxes at the base of the booth ready for their interment to another world. 'It's OK, I've got this,' he sarcastically declared as he stacked the last box on the ground. 'OK, let the fun commence.' He dramatically held aloft the first book from the top of the uppermost box and in a mock theatrical tone, announced 'goodbye...goodbye...er...hold on that can't be right. No, this is a mistake surely?' The book was titled *The Dreamy*

Canalways of Great Britain and was a hardback with an old-fashioned loose-leaf cover and with a black and white photo of a couple standing side by side at the helm of a barge as it approached the first of a row of locks. It must have been quite old, thought Ellie, as the man wasn't just *black and white* but was smoking a cigarette and that sort of thing stopped being allowed decades ago didn't it? His female companion seemed to be having the best holiday of her life as she was tossing her head back and her inconceivably blonde hair flapped in the wind. She was a picture of happiness, wearing strange tight denim shorts that came all the way down to her calf muscles from a waist that was so small that she couldn't really have eaten anything on the holiday; her hysterical happiness must have been due to drugs or something.

'Darling,' began Anne, with a school-marmish undertone of admonishment, 'Come on now. You bought that book ten years ago when we visited the Haye-On-Wye festival and: have we ever been anywhere *near* a canal?'

'Yes you see but that's because we go to book the barge holiday and then I am always so considerate that I give you a choice, you know like the *alternative mystery house* and you are always seduced by the inglenook or the butcher's, or is it butler's, sink-block thingy and so despite my best efforts we never get to go. So look, here's the new rule: we're all allowed to rescue one book each from oblivion. And this is mine.' Paul gingerly retraced his steps to the boot of the car and guiltily placed it inside, to the displeasure of a scowling Anne who registered her discontent yet further by walking a few yards away to light up a cigarette. She rarely lit up in the day, unless she was in a pub garden, and Paul knew that he would have to act as expediently as possible for the remainder of the exercise. He was relieved to find that the next book was an inane and thoroughly anachronistic title called *DOS for Dummies* and he proudly held it aloft before attempting to plunge it into the book booth. He pushed it against the chrome letterbox but nothing happened, so he tried it again. Resistance.

'No Dad, it's like this,' asserted Ellie. Oh how she loved to be the wise one on these occasions. She walked up to the booth and pulled the small handle that adorned the letterbox-like door, swinging it towards them in a contrary fashion to that attempted by Paul, and there it was revealed: a sort of wedge-shaped inner box where you placed the book ('give it to me Dad, I'll show you how') and, here was the trick. You pushed the handle of the letterbox back to its original position and *ploompf*, there was the sound of *DOS For Dummies* falling into eternity. Would it be burned or still find landfill? In another millennium, be the focus of archaeologists trying to make sense of a thousand years ago?

'Blimers Ellie, how the hell did you know how to do that? Very impressive. Thank you. What a clever daughter I have created.' And for once Ellie didn't mind one bit the crushingly embarrassing reference to some kind of genetic link between them.

By the time Anne returned, ominously not attempting to make eye contact with him, Paul was nearing the bottom of the first box. He hesitated, how could he not? For the first of his favourite *Nordic Noire* trilogy was staring up at him. But with a stony silence emanating from Ann he realised that there was nothing else for it but to dispatch it with the same perceived contempt as he had shown for the previous book. He pulled the swing door towards him and put all three books of the trilogy in at once, as if by so doing he would reduce his inner anguish by two thirds. Acutely aware of the prevailing *sang-froid* that lurked in his immediate vicinity, he looked back at Anne, to meet her eyes, to show her that on this day he *did* mean business, that he had strength in their relationship after all, in more ways than one.

And with a flick of his wrist, he binned them.

But Anne was not returning his gaze and instead was staring intensely at the space where the books had, moments ago, left the pannier. Paul coughed dramatically to demand her attention but to no avail. It was a frozen, mournful stare that was utterly motionless. Anne's eyes then widened fractionally. 'Oh no…'

'Darling, what is it? Look, look that was painful for me too, you must know that. But I thought we'd decided that they could go. Yes we enjoyed them so much but didn't we agree that they are in almost every charity shop that you ever visit? And and, look, tell you what, once we've cleared the house and the dust has settled, this is what we'll do: we'll go onto a specialist book website and order a *proper* set. Not one like you'd find in Oxfam but a genuine early hardback edition. We'd jolly well put it in the classics bookcase on the landing, in with the Byrons and the Brontes.'

'It's OK, it's OK,' said Anne snapping out of her reverie, 'Sorry I just don't know what came over me; I think, I think I feel a little sick, it's OK, I'm fine. Gosh that old trilogy, hey? Ha, all good things come to an end,' she finished her sentence, feebly.

'Look love, you go get yourself into the café section round by the deli counter; take the weight off your feet. Ellie and I will finish up here. You never know, we might even surprise you with a rescued book in the boot when we go home…'

Anne smiled at him. 'That, that would be lovely, thank you, if you're sure you don't mind? I feel dreadfully guilty now.'

Ellie and he soon finished what quickly became an almost cathartic exercise, as their mastery of the hidden pannier swing system developed its own rhythm, Ellie gleefully proclaiming her one rescue book by deftly snatching *50 Things Your Cat Tries To Tell You* away from Paul's hands. For Anne they settled on *Daily Prayers For Slightly Sacred Ladies* before they jointly slammed the boot shut. 'No point you getting in the car Ellie,' said Paul as he eased himself into the driver's seat.

As he drove around trying to find a parking space nearer the farm shop, Ellie began to make her own way there. She strolled the long way around the central block of parked cars. She was at an age where she felt acute embarrassment at the prospect of interaction with other humans and it was always so busy there on Saturday mornings that negotiating the parked cars would almost certainly lead to an episode of a family exiting their car and one of them saying, 'Sorry, didn't see you there.' Or the excruciatingly worse older teenage boy glancing at her with...with what? The blank gaze of a nearly-man to whom she was some gangly child or the subtle raising of an eyebrow at the burgeoning, sullen beauty of a child yet years from maturity. She never knew because the very thought of making eye contact was pulverisingly awful, anathema, the lowest circle surely of anyone's version of Hell.

No, life was simpler this way. She could act like an impish *femme fatale* with her school mates, passing a group of boys in the street next to her school, indignant smirking faces giving way to raucous shrieks of derision when the brief, unrequited, and if she were totally honest from the boys' perspectives, unknown encounter was over. But here at the edge of Lounsley, miles from the machinations of boastful and boisterous teenage grandstanding, the shocking truth was that this was it, this is who she was: a brooding, introverted, vexatious being, who, if the cat didn't snuggle up to her legs in bed at night, would reach for her teddy bear and kiss him gently on his forehead and hug him all night long.

But at least existing as herself gave her time to relax and not try so hard all the time to *be* someone. No matter how much she rolled her eyes at her dad's inane predisposition to treating her like someone even younger, and no matter how many times she would mumble a sullen thank you to Anne as she served her a piping hot bowl of Mulligatawny soup with homemade bread on a lazy Sunday afternoon, she was secretly glad of it, all of it really. Because she could be a child and she felt protected and the thought of growing up and leaving all that behind represented a sort of black hole of nothingness, a frightening malevolence of change, an irreversible blooming of petals, never again to close in on themselves.

As she skirted the last car of the first row that faced the farm shop, she felt a drop of rain. And then another. She loved the rain, its certainty of being, its arbitrary habit of not caring when and on whom it dashed. It seemed to her opinionless and without self-consciousness and as it quickened its downward pace she imagined that the small puddles which would soon begin to form, would slowly join up and create a vast muddy sea. She would be swept away from everything that was human awkwardness, for without other humans she was everything she could ever be, or want to be, which in her imagined murky sub-aquatic ocean, were the same thing really.

Her involuntary daydreaming was invaded suddenly by a face that she recognised. It was rather like the way that Bernie had stared at her that time at The Old Vicarage, but not stare at her at the same time, vacant and through her.

But it wasn't Bernie.

It was the face of Anne staring out of the café window.

At first she thought that the raindrops on the windowpane distorted the features of her face slightly, but then she realised that Anne was crying. Completely unaware of Ellie's existence so near to her, and crying. And yet the rain upon the window added a melancholy to her, real or imagined. Ellie was frightened but she did not know why. The day had started poorly but she felt that things had improved with the book-clearing process; and now this. She'd seen plenty of tears in the house, she'd often *been* those plenty of tears, but it wasn't that that bothered her. It wasn't like Dad's tears of joy when a footballer chipped the goalkeeper from distance on Match Of The Day ('Ellie, Ellie, my god you have to see this.') or a bit more embarrassingly when the couple got back together at the end of one of those RomComs that they kept in the cabinet beneath the TV. Or Anne's tears of indignation as she stormed off upstairs, Dad's words of apology always too late.

No these were silent, mournful tears: intangible and therefore astride some involuntary emotion of incongruence of being, of other self, of incompleteness. And she dared to think it: *the tears of not being with Dad anymore*.

But Ellie would not let that happen. She'd been through all that shit with Mum and you can't just go through life splitting up with long-term partners all the time because, frankly, the next one might just simply be ghastly and not bring you steaming bowls of Mulligatawny soup and homemade bread.

She spun around in the now heavily pouring rain to see Paul, umbrellaless, make a final lunge for the shop entrance with his jacket above his head. Would he make straight for the café? Yes, he's a bit clingy and that's exactly what he'll do, she thought. But then she remembered the side door - the one that the staff mostly used to run outside and throw plastic milk bottles into a smaller temporary recycle bin and sometimes ferry large drained vats of olive oil to add to the stack outside.

She was surprised to find the strength of purpose to toss aside her customary fear of self-conscious human interaction, and launched herself at the slightly opened door before she could think to change her mind. A seemingly indolent and blissfully uncomprehending face of a kitchen cook chopping something up on a board surrounded by metal pots and pans all askew a giant range, looked up at her. She smiled the most ridiculous smile she had ever smiled and instinctively pushed open another door to her right whereupon she skirted around a column to her left and...She was there, she was there, standing right behind Anne's gently trembling hair, her fingers impassively clutching a coffee cup with bits of sugar and paper and a collection of small wooden stirry things on the table in front of her.

'Anne...Anne, it's Ellie,' she said. But there was no answer. She looked to her right and through the small window of the door at the far end of the café, that led to the main part of the farm shop, she could see her dad approaching, ruffling the damp hair on his head with his fingers, his demeanour his usual sheepishness, yet somehow confident and purposeful.

Ellie walked around to the side of the table and did something that she never thought she could be capable of doing. She pulled Anne's face upwards and sideways towards her with her right hand and with a confidence that she did not recognise and with a voice that barely seemed to be coming from her at all, said, 'Anne, I have to show you something and I have to show it to you right now. It's outside and it's very important and you have to come *now*.' In the single second that followed, it seemed that time stood still. She was acutely aware of two things in that split moment. The certainty of the rain upon the window beside her, its couldn't-care-less-ness, its ambivalence toward human life and its underwhelming dramas. And the table beside her, where two chatting middle-aged women just stopped, stopped completely what they were saying, doing, being. And stared at her. Stared at her like she was not-of-this-place, not-of-this-world, not-of-this-humanity and she stared right back at them and in that split second that was nearing its close, her eyes flashed the defiance of a girl that had lived for years beneath the ocean and seen amazing and other-worldly creatures and creations. '*And?*'

With that single word, the women looked away from her, cravenly; for the first time in her life Ellie knew the power of certainty and purpose and for that moment in time it seemed she no longer feared the future at all. But that eternal second was over and Ellie's hand was already upon Anne's arm and already Anne was rising upwards to her feet, to Ellie's Will.

'But...but...what?' she heard Anne say as they rounded the pillar and moved leftwards to the inner door. She was dragging Anne now, compliant to her wishes in a way which seemed surreal, as the kitchen cook with sawing knife, looked upwards once more, his face still its unrelenting facade of contented ignorance upon this bit-part detraction of his day. Through the main side door they went and into the rain they emerged.

'What, what is it?' asked a suddenly awakened Anne.

'Look, look…' said Ellie pointing upwards, 'Isn't it all so beautiful?'

Anne looked up into the slanting, driving rain which cascaded over her face, her eyes and, whether tears looked like rain or were simply washed away it really didn't seem to matter. 'Oh yes, yes, it is, it's all so beautiful.' Ellie raised her face to the clouds also and it *was* beautiful. They stood there together, becoming soaked together, two faces lifted up to the sky as if the rain was just tiny watery magnates drawing upon their souls.

And then Paul was there too.

As he had pushed through the door from the shop to the café, he just had time to notice the two female figures lurch from the table and round to the inner side door; he had assumed that Anne was going to be sick after all. But he was beside them now. 'You bloody nutters. What are you like?' They turned and smiled at him and he stretched his arms around them, hugging them to him closely.

Putting his jacket over his head suddenly seemed the last thing on his mind as small rivulets of water saturated his neck.

Chapter Five

Paul indicated left as if to exit the A2 at the next junction marked Canterbury but, instead of slowing down, accelerated hard into the outside lane and overtook the white van with the words *It's this dirty as I washed it with your wife's knickers* etched onto the rear doors, before dramatically swinging the car into the nearside lane again and, keeping his indicator continuing to flash left, swept he thought rather majestically into the slip road.

'Saturday drivers,' he laughed, to deflect more than anything from Ellie sensing any gratuitous risk-taking on his part.

After last week's drama at the farm shop Ellie had supposed that this one, the one Saturday in four when Anne attended her yoga class and she and Dad passed the time by lunching in a restaurant in Canterbury, would be a welcome respite, yet she felt herself wishing that all three of them would be together again. It wasn't that she was worried about Dad and Anne in the same way as last time, it was just that she found that Dad didn't try quite so hard to engage her in conversation when Anne was around - on those occasions they all talked rather than conversed (and laughed and just were generally very silly).

'What ya reckon?' asked Paul, as he always did halfway along the Rheims Way, in anticipation of the next roundabout where they could either continue straight on by skirting the east of the city or cutting left towards St Dunstans and circumnavigating it by the west. 'Zanda's again?'

'I don't mind,' she answered, as she always did.

'Or one of the Italians? You can never go wrong with Italian.'

'I think I fancy pasta, but, oh I don't know, I just can't *think*.'

Which was all part of the well-rehearsed play that they trotted out once a month and culminated, as it always did, with Paul cutting left at the roundabout towards St Dunstans.

'Zanda's it is then.'

The reason they seemed always to go there, just the two of them, was actually two-fold. Firstly it was because it was really two restaurants in one, in that it had both a Moroccan and an Italian menu. For Paul this meant that it avoided the risk of Ellie going all quiet on him as thirteen-year-olds, it had dawned on him within the last nine months, are prone to do if things do not go their way, for example if the choice of menu before them suddenly becomes the most wretched imaginable. He prided himself on being a traditional disciplinarian but if he was very honest, he hated confrontation and sought to avoid it at all costs. What, he often thought to himself, is the point of a weekend when you have to spend it being miserably *right* all the time? Secondly it was because Anne hated restaurants 'that don't know what they are.' Paul and Ellie sometimes sniggered about the original incident that had started it all off. An already indignant Anne had agreed not to get up and leave the restaurant, right there and right then, when they were each handed the two quite separate menus, as it fast-dawned on her the duplicity of it all. But then Paul, subconsciously or otherwise he honestly could not recall, stated his order as a starter of prosciutto-wrapped grissini breadsticks with a

Gorgonzola Dolce sauce, followed by a main course of slow-cooked Moroccan ribs in an apricot and ginger sauce. Anne had gone very quiet and not spoken throughout the first course save for a barbed comment to the waiter who attempted to take the wine order: 'I have no idea - ask my *sommelier* husband.'

As the car wormed its way past the parked cars on the narrow lane to St Dunstans, Ellie could finally relax. They both knew the lines of the play by heart, but it was as if there was always the threat of a new method-acting, improvise-loving director jumping on stage and tearing up the script to cries of 'Throw away your preconceptions, speak from the heart…' Paul felt the same and they soon embarked upon their favourite game of inventing lives for other people that they passed upon the pavement.

A shuffling middle-aged woman with a pinky-purple washed-out head-scarf and holding three carrier bags stuffed full of shopping on one arm and an enormous brown faux-leather handbag on the other was nearly knocked over by a sudden gust of wind that shook the car as it limped past her in the slow traffic.

'Off to meet her lover in the rear car park of The Plough, that one,' said Paul.

'Yeah but she best be careful when she opens one of those wine bottles Dad. The bouncers will throw her out for not ordering the in-house stuff.'

A young pretty girl with Slavic features and black ripped jeans passed the lady walking the other way, seemingly impervious to the wind. 'You on to Pascals yet?' asked Paul.

'Hmm, I don't think she's a Pascal Dad, more a Titziana.'

'Wooahh, steady on my girl, that's enough of that talk. I was only looking at her legs. No dummy: Pascals. You haven't started that in Physics yet? The pressure on an object being proportional to its surface area when acted upon by a certain force.' Like most things since he had taken his science degree decades ago, he had no idea anymore if he was making it all up but he had long discerned, ever since his daughter could form a sentence and had asked him why the sky was blue, that they pretty much believed anything you said, if you said it with authority. 'You see, the lady off to The Plough - she's not exactly slim is she? And with all those bags she presents this large surface area to the molecules of air that are battering her. But you see Pascal, I mean Titziana, she's all slender and she confidently cuts through those molecules like a knife through butter.'

'Or but yeah Dad, Pascal, she just came from the car park and is in a hurry because she, like, *snogged* Barry—'

'Who the f...who the hell is Barry?'

'Keep up Dad. That's Elsie's boyfriend.'

'Oh right Elsie. I get it now. Elsie who just passed Pasciana—'

'And who's gonna run back when she sees Pasky's lipstick on Barry's neck and *stab her up, innit.*'

They both roared with laughter as Ellie stole the show with her deliberately South London white girl patois.

They reached Zanda's at just after half one, having finally found a parking spot in the Pound Lane car park. Paul was annoyed as a small group of shuffling tourists just managed to extricate themselves from the outside menu and enter the restaurant almost immediately in front of him. He hated it when that happened, as if they would all be deemed to be together. He could tell that they were tourists, without hearing any of them speak, as the three women of the party had those slightly shiny, light coppery puffa jackets that the Europeans wear, accompanied by short well-coiffured hair.

What completely sealed this conclusion, for Paul, was that extraordinary continental ability to show absolutely no sign whatsoever of self-consciousness. The English were all 'oh gosh do I stand here?' or 'oh hello, we were wondering if...?' But these Europeans, for whom restaurant lunches were part of their very being, just *existed* in restaurant entrances. It was completely logical really, if you thought about it. This is a restaurant and you have just walked in. What is there not to know about why you are there? Conceivably one variable was if you were asked if you had booked a table or not. But this lot would just say no and not smile and they would be seated probably a lot quicker and with more reverence than frequent Zanda-diner Paul could ever expect.

The foreign throng having dissipated from his intended line of sight, he tried to muster acknowledgement from the senior member of staff whom he had always imagined to be the owner, or maybe the owner's brother or son, as surely if you owned a restaurant you wouldn't be the front of house person, would you? Paul was convinced that the man would know his name by now and often fantasised if it could ever be like the films. 'Ah Mr Fewings, welcome, welcome. I have nice table for you today.' But it never really happened like that.

Paul, who struggled sometimes to understand what was and was not allowed in modern conventional human conversational intercourse, had recently formulated the theory that for a business owner to greet a customer by name might, for the politically correct, be a form of abuse, assault even. 'Hold on, you said my name. I'm uncomfortable with that. I feel violated.'

The restaurant was nearly full and naturally they had not booked because of the choices game they always played on the way there, so Paul's masculinity was restored as the *important* member of staff went to considerable lengths to walk them upstairs and seat them by a window overlooking the narrow cobbled street below.

'You OK that way Ellie?' he asked as he went to sit with his back to the window. He was an unashamed people-watcher, they both were, but Paul could never quite choose between unsuspecting street walkers and the curious intimacy of glancing at people on nearby tables, whose conversations were almost tangible. Ellie didn't mind one bit. She shared her dad's imaginative powers of creative people fantasy, but would rather there was a bit of a distance going on and the people in the street below didn't seem to know that she was up there looking down on them.

There was no window blind where they were sitting and the sun had just crept around the side of an opposite building, its rays beginning to burn the back of Paul's neck, as the waiter handed over the two sets of menus.

By the time the drinks arrived, the sun was now so hot on his neck that he guzzled his beer until only half was left, which niggled him. The seed of a possibility had entered his head, and it would not go away: *I cannot possibly ask to be seated at a different table away from the window because this is the best one in the house since it's by said window and the English are always complaining about how terrible the weather is here. But I'm not going to enjoy myself because I'll know deep down that I'm not a real man, or even like the personality-less Europeans that preceded us, because they have no fear of anything outside of getting what they are paying for.*

Ellie could see for herself the inevitability of what was going to happen and she resigned herself to it, as the waiter reappeared with his note-pad to take their food order.

'I'm really sorry but it's simply too hot here - please can we be seated elsewhere?' Paul asked.

Most people, certainly the foreigners thought Paul, would have left it at that but he was particularly sensitive to the fact that small children were sitting at the adjacent table. The reason this troubled him was because he particularly disliked being anywhere near small children in restaurants. Despite the partial loss of hearing in his right ear, it was still nevertheless sensitive and inevitably these sorts of small primates, as he thought of them, seemed to have a free license to create a cacophony of sound against the back-drop of something akin to a parliamentary privilege.

And of course he thought too much; he was aware of that and whilst he realised that the people at the next table could not possibly have known about his aversion to the concept of freedom of expression of small humans, he now felt a peculiar need to reiterate absolutely the *only* reason he wished for them to be reseated. 'Great position this, really probably the best table in the house, but can you believe a typical whingeing Brit thinking the sun on his neck is too hot,' Paul continued a little too loudly to the waiter as if to impart his message to a wider circle.

All completely unnecessary thought Ellie, a view validated she realised by the waiter simply politely acknowledging the request and saying that it was no problem and please would they come this way. Ellie picked up her jacket from the back of her chair and began to rise from the table. The ordeal was over and soon they would be in a quiet little darkened corner and Dad could relax and sip his beer and all would be well.

Only it didn't happen that way and she soon found herself involuntarily reaching for her mobile phone. If in doubt, as a cat might pull out of a stare with another and begin to wash its own fur, a teenager will reach for her phone and feign utter ignorance of any unfolding drama. By the time that she started tapping the pretend characters into the small device, it was now obvious that Paul was concluding their exit with one final, awful flourish of justification.

For Paul, what happened next went like this. The truth was that the children at the table next to him appeared to be very well-behaved indeed in his opinion. One, a girl of ten or so, was evidently called Olivia, a name he thought that could have gone either way. True, Courtney or Ashleigh even, would have been an instant alarm bell, as those sorts of parents would have had virtually no social self-awareness and, to numbingly high volumes of conversation, you might also begin to fear shouting, well-meaning but unbearable shouting, in the sense that it would be intended to control their offspring in what they vaguely realised *was* a social situation. Or worse yet: the fear of food being hurled to the floor and strange nappy-like smells spreading via osmosis through the increasingly fetid air. But equally there would be Olivias in the world, perfectly presentable with thick grey tights and Mongolian-themed knit-wear, whose middle-class-aspirational parents had not got to this stage of life's great preparation without imbuing in their daughter the gift of sharing her intelligence with the world. The quiet, downturned pig-tailed head could easily emerge from its silent machinations upon a colouring book and declare loudly to the world, 'Mummy, in history we're studying Elizabeth The First and she wouldn't have known what these chips were.' But Olivia wasn't declaring anything to the world, in fact she appeared not to be entertaining any latent thoughts of impertinence at all and if, as he assumed, that was her younger brother opposite her, he bore no signs of imminent rapture either. In fact, so impressed was Paul with this fleetingly adjacent serenity, that it further propelled him towards his departing remark. 'Nothing personal you understand, and um, what well behaved children you have.'

But as he turned to deliver his departing declaration of simultaneous approval and mollification to the nearest adult, the mother he assumed, he froze.

He realised that here before him was the woman in the photograph on the Palmers' living room wall.

He quickly made the decision, mildly awkward though the inevitable brevity of the exchange might be, to acknowledge the fact, much to Ellie's now complete abandonment of hope to escape what was clearly developing into a new nadir, to arrive at a level of Hell that even Dante could not have foreseen in his grand tour of the underworld.

'Oh hello,' he simply said to an initially smiling yet blank-faced mother, 'sorry, sorry, you don't know me, or my daughter for that matter...'

Ellie feigned yet further ignorance. Sudden survival was required. This was *quietly climbing a tree to escape a charging tiger territory*, she thought as she subtly edged herself along the remainder of the table, smoothly to pirouette silently past the immediate ally of a coat-stand that stood beside her.

'But we know your parents!' The mother's face at this stage appeared normal, revealing neither bafflement nor annoyance. 'Your parents, Patrick and Bernie. We were over there just...ooh two, three months ago it must have been. Such charming people. Such a small world isn't it?'

Ellie, with the cover of the hat-stand protecting her from the merciless cruelty of the episode, found that she was now prepared to glance up from her darkened phone screen and scrutinise proceedings as a hidden voyeur of some ghastly, unfolding social snuff movie. And there was no mistaking it: the mother's complexion now showed the slightest, tiniest sign of situation-assessment, risk-computation. Ellie knew this, as the mother cleverly, as only a mother protecting her young can, prevaricated her intentions beautifully by opening her mouth as if to reply, holding her smile and turning her eyes momentarily but with geometrical calculations of all distances and permutations of eventuality between this man before her and her children. She then looked at Paul and said, 'I'm sorry but I think you are mistaken.'

Paul said nothing but just looked back at her and Ellie edged her face into complete strangers' coats as it slowly dawned on her that *there was now a wider audience*. Though she could no longer see her dad, she recognised the terribleness of his situation in the tone of the words that she knew would eventually tumble from his mouth.

'Ha ha. Really?' A momentary silence. She could feel the audience spreading. It would soon include *people she would have to walk past*. 'In that case, I'm so very sorry. Please believe me when I say that you really do look like a doppelganger of the photo…'

Nothing.

'…in question.'

The woman's silence was tangible and as Ellie extricated her face from the strangers' coats, her sense of shame further compounded by the realisation that the *primary coat* had the scent of *older men's aftershave and cigars,* she made the bold decision to turn around and face the *audience*, all pretences of the smartphone as prop having quietly tiptoed away, vanished.

For Paul, his chronic sensitivity of all social situations now reaching fruition in this instance, he suddenly felt like a menacing child-snatcher, a day-release father granted a court-ordered, rare visitation right to his daughter, gulping his beer as quickly as would any man deprived of it during incarceration. A deluded sociopath preying on the quiet and private culinary gathering of a loving family on an early Saturday afternoon in a city whose only great crime to date was the murder of Thomas-a-Becket some 850 years earlier.

The two social fugitives, a metaphor that they both felt in common at this point but for quite different reasons, were then hurriedly reseated in an almost exclusively private annexe with no other diners in it. Paul tried to take his mind away from what just had, or in a sense, hadn't happened; Ellie's brooding catatonia like an icy lake enveloping him.

This new dining area seemed somehow to be an experimental business plan of sorts, the *Moroccan Quarter*, with naive watercolours upon the walls, of what he supposed to be the little charming alleyways of Marrakesh, not particularly dissimilar Paul noted, to the little charming alleyways of Mousehole in Cornwall. And ornate elephants, multi-coloured and diligently placed within enchanting little adjacent alcoves - what were they: receptacles for expensive and seductive candles? And actually: were there elephants in Morocco at all? He doubted it.

No, what would normally have passed for exclusivity, the preserve of the rich and famous, for both of them now took on the taint of the unwanted, the hidden, the superfluous, the slightly, insufferably, awkwardly damned. And the courses came and went in almost complete and mutual sience.

Chapter Six

'That's why I was a bit quiet with you when we picked you up from yoga.' Paul had decided to delay relaying the theatrics of Saturday lunchtime to Anne until the following Monday evening when Ellie was safely back in London with her mother.

'Oh, I see,' said Anne, half listening as she started loading the dishwasher. They could never quite bring themselves to tidy the kitchen up after dinner the night before: it seemed such a boring idea. She was slightly annoyed that Paul was engaging her in conversation at this point as the convention was that he would unload the washing machine adjacent to her, pour himself an aperitif and bugger off upstairs for half an hour, delicately and scientifically to arrange the damp laundry upon the various drying racks that were sprawled throughout the guest room. She never ceased to be amazed at the fastidiousness of his system of drying clothes which verged, she sometimes wondered, on being some weird hobby of his. He seemed particularly delighted with his multi-rack system of drying whole duvet covers, stretched halfway across the room. She put her foot down only once, when he attempted to secure one side of an undersheet between the back of the delicately reupholstered chaise longue and the wall behind it. He in turn suspected that her fabric-discolouration theory was bogus but decided not to contest the position for fear of losing his hegemony over the top floor clothes-drying business. Perhaps the first drink of the evening would cause the most anodyne of activities to acquire a frisson of satisfaction between icy sips of gin and tonic, she sometimes wondered.

Only once had there been a slightly awkward moment when she went to fetch her laptop lead from Ellie's room next door and across the small landing saw him holding up a pair of her knickers to the light as if the translucence of the material would decide their long-term fate.

'So that's what you get up to up here,' she had teased him. But before he broke into his usual raucous smile she detected a hint of...what...embarrassment? This the man that openly worshipped her pants upon her curves yet momentarily cowed into a sullen and furtive assessor of female undergarments upon a drying rack.

As Paul spoke to her whilst she rinsed the plates of caked-in debris before inserting them into the dishwasher (he didn't necessarily need to know that she had her own curiously satisfying *system* of loading the machine, a private and, she prided herself, scientifically miraculous way of maximising spare space, gin fizz capturing her veins as she did so), she rather wished that he would study her underwear all he liked upstairs, thank you very much.

But it was clear that he wasn't going anywhere until she had listened to whatever it was that he had to say.

Conceding defeat, she stood erect and turned on the cooker's extraction fan. She was down to her last five cigarettes and fretted that she might have to tease them out a little conservatively before bedtime. Drawing in her first draft of nicotine deeply, she fixed her eyes earnestly upon Paul's and he began what she conceded was a fascinating story, clearly she thought, an hilarious case of mistaken identity. 'Oh darling you are funny. That's your thing isn't it. Getting people all mixed up.' It was a reference to his confusing famous old actors and he knew it.

'Darling this is not the same as confusing Tom Courtenay and Albert Finney. *Clearly* they don't even look alike - that's just the phenomenon of cross-contextualising contemporary actors, you know, who were part of my upbringing, the substructure of popular culture and all that.

'The woman in the photo on the wall *was* the woman in the restaurant. There is no element of *cross-contextualisation* here is there?' His annoyance with her was palpable: it had been a typically long and trying day. 'Always good to get Monday over and done with,' was their often repeated clichéd mantra of such evenings. But for Anne the sentiment did not extend to the evening itself which provided a very welcome buffer to the rest of the inevitable working week and she sought to avoid even the slightest hint of conflict because of it.

'Well, yes I suppose, it's possible. I mean if you are absolutely sure.' She delivered her becalming words within an admixture of sympathetic tones, sufficient she thought, to tread the fine line between dismissiveness and acceptance. The truth was that her mind was in a rather strange place this evening. As they both left the house quite early for the morning commute, they only ever discovered what mail had been delivered when they returned home in the evenings. Tonight's pile was just beside her on the main kitchen work surface. She had a tendency to avoid unopened post that hinted at things like monthly credit card statements or hospital check-up invitations. Bills themselves were anathema, not because they needed paying as everything was by direct debits these days, rather they had a tendency continually to reinforce the gravity of their finances, dragging down her myriad ideas to escape her salaried life. Over the years her brain had developed a fantastic recognition database of envelope types, postmarks and address fonts, for she very rarely got it wrong. Occasionally during one of Paul's infamous paper clear-out days, he would thrust a pile of unopened post onto her lap and demand that she opened them 'right now.' Her finely honed intuitive mail-recognition skill-set worked even better the other way round. Rarely would a hand-written address be the harbinger of doom; final demands and exorbitant bills being the domain of faceless office bureaucrats and their systems of ruthless administrative homogeneity. A tax rebate cheque would always come with a very slightly off-white page colour peeking through the window and as for freebie invites to exclusive brocante fairs...well there could be no greater mind than hers in detecting them.

No, the letter in question completely threw her, as she recognised the name on the postmark almost immediately, though it had been many years since she had last seen its like. Galway was the location of her family's solicitors: Burke, Harvey and De Burgo. When her parents both died in fairly quick succession some thirteen years ago, barely elderly, having conceived Anne quite late in life, it had been left to the legal firm to act as executors to both estates, which by virtue of acceptable Christian tradition, were practically one and the same. Indeed whilst Padraig De Burgo was a co-executor, the final Will, that of her father's, was drafted in such a way that Dermott Burke, as close to the family over the years as some visiting uncle might be, was able to make decisions exclusively. In practical terms this meant that the estate was wound up rather efficiently and quickly. Though he had left fairly decent funds for the charities that he had supported because of his relatively senior clerical position within the Church of Ireland, and his collection of antique renaissance musical instruments to his brother in Cork, he had nevertheless bequeathed the reasonably significant remainder to his sole surviving issue, Anne.

Gratitude and grief had been strange bedfellows to her a decade ago not least because she had never felt quite so close to her parents as her contemporaries at school seemed to be to theirs. She had always explained this to herself by referencing the more stoic cultural familiarities of the Anglican Church to what she had always perceived to be the more tactile and emotional mores of Catholic life, but she could never be sure. Her older brother had died when she was still very young and so she had never really had anyone else in her peer group with whom she could talk these sorts of thing through. In her early teens she often felt herself guiltily clinging to the domestic normality of her friend Dana's mother, Mrs Clery, who would fuss over them and run around the small family kitchen uttering all manner of quaint Irish colloquialisms, like 'Three o'clock and not a child in the house washed…' Sometimes their early evening meal there would consist of delightfully forbidden foodstuffs like spam from a tin or crispy pancakes from a packet, forms of cuisine which would have disgusted her parents if she had been honest enough to tell them.

She loved her parents more than she could say and when her father, the retired Dean of Tuam died, her geographical distance from him across the Irish Sea as she was by then, failed to mitigate in the slightest a very deep and dark hole that opened up before her as it dawned on her that her family was now completely gone. Her new-found freedom in England rapidly became the chains of incarceration in a distant foreign land.

She'd met Paul not long after this, an innocent and random client relationship fast-becoming a furious love affair, followed by romantic declarations of life-long devotion and monogamy, the existence of his then three-year-old daughter, innocent and dependent upon him in so many ways, a further catalyst towards cementing her commitment towards him. Had her parents' deaths, so close together, been an even greater and more unconscious facilitator in fomenting this whirlwind of affection that seemed always to be so beautifully and conveniently mutual? Paul had always known of her modest legacy. Might she have even joked about how it had allowed her to start up her own business, before they had gone to bed for the first time? she now wondered in a sort of retrospective horror. But Paul was the most unmaterialistic man she had ever met, a very sweet and important thing to her at the time, occasionally maddeningly infuriating. Particularly in the aftermath of his annual reviews, which had convinced her that his boss was a mean piece of work, whilst admitting to herself that Paul clearly contributed to this innate and chronic sense of diffidence, borne of lack of ambition.

'So clearly you don't believe a word I'm saying and that's fine,' smarted Paul as she realised that her mind had wandered and she had utterly failed to undertake the one simple task she had set herself only a few moments ago: to be nice to her sweet and evidently demented partner. It quickly dawned on her that what had seemed her preference only a few minutes ago, for Paul to climb the stairs and compose his latest artwork of damp clothing arrangements; that this prospect now filled her with a terrible sense of impending loneliness and regret. She realised that she really had to, wanted to, say something.

'Darling, darling, look, I'm so sorry, but...it's just that...a letter arrived today.'

Paul span back around to face her, his pique momentarily becalmed to a state somewhere between intrigue and anxiety.

'It's silly really because I haven't actually opened it yet.'

Paul's face was now one of mild exasperation.

'It's just that I think it's from…' she paused, not for effect but through some anxiety that she had yet to identify, 'Mr Burke's office…I think.'

Paul detected her apprehension immediately and changed his tack in turn. 'Darling, it's best not to worry about it and, just well, open it really. It's probably some sort of obligation they have to you. It'll be fine.'

Anne smiled at him gratefully and picked up the envelope, gently peeling back the flap. Inside was a single-page letter and as she lay it out before her she steadied herself with a sip of gin.

```
Dear Mrs Fewings

I regret to inform you of the sad passing of Mr Dermott Burke who was
a much-loved partner of this firm.

Whilst it is a difficult time for all who knew him, I am nonetheless
obliged as designated sole remaining executor of your late father's
estate to assist you in completing any remaining tasks in winding up
the estate completely and absolutely. Reviewing the existing remaining
estate documentation, correspondence and accounts, it is unclear to me
as to why Mr Burke did not conclude this matter some time ago, though
I stress that I am sure he had always had your very best interests at
heart.

To this end I would be grateful if you could arrange collection of what
in practice are a number of boxes containing all remaining paperwork
and sundry assets. I regret that due to one of the winding-up clauses
these items are required to be collected in person upon signature, the
latter of which simultaneously authorises this firm to make final
payment to you of any residual funds.

Thank you for your co-operation in this matter.

Your sincerely

Mr Padraig De Burgo
```

Anne let out a stream of air from her lungs and looked up at the ceiling where her eyes remained as she spoke to Paul. 'Burke. End of an era. Feels like that was my last link to everything really.'

Paul went to her and gently turned her to him. Her eyes were slightly cloudy and her softly quivering lips braved a smile of sorts. 'You knew him well?'

'No, not really. Just more that he was Father's ultimate confidante and he's gone and I suppose things, little things, unknown things, I suppose they're all gone now too, aren't they?'

'Maybe darling, but maybe he's up there…your father I mean and…' And he immediately began to regret this direction of unnecessary platitude. An atheist himself, or so he liked occasionally to declare himself, he was perfectly content with the idea of his dead relatives *being up there* somewhere in some indefinable stratum of spirituality, sort of bumbling but well-meaning guiding forces from beyond the grave. But such fanciful and supernaturally speculative whimsy had never sat well with Anne and her rigorously religious upbringing, no matter how much she had left it behind, literally when she moved away from the isle of her birth all those years ago. The truth was that Paul had always detected a dull sense of foreboding when broaching the subject of her familial past, nothing quite tangible and yet sufficiently unsettling in some unknown way, that they never really spoke much about it. Whether it was a retrospective sadness on Anne's part that she had had to rid herself of the formal shackles that were inevitable in being the daughter of a dean of the Church of Ireland and her subsequent struggle to make her own way in life, or whether it had something to do with an even more poignant sadness at the sudden loss of her older brother at such a young age, he never really knew. All he did know as her quietness descended upon him beneath the bleak glare of the industrial kitchen lights, was that he somehow had to take charge of it all.

'I shouldn't have said that sweetheart, I'm sorry.'

And she knew it and smiled at him.

'Right, Anne, darling. This is what's going to happen next, OK?'

She liked this very much, it's what she craved and she meekly nodded at him.

'I know a bit about this sort of thing because of Work you see. I am going to get Legal to print me off a Power of Attorney letter; you sign it and then you don't need to worry about anything anymore. I have to go to the Dublin office in the next month or so anyway - I keep putting it off and this is the perfect excuse to conclude some stuff that I should really have done at the end of last year. Stay the night. Drive across to Galway the next morning and maybe one more night in Dublin and home to you and it'll all be over...OK? Oh and I'll make sure it's all on the company, hire car and everything.'

Anne wrapped her arms around his waist and buried her teary face into his chest. 'Oh baby, thank you, thank you. You really are the best. What would I do without you?'

And Paul felt all giddy with his new-found masculinity, his taking control like this and the mild sense that he really was going to be *Attorney for a day*, the concluder of probate with its gravitas and machinations of finality.

Even the mystery of the Palmers' daughter's doppelganger had receded in his mind a little.

But not for long.

Chapter Seven

Returning from work the next evening, Paul felt uneasy as he marched his way along his usual route from the train station. It had been a busy day for him as he liaised extensively with the Business Development team in Dublin and diaries were cross-checked repeatedly against the availability of the potential business leaders whom they would seek to impress within the next few weeks. His originally slightly urbane ambitions for the Dublin trip had now been overtaken by the fact that there had been an approach to the company from a potentially very significant client indeed and it both exhilarated and frightened him that he was to play a major role in negotiating the deal. Finally there materialised a choice of two dates and he'd made a note of them on a piece of paper so that he could run them past Anne.

But he was also a little apprehensive about raising the subject of Ireland again so soon after last night's conversation and exchange of emotions. He took his coat and boots off in the lobby before entering the living room: he quickly realised that he needn't have worried. Anne bounded up to him, not something she normally did, her warm and energetic smile from the other end of the open plan ground floor usually sufficient to reassure him that everything between them was fine.

Not only did she spring towards him, but she effected a sort of comic shuffle of a gait as she approached, grabbed his cheeks ostentatiously between thumbs and forefingers and placed her lips firmly upon his, lingering longer than her customary, he often feared, nominal contact of academically-signalled love. No this was a kiss of un-calculated and insinuated meaning, physical and full of want. It aroused him in a way that was beyond its baseness of meaning and its pledge of yet deeper physical affection to come. It spoke of unrequited and retrospective longing. Longing lost in gaps in her previous existence but now all thrust up to the surface of life to smother her sensible, conscious mind. He responded in kind, how could he not, how could there be any decision-making right now in any of this? But there was a mischievous element within him which slowly came to the fore as they embraced and he reluctantly declined to consummate immediately this unexpected, savage and unsolicited attrition upon his physical being.

'Oh my god, you absolutely delicious and sluttish whore,' was all he could muster and tempered his feeble attempt to delay in some way his organic desire for gratification, by seizing her from behind and gently biting one of her ear lobes. Her favourite, slightly blokey and hideously expensive perfume, which was always his perfect lazy birthday or Christmas present to her, infiltrated his nostrils and assaulted the ardour of his fervency yet further.

She giggled and dragged him by his hand to the kitchen where a bottle of sparkling wine was already opened, her glass more than half empty, as appeared the bottle, and his waiting glass all full and effervescent, as she appeared to him herself right now.

'Have we won something?' he mocked her.

'Yes,' she slurred very slightly, 'I won the most wonderful man of my dreams.'

Is this the sort of slurred voice, thought Paul, that every hard-working man dreams of when he comes home? Not the slur of domestic indolence and habitual daytime inebriation, which leads to rows and inevitable divorce, but the happy slur of wild, abandoned adventure and lust for life itself.

'I actually rather think I adore you,' he said.

'Oh, so you've finished chatting up young gals in restaurants now have you, and have time for lil' ol' me?' She pulled a mock face of Victorian modesty set in the grounds of some Deep South Southern States ranch. Cheap Champagne, controlled slurring and now the affectation of an Alabama Belle. Could the evening be yet more alive with possibilities? wondered Paul.

'Well yes only if you have finished lardy-dardy-ing around with the Lord of The Manor.'

'Say what?' she continued with her faux-Confederate drawl.

'I saw the way you were with Colonel Palmer some, some ...three months previously.'

They both stopped their absurdly amateurish pretensions; it was Paul who momentarily came out of character first and said in his perfectly normal voice, 'Gosh, crikers, was it really three months ago that we went to the Old...Vicarage?'

'Yes, I've been thinking the same,' she replied pensively and all Anne-of-Lounsley again, 'You, erm, think it's all a bit strange?'

'Forget strange, it's outright bloody disrespectful, I mean who do they think they are?'

'Yes, I know what you mean. I'm a bit hacked off with it, the fuckers.'

'But in all seriousness darling, there was no *drink* was there? I mean yes there was *tea* so for once I couldn't have made a complete arse of myself.'

'No, no you were fine darling, honestly. I mean it was almost like the perfect visit really wasn't it? They *hugged* us for god's sake when we left. And the bloody cow, it was her that knocked on our door on my day off, so she can basically... Fuck. Right. Off.'

'Unless,' began Paul. He moved towards her in a theatrically menacing way, 'you...erm...did something to make Mrs Palmer...jealous?'

'I say! What can you possibly mean?' and now it was Anne the actress again, all giggling and a priggish Victorian English school marm, Anne of a thousand guises and the one to bust him all up and libidinous again as she detected within him the frisson of mild cuckoldry, which drove him to a sort of morbid fascination with Anne the adulteress.

'He, he...Colonel Palmer...he, *touched* you didn't he, as the devil took you off on that so-called tour. I knew it and you know it.'

'Oh he did more than touch me, feeble husband of mine,' she retorted. 'Why he may be old enough to be my father, but he was as manly as a man can be.'

It was too much for Paul: he grabbed her and spun her around and pushed her forward against the kitchen counter. He wrenched aside the futile modesty of her knickers and unbuckled his belt in one grand flurry of intent before he was fully in possession of her.

'You must know that I cannot allow such insubordination to continue unpunished,' he panted.

'Beast. He was a man. But you, you are. A. Beast.'

'Act like that in the Manor House again and I will beast you again. And. Again. And. Again'.

'And. Again. And. Again.'

'And. Again. And. Again.'

And they took it in turns to say the words. Words that soon came together at the same time, like streams of water converging into a gushing river.

And then there was silence.

Paul looked up at the ceiling and as he stepped backwards, the top of his left heel brushed something cold that rolled around inside a carrier bag. So there was another bottle of Champagne to come and they hadn't even finished the first. For Paul the evening had become almost flawless. If nothing else he thought, as Anne waddled away from him, her ankles all beknickered, the curious knock on the door from that strange lady some ten weeks ago, mystery daughter or not, had contrived to open doors of an unexpected kind and he was glad of it.

The next evening life was passably normal again in the house. Paul seemed content with his top floor damp clothes-arranging detail and Anne her dishwashing-solutions assignment. As Paul descended the final few steps of the bottom staircase, Anne dramatically slammed the dishwasher door shut and punched the flashing red light as if to fire up the next phase of their evening together. Paul knew that the excitement of the previous night was most unlikely to be repeated and therefore was not in the slightest bothered by Anne's question.

'So now darling, in the cold light of day, it is that I have to disappoint you by revealing that Patrick—'

'You mean the Colonel—' he began to interrupt her before she cut him off in turn.

'No, there'll be no Colonel Palmer tonight, OK.'

'Oh…kay...'

'…did not molest me in the corridor…alas...'

'Oi, unfair. You can't say that!'

'Sorry, that was naughty of me. Of course I didn't want him to, don't be silly. But in all seriousness what do you think did or didn't happen. I mean in their heads?'

Paul went to venture that the restaurant doppelganger incident meant that they really should investigate it all properly but something made him change his mind. The down and up of the last two evenings maybe, or the need to get Galway over and done with so that they could all relax and move on with their lives. He instead chose the path of levity and started up a new game, not to court physical gratification, but to be with her: all silly, childish and irreverent.

'Can you imagine...?' he started, and Anne knew this game and lit up in anticipation: both her face and a cigarette, '…that we just turned up one day uninvited and knocked on the door?'

'Aaarrgghhh. No, no stop it, I can't deal with that. Hideous, hideous,' and she went to put her fingers in her ears, but clearly had something even nastier, she thought, to lob right back at him. 'No imagine, imagine this. We go up to the door and knock on it. And a completely different couple open it. And they just stand there and say "Hello, can we help you?"'

The awfulness of it was too much for Paul. 'No, that's low. You cannot be going there—'

'And there's this awful silence. And we ask them where the Palmers are—'

'Nooo. That's enough. Ah come on love, there are limits—'

'And they say "Sorry we don't understand. There's no parking here." They're a bit old and deaf you see. And we say "No not parking, we don't want parking, we want the *Palmers.*"'

'Please Anne, I beg you—'

'And we describe them but it's no good and they don't know what we are talking about and say that they are terribly sorry but cannot help us—'

'Evil, pure evil—'

'Because my darling: *The Palmers don't exist and have never lived there and we were entertained by weird opportunistic artifice burglars in some way who knew when The Old Vicarage would be unoccupied and invited us on that exact day.*'

'OK OK OK, you win, you win.' He'd lost the game, but he couldn't resist a final parting volley in defeat. 'In all honesty darlers, did you check your jewellery boxes after she called on you that day?'

The evening had become diverting and they both felt relaxed with each other. But little secret thoughts were already beginning to enter Paul's head as they chatted away about all sorts of things: work and the impending school holiday (that was news to Paul - he was sure he was thinking of the Galway trip for that week and Ellie's mum would be pushing for her to come down for a few days, to "give me a break"). The fact of the matter was, all their puerile fantasies aside, that the Palmers really must have lived in their house all those years ago, unless one considered the hugely contrived scenario whereby the fake Palmers' artifice involved discovering the old photos on an earlier *visit* to the unoccupied premises. *And* having the foresight to pretend to be who they weren't (given that they did not look dissimilar to the people in the photos, factoring in decades of facial physical metamorphosis) and knock on their door in Lounsley...but for what? The Fewings were not wealthy. That degree of artifice, that *brilliance of artistry* would be reserved, surely, for film plots where people steal very expensive paintings. No, the fact of the matter was he thought, as Anne pointed to a print-out of a desk calendar and shook her head for some reason, that the Palmers, former residents of their current house in Lounsley, really did live at The Old Vicarage, claimed to have a daughter whom probably was not theirs, failed to send them all the things they had gleefully promised them and Paul developed a niggling feeling that he could not let it lie. Not one bit of it.

'...Last week in July...Are you listening to any of this?' Anne stared accusingly at him.

'Ah, sorry, no I wasn't. I was momentarily you see, intoxicated by your sheer facial beauty, forgive me.'

'Any more bollox like that, and I'll give *your* face a right old back-hand, OK,' she said sardonically, because she was a little annoyed that he wasn't taking the subject of Ellie and the school holidays at all seriously. She was *his* daughter after all and why should she bother, if he didn't? 'Look darling the point is that yes I am so very grateful for you adding Galway to Dublin, really I am, but won't her mum expect her to come down at least for half the first week of the summer holiday? But you know what she's like, she might be a bit funny if it was just she and I together, I mean without you.' What she dared not say, though Paul was not stupid and suspected it, was that she was fine playing the supportive role of *rural stepmum* but it was just that: *supportive*. Without Paul there it was liable to be a bit much really - she had so little time to herself and her creative projects these days as it was. Her words were pregnant with the implication but she was satisfied that they were nonetheless diplomatic enough.

'Hmmm,' began Paul slowly, wondering if what he was about to say might become an *a priori* fact if he were not too careful. 'But what if she came *with* me?'

Anne tried not to look too supportive of the idea and stayed, she hoped, within role. 'Oh, I see; what a novel idea. But what about the extra cost? And would she even, I mean, would she even be *up* for that?'

'Well, here's the thing: I've looked at options in the past and from memory, car plus ferry, if you factor in personal mileage being far less than car-hire the other end and things like airport parking: sort of the same really. I mean, I'd still let Work know she was coming with me, but it's like that time you came with me to Dublin: they don't seem to mind what I get up to in the evenings so long as I get the job done. I don't think they see it like the England team Wives and Wags thing; are they a distraction or not? A double room is the same cost as a single and all that. You remember we just paid extra for your air fare and that was the end of it.'

'Yes but with the greatest will in the world sweetheart: you and I, hotels, hard day in the office and all that. I was, I think it's fair to say, a rather *pleasurable* distraction, Wife or Wag...I mean I'm not being funny but I don't think we could stretch to paying for a single room for her out of *our* money could we? And besides, I know she likes to be all independent, but she is still only thirteen and wouldn't you fret if she was in another room, you know what you're like.'

'Not sure. I have a hunch those family rooms can sometimes kick in cheaper. The hotel might have under-occupancy: didn't we stay in one once, just the two of us, and you said the bunk beds in the far corner made you feel like we were spending the night in some sort of quasi-luxurious social housing?'

'Well she might go for it if it was as large as that one. But you know that age, thirteen, I mean she isn't going to be happy; *private* doesn't even come close. Her bath last Saturday evening took two hours; I had to bang on the door to see if she was alright!'

'Look how about I just ask? I could sell it to her by saying yes; Dad in pants walking from bathroom to bed: not a good look, but I do that all the time here don't I?' and they both laughed as he gave his rendition of 'Fat Dad in Pants Alert' as he swept down the stairs on a Saturday evening to pour himself a drink with the bath running above. 'OK so I'll give you a small cross there. But trade that off against: me in the office all day and she...well what do they do at that age? I don't want her wandering off outside the hotel, but she wouldn't anyway. All that *stuff* they throw in, at hotels. The paraphernalia they bang on about when they show me to the room or serenade me at check-in, all the stuff that goes completely over my head because I just don't *get* it.'

'What sort of stuff?'

'Ha, you tell me. Don't they have these ghastly gyms that real business people go to in the morning before they take their breakfast of muesli and apricots? Ok, so she might not go for that. But all the pampering stuff. Don't they have that sort of thing at the place I stay in; the Marritone thingy? I'm sure they do. I think I saw it on the welcome screen on the TV in the room. I was trying to find RTÉ One but none of the buttons on the clicker could get me away from this tortuous video of the hotel's facilities and I'm convinced there was a shot of a betoweled woman with cucumbers for eyes and a racially stereotypical Middle Eastern masseur bearing down upon her. That was it; and a smoothie bar. I mean come on, tell her she can make free smoothies? The company sees smoothies on my bill instead of half bottles of wine from the minibar and they'll think: that Paul - he's turned the corner.'

Anne was warming to the possibility and thought that she could now safely ditch her pretence of consternation. 'Swimming pool?'

'There is, oh my *God*. Sorry didn't mean to blaspheme, just slipped out. There's a swimming pool if I can get the Queen's Hotel alright. My body dysmorphia prevents me going anywhere near the place. No, tell a lie, I tried it really late one night a few trips ago. I was absolutely bricking it. I didn't even know what the procedure was, me a man of my age. I took everything I needed in a sports bag down there with me - it was in the basement - and the coast was clear. I found this cubicle and came out in my trunks, trying to look all cool, just in case a *real* business person appeared with cucumbers strapped to their eyes or nipples or something, but I was on my own. Did I not tell you all this?'

'No you bloody well didn't! Midnight drunken swims with girls in bikinis, is this where we're going here?'

'Ha. If only - *only joking* - no. It was worse than that. So embarrassing. I dived into the pool and as soon as I surfaced I saw that one of the receptionists was marching in looking at her watch and shaking her head. "Everything OK?" I asked her and she replied through gritted teeth that it was not and that the pool facility had closed an hour ago. So much for twenty-four hour service. She muttered something about Health and Safety and poolside supervision. I told her to give me five minutes, I mean I *tried* to assert the big important customer is king shit, but she wasn't having it. It was awful; I got out feeling like a beached whale as it was, but then had to dry myself off in the cubicle knowing that she was *waiting* for me outside.'

'Hmmm, so it wasn't like when you were in Cannes that time then, eh?'

'Whaddaya mean?'

'You know. The "young pretty girl" as you insisted on calling her - too much detail thank you - who said that you could have a massage in your *room* for heaven's sake.'

'Oh yeah, so right. This is Ireland we're talking about, not France - nothing happened in France by the way - she's not going to reprimand me for jumping in the pool unsupervised and then *offer* me some sort of cubicle-based furtive relaxation therapy is she?...I mean did she?'

'You're asking *me* what happened?'

'Enough! Nothing happened in Cannes and nothing happened in Dublin...gosh why can't I just be like normal blokes and have a lovely wife stuck at home doing designy things whilst I get laid by prostitutes whilst away on business?'

'You actually mean that. I cannot believe it: the truth is out, at last—'

'Ok, yes you win. I can't take the guilt anymore. I had a massage lying on my back in my hotel room in Cannes. I started on my front honest I did but she said, "*Monsieur, sur le dos, s'il vous plait*" and I complied. This is such a *relief* to confess. And yes in the pool in Dublin, it was more like blackmail. She said, "If you don't expose yourself to me now I will call the night concierge and tell him that you tried to touch me."'

Anne tried to be outraged further but instead found herself in a hopeless fit of giggles and hugged him to her; he was suddenly exonerated of all charges.

Chapter Eight

'Oh and darling.'

Paul tried to pull the pillow more tightly over his ears, but it was no good. Anne's train into London each morning was nearly an hour earlier than his which meant he could normally fall back to sleep as soon as she slammed the old heavy front door behind her. But this process might be put in jeopardy if, god forbid, a last minute *instruction* were given to him as she left. Dancing images of waterfalls and mathematically absurd physical constructs, the sorts of abstractions that allowed him to drift off into last-minute reveries before his alarm pronounced its dreadful cadenzas of chirpiness, would be at risk. A simple instruction such as remembering to give one of the cats its medication, could promote itself to a full-scale worry of it bolting off into the garden, Paul's body language as he held the pill-dispenser aloft, a signal of dastardly intent. And then his waterfalls and metamorphosing shapes would quickly gain purpose, rationale, definition and all opportunity of slumber would be lost for another day.

'Darling!' she reasserted. She leaned over him and her perfume and hair and lipstick consumed him and his masculinity alike. Suddenly he just wanted them to take the day off together and replace the waterfalls and Escher paradoxes with passions interspersed with old films. 'I've left the cash for Aaron by the telephone. You must remember to pay him as you leave. I told him to clean the windows at exactly the right time so you won't miss each other. We owe him a whole month and bless him, he never asks us for it, which is why you absolutely *cannot* forget OK? He's very good, much better than the last one. Thank God for the Poles.'

'I'll give you…pole…carry on…' he slurred and she was amazed that he could be so obsessively suggestive whilst not even being properly awake.

'Well if you must darling, but it will have to be all in your head for now; my part in your fantasy is over. Have a nice day. Love you darling.'

'Nas dee, luff youtoo...' he managed and her face and her perfume and her loveliness were no longer there and he was all alone as waterfalls and mathematical paradoxes swirled around his head. He was vaguely aware that a sort of Polish river god called Aaron stood at the top of it all, that of his Creation, his cleansing the world, causing these glorious bejewelled cascades of aquatic light all around him and reverse rainbows, defying all natural laws of refraction. And he knew that the Grand Instruction was good. Then there was this sense of him drooling upon the pillow - and he knew that he was already slumbering.

'Farewell cattings, have a gloriously lazy day,' he said over his shoulder as he swiped Aaron's wages from beneath the phone and entered the little hallway. Curious name, he thought not for the first time, for a Polish man. It wasn't as if the current European debate about the free movement of people was up there with the threat of internment of Germans during the war; or the post-war decision of German-born naturalised Americans to drop the 'C' from Fischer in order to anglicise themselves a bit. Aaron didn't strike him as one little bit coy of his Polishness – and besides Paul had heard him speak on his mobile phone several times in his native language; it could just as easily be Hungarian for all Paul knew, but it certainly wasn't English.

'Here you go mate,' Paul shouted up at the ladder as a large lorry thundered by. Aaron descended a few rungs and gratefully took the envelope from him.

'Cheers mate,' said Aaron in reply, with a glint in his eye, not without some intentional parody of English chirpiness, which Paul thought was hilarious. 'Laters!' And they both laughed.

'See you anon...Aaron.' That will be too nuanced even for our dear Polish friend, he thought and off he marched. Suddenly a thought entered his mind and it grew with such alarming persuasiveness that he made a conscious decision to be late for work and catch the train following his usual one.

'No wait, Aaron,' he started again as he quickly retraced his steps at a jog. Aaron looked across at him, momentarily fearful of his employer's terrible mistake in realising that he had inadvertently, perhaps, included his daughter's dinner money in the envelope. 'Aaron!'

'Yes, yes Paul, I can hear you. What is it that is up with you?'

'Look could you do me a favour?' Aaron looked a little doubtful but smiled nonetheless. 'Well it could be a favour, if nothing else, but equally it might mean more business for you. I mean, how do you generate new business around here. How does it work?'

'Leaflets Paul,' began Aaron, with doubt still registered within it seemed, 'You remember what made you call me last year?'

'Ah yes, aha. So it was. But for example, do you know The Old Vicarage on the other side of Lounsley, in Brenham? Up that steep windy road from the pond, on the left? It's set back a bit.'

Aaron thought for a moment. 'Yes I think I know that road. But I agreed with Tomasz: that was his side of town.'

'Tomasz?'

'Yes my friend Tomasz. Friend I live with.'

'Oh like so you split the business in two geographically?'

'Yes, I think that's it.'

'Well my favour still stands but, either way, look take this tenner.' Aaron instinctively reached down to take it suddenly wondering if that was rather tying him in to something to be later regretted. 'All you need to do is first ask Tomasz if he does that one; The Old Vicarage. If he does, ask him what sort of relationship he has with the owners. Actually who are the owners; what do they look like and does he know their names?'

'OK.'

'But if he doesn't do that one, please could you yourself actually go and knock on the door tomorrow and ask them if they want the business?'

Aaron smiled sheepishly, tilting his head in the process, in what Paul considered to be a Slavic gesture of uncertainty of some sort. He dug into his pocket and fished out a five-pound note and a couple of pound coins, guiltily realising that the needs of the Big Issue seller on Blackfriars later that morning would be subjugated beneath his thirst for arbitrary knowledge. 'Look take that Aaron and I'd really appreciate you doing that for me, really I would. Just between us OK? No need to say anything to Anne for now.'

'OK Paul. I am going to do that for you no problem.'

Paul smiled and turned to walk on again towards the station but thought he'd best obliterate any lingering awkwardness between them and shouted over his shoulder, 'You get the business mind, I'll have that money back!'

And he was sure that he could hear Aaron laughing as he strode away.

Arriving at work later than usual propelled Paul into his favourite mode: working flat out to get everything done that he had set out to. He even managed to agree the Dublin dates for his trip next week. Ellie had surprised him by her enthusiasm in wishing to accompany him and he was quite excited about the prospect. He was immensely proud of her for no other reason than that she existed; he was even playing with the idea of taking her into the Dublin office itself for an hour or so, to show her off to the staff there. I mean, he thought, the Irish love all that sort of thing don't they: family stuff? Anne was some sort of exception to this; her past strange and unfamiliar. Had he never offered to take her into the office there, he wondered, aghast at the idea that his partner was after all Irish and he had never paraded her around the company or even offered to do so, even when she had stayed with him at the hotel on one of his trips there. Surely they must have discussed it at some point? Perhaps they had but Anne had been lukewarm. He knew that Ireland itself, if not anathema, certainly held a peculiar place in her heart. He remembered that he was greatly taken aback on their third date to find out that she wasn't even English, as she spoke with what he regarded as a received pronunciation, a huge bonus he felt at the time; the sort of girl you could introduce to your parents gleefully.

'Ah Paul,' his mother had said upon their first introduction, 'you've found someone, well she's lovely, really she is.'

Of course third dates were notorious for something else, he recalled with a grin, and might her sudden Celtic-ness have driven him on yet more fiercely that evening to consummate their mutual and sudden longing?

His fleeting nostalgic reverie was pierced by his private mobile vibrating upon his desk. Probably Ellie with a characteristic change of mind regarding Dublin, he pessimistically thought.

'Hey Paul. It's Aaron.'

'Oh hi,' gasped Paul, nearly knocking his cup of coffee from the table as he staggered to his feet, quickly closing his office door, as if a conversation with a window cleaner should constitute something absurdly clandestine.

'I decide not to wait as I found out it for you.'

'Go on.'

'Neither scenarios is like you thought. Tomasz not his house. So I go past there early. I don't like having the money without result for you.'

'No, no, I appreciate that Aaron.'

'I went to knock on the door but suddenly I hear someone shout under at me.'

'You mean *over*?'

'No, under. There's some cellar steps outside main house half way up he was speaking. This man is Polish I know suddenly.'

'You what?'

'Yes, can tell. Before I know it I say "*Dzien dobry*" which is *hello* and we are now talking with Polish.'

'With *whom* are you speaking Polish Aaron?' asked Paul, fearful that a change in tense might jeopardise any mutual understanding.

'His name is Lech and he is working for the owners. And he tells me that the man is Patrick Palmer and his lady is Bernie Palmer.'

Paul felt the faintest of diminutions of the lurid conspiracy fantasist within him and was embarrassed to find himself regretting parting with his £17 before Aaron had even enlarged upon this unexpectedly early filing of his report.

'But he says they are away all week. He says he prefers as the lady she likes conversations and he wants to finish the tank.'

'Tank?' Paul spluttered, with a sudden diabolical image of Patrick, the military collector, rear North Wing obstructed maliciously to casual visitors such as Paul and Anne, by virtue of walls of Nazi memorabilia and corridors awash with old Russian grenade sticks.

'Sorry "tanking". It's what....er....the English say for desiccate damp cellar.'

'Ah, *tanking*, I got it.'

'So, sorry Paul for not much to report you. Lech he says he will ask if there is to be a windows job when they come back.'

'Does he know when that would be Aaron?'

'Yes, Saturday. They are returning Saturday. Two days' time on this Saturday.'

'Thanks Aaron, really appreciated.'

'OK Paul see you next time—'

'Wait! Aaron.' Paul felt that he didn't want to give in just yet. It was an uneasy feeling. 'This Lech. You get on?'

'Ha ha, well I didn't want to say Paul, because last time you asked me if I knew that family of the Polish man at your work and I told you that Poland is quite a large country, you remember?'

'Oh blimey, that was embarrassing. But I wasn't really being that serious, you know?'

'Well it's for me to be embarrassing now. This Lech, his family is ten kilometres Lublin and I am sort of knowing his uncle, or what I mean is that my father knows his uncle...*maybe*.'

'OK, so Lech likes a beer right?'

'There is Catholic joke Paul—'

'*OK* Aaron, yeah yeah I get it...rhetorical question.'

'Question not horrible. Just fun.'

'Ha ha. Look Aaron, seriously, what would you say if I offered to pay for all the beers you could both drink say lunchtime tomorrow, Friday? A whole hour. Nearest pub would be...' Paul's pub crawl days were long-gone but town planning in his head was still predicated on the distance of anything to a pub. 'Yes, The Anchor - at the bottom of the hill, turn left. They do at least five ales.'

Paul mistook Aaron's silence as a terrible rejection of his sudden and peculiar masterplan that had hatched irresistibly within him. But it wasn't the plan itself that was awry but the detail within.

'Ah *ale*. Brown drink?'

'Doh,' ejaculated Paul, realising his error. 'No not The Anchor. What was I thinking? The Castle Inn, further down. Not a cask-conditioned ale in sight. Just a row of shiny electric lager pumps.'

'I know Castle Inn. Nice beer there Paul. Thanks, very kind. Lech and me we talk plenty.'

'But...' Paul realised that this sudden and unsolicited altruism really did require a modicum of explanation, 'Aaron, you know that I am not a *bad man*. I am silly Englishman, *Work For The Man*, and all that?'

'Paul. We all *Work For The Man*. You are The Man yourself don't you forget.'

'Crikey never thought of it like that. But you know what I mean. I'm not. A criminal.' He wondered if he had said too much, but he'd started and had to extricate himself somehow. 'Look Aaron, I just need you to trust me on this. I won't do anything to harm Lech and his business. I just need to...' he realised this was not the right time accidentally on purpose to lose something in translation. Aaron's English was not of an academic standard but he detected within the young man a sense of the real language of life being a universal truth in some way, not to be messed with. '...*confirm* something about the people that live there.'

'OK Paul. I take Lech drink. It's no problem. And...' The pause was brief but palpable and if it were at all awkward, then it was considerably less so, thought Paul, than the brief remainder of his sentence: '...I think you are a good man Paul.'

Paul pressed the red button on his mobile, and settled back with difficulty into his ergonomically-assessed office chair. He wondered quite in what way that removing a Polish man with guile from his valid and legal place of work under inducement of beer, in order for he himself surreptitiously to *confirm* anything, notwithstanding the very basis of the law of trespass, could in any way be interpreted as the actions of good man.

Chapter Nine

Paul glanced at his watch as he reached Brenham town's pond. It was 12:48. It had been just a day since his telephone conversation with Aaron. Any dissipation of feelings of ethical misadventure from that episode had however been supplanted by a whole new set of guilty sensitivities, for that same evening he had casually announced to Anne that he was indeed *working from home* on Friday. He'd already agreed it with his Managing Director that his preparation for the following week in Dublin should include at least a day of uninterrupted contemplation of how to approach the meetings there, at least one of which he described, to Paul's dismay, as a *potential game-changer*. A phrase impregnated, to a corporately insecure Paul, with a sinister sense of finality: that of his job if he got it all wrong.

As he began his slow but deliberate amble up the hill, mathematically timed he was sure, to secure his arrival at the exact moment that the Poles would depart, he wondered upon the recklessness of allowing potential game-changing moments in his life to run congruently alongside spuriously amateur-sleuth investigations of any kind. Especially any that might compound his yearly review with 'the small and unfortunate matter of the trespassing episode as reported in The Brenham Chronicle,' as he imagined his MD putting it, with his bushy raised eyebrows, no doubt adding, 'It's all online these days Paul old fellow you know.

It's all *Google-able*.' And what would Anne have to say about it all? He could hear her now, as they withdrew themselves from the community, the enormity of which being no less mitigated by their not *being* part of any community. Because, he was sure, for the purposes of his public censure, one would very much be created abruptly in a sort of collective group-think to his heinous trespassing crime. Village voices. 'The New Year street party may be long-gone, but the people of Lounsley, we just don't tolerate that sort of thing around here.' For Anne it would be much simpler and far more devastating: 'It's not that you were caught snooping around someone's property, someone God forbid that we actually *knew*, it's because you *lied* to me about working from home. If you can lie to me about that, what else can you lie to me about?'

His knees wobbled slightly at the thought of it and at the same moment a car sped past him from behind so that he was forced to cling like a free-climber to the old Victorian brick wall that encased the whole street on either side. He had thought the narrow road to be one-way so that he could see any car coming towards him; well it had been, he was sure, when they first moved to Lounsley. But now he saw a sign ahead asking for traffic coming down the hill to give way to that going up it and he realised how lucky he was that the Brenham Chronicle did not instead wryly report that the game had indeed changed for local man Paul Fewings.

He was working from home that day, said his bereaved partner. *I suppose we shall never know what he was doing upon that hill, a mile from home. He has taken it to his grave.*

What he would not do now for a stiff drink, Paul thought as he approached the large iron gates of The Old Vicarage. He thought of a Plan B, whereby he would abandon Plan A altogether and join Aaron and Lech in The Castle. But then his prevarication to Anne would surely be so much the more awful. What next: a strip club?

The mathematics of his timing were now almost too perfect because he had quite omitted to predetermine how the *changeover* would occur in practice. The pavementless, highwalled lane afforded no opportunity for a pedestrian to feign indifference to his surroundings and loiter convincingly within a storefront window or sidle up to a random tree. This was not a road where anyone in their right mind would look anything other than *suspicious* in taking a fake phone call to portray a sense of invisibility.

At exactly the moment that Aaron and the man he supposed to be Lech, stouter and he thought a slightly older fellow by about a decade, and from his louder voice, the *back-slapper* of the two, began to swing the large gates open, Paul found himself fully opposite them on the other side of the thin road. He brought himself to an awkward standstill, realising his exposure. He hoped, as the two Poles stepped onto the lane that, the complicit Aaron aside, he did not appear very slightly strange as he made a self-conscious turn to his left: attempting to convince the entire world that he was a man that was always only ever marching up the hill, without the faintest vacillation of purpose.

He could not be sure if Aaron had acknowledged his awkwardness with a sideways glance. When he determined that the volume of Lech's enthusiasm towards his impending liquid lunch had abated according to the inverse proportional laws of distance and sound, he pretended that he had forgotten something from his fictional existence at the bottom of the hill. He span round, realising that there was now no audience, no paying public to this pinnacle of acting perfection.

He was immediately grateful that Aaron had left one of the gates ajar and, unnecessarily checking his watch to determine that it was now exactly one minute past one o'clock, he moved silently through it and onto the long gravelled driveway. As he glided towards the house, now so recently familiar, he felt slightly elated that the plan had commenced, the incident of the unexpected car notwithstanding, so very smoothly. He had already prepared in his mind a series of plausible explanations should the unlikely offices of law rear their unwelcome heads at that very moment. That would have been just his luck really as one rarely saw a police officer in Brenham let alone Lounsley these days.

The village joke was that you would only ever espy a whole phalanx of them on Carnival Night or upon the occasion of *an 'orrible murder,* the last one of which had been recorded in 1969 at the now extinct Chandler's Arms in the market place. A man with a sawn-off shot gun from London had demanded respect from one of the locals. The good people of Brenham have since rather enjoyed an historical sense of *Schadenfreude* as the tale became infamous: for the murderer was in fact not that at all, but a man convicted of manslaughter.

The pub's resident idiot, Terrence, was not a village idiot, but a man of facial disfiguration, blind and with a white stick, which in 1969 in certain quarters of working-class Brenham was cause enough unfortunately to be branded *idiot*. He had defied his lack of vision and shuffled past the grinning gangster who was already beginning to squeeze the trigger of his abominably modified weapon in the direction of his alleged slighter. Seemingly to have his tankard refilled with his favourite brown ale, promptly, it is generally agreed among the old boys of Brenham, Terence superbly and accurately swung his pint glass around, smashing it down and upon the side of the neck of the would-be assassin, severing his jugular immediately. The sawn-off gun fired its potentially deadly particles of metal harmlessly into the expendable, it was reluctantly generally agreed by the locals on this occasion, pub optics, creating a climactic explosion of blood, rum and whisky all across the saloon bar.

Five years later Terrence's manslaughter conviction was overturned when the dependable old boys of Brenham, in a decades-long anticipation of crowdfunding, all clubbed together for a top London lawyer, who easily argued, now that Britain was part of the greater good of the European Common Market, that Terrence's Human Rights had been violated because a man with a gun had maliciously blocked his way to the bar for his pint of brown ale that terrible evening.

With respect to his own potential interface with the constabulary that day, Paul's main defence upon such an unlikely intervention would have been a technically correct one: namely that he was paying a visit to his friends, the Palmers. Which court of law in the land would treat with contempt the fact that he and his family had recently taken tea with the Palmers after all? He'd thought about the extent to which he could stretch this theme should his incursion upon the premises be much more advanced than knocking on the door; he was vaguely aware of the all-too-common occurrence of *concerned* neighbours or friends not having heard from someone whom they later found, through forcible entry, to have died an horrific and lonely death between their armchair and the coffee table.

They are getting on a bit officer; I was worried...It's just so sad.

He gingerly knocked on the front door as a precaution and almost dreaded the possibility of a shadowy blurred figure approaching the door from the other side. It would have been excruciating.

Oh hi, Patrick, Bernie: just passing...how's things..ha ha...

But of course there was no answer, no evidence that Lech was a liar, an imposter. He glanced around the front lawn, driveway, shrubs. Just birdsong and bright sunlight filtering from the south through the silent vastness of the giant cedar. He walked over to the exterior cellar steps and cursed the fact that they were at the front of the house; surely the coal and ale delivery men a century ago would have been encouraged to be out of sight on the eastern side? Or was it like a church all those years ago; the East was holy and unworthy a place to visit by a mere member of the working congregation?

Lech's discarded cigarette butts belied the entrance to the cellar steps which was a square wooden horizontal door, about three feet across. Paul stared at it now, aware that he was about to pass into the realm of technical trespass, historic cream tea or no cream tea. At that moment the sun shifted imperceptibly to the right of some branch of the cedar tree and cast a burning tube of incandescence upon the earth-bound gateway and, whether unconsciously or not, this seeming celestial direction from above spurred him to lean down and pull upwards upon the iron handle, painted the same ash colour as the door. The coward within him prayed that it would not give, but the intrepid explorer showed a hint of a smile as the door lifted upwards with a reassuringly clichéd creaking sound. He scanned the lawn and driveway behind him one last time but nothing had changed and he began his descent of the steps. As he lowered the door back down above his head he pulled out his smartphone, illuminating the remaining three or four steps: he found himself by a relatively small door, presumably to the cellar itself. He turned the door handle and gently pushed: nothing. He tried the manoeuvre again, nudging the door with more exertion from his right shoulder; it bowed in the middle and the latch creaked; he was sure that it could be breached with a little more effort. He reached into his inside jacket pocket and retrieved the slim flathead screwdriver, an item that if stopped and searched by the only police officer to have graced the streets of Brenham in years could hardly have been deemed fit to perpetrate an act of Actual Bodily Harm upon even the most vulnerable in society. In Sweden ordinary men carry hunting knives strapped to the exterior of their belts as they walk the aisles of their local ICA store with impunity. In England a man is not a man without a screwdriver in his pocket. A nation of shopkeepers indeed, but a merry band of marching DIYers to boot.

He slipped the head into the gap and gently levered it. A creaking, straining sound. It was still holding fast towards the top so he really jammed it in further now up to the handle and pulled hard. *Thwack*. Something gave and the door opened for him. He gingerly glanced within but it was very dark indeed. Propping open the main hatchway above to let in some light was not an option and he contemplated navigating his way, with the smartphone's complimentary torch, through the secrecies of the troglodytic world before him. But it was unnecessary because there was a light switch on the wall to his left. With the hatchway closed above and pulling the main cellar door to behind him he decided that there was little risk in trying it and unsurprisingly the cellar lit up before him. It was about twice the size of the cellar in Lounsley, but seemed not dissimilar in density of content. Storage boxes, a pile of old LPs, what looked like a timeworn musical amplifier of some kind, an unusually large model of an elephant's head, presumably a stage prop of some sort. He might have time to investigate all this later, he thought, and moved towards what were clearly the stairs to the inside of the main house above. As he neared them he realised that this quarter of the cellar was empty and a pungent tarry smell invaded his nostrils - so Lech was tanking in phases. That made sense: why have to carry all this junk up into the main house at their age when it could be moved around in stages as Lech progressed?

As Paul mounted the staircase he noticed a small gap between it and the north wall of the cellar and observed a vertical stack of old picture frames, design boards, a hoary set of architectural paraphernalia he wondered, unconsciously lending weight to the concept that he really shouldn't be there at all. So much so that he resolved that if the door at the top of the stairs were locked, which surely it must be, then that would be it. He would stick to the cellar; find out what he could. If he were caught, a wary Lech and policeman before him, why, what little England village bobby on the beat would not be placated with a little guile. 'Officer, careful how I put this, but when my dear friends the Palmers told me about the tanking, well you never know, great workers the Polish, but I thought there was no harm in swinging by and checking all was well.' A *Brexiteer* wink between local old timers and he'd be on his way.

But to his surprise it wasn't locked and Paul almost reluctantly found himself within a very familiar hallway indeed. It was the one through which the caddish Patrick, as he had perceived it at the time, had steered a giggling Anne off, as he had masochistically imagined at the time, to show her some other corner of the house *in camera*. It seemed like yesterday. He looked down at his phone to turn the tiny torch off and as he did so he noticed the time. 1:20 p.m. Forty minutes left.

Keep those pints coming Aaron. Time to be a gratuitous Slavic stereotype...please.

He easily remembered the location of the conservatory and gently turned the door handle, all too aware that it faced southwards onto the still silent and guiltless garden. He was sure the cedar tree was no fool though and as he entered he gently nodded at it now to pay homage to its all-seeing wisdom. Only one thing really to check here and he looked up at the wall: to the photo of the Palmers' daughter.

It was gone.

His heart was racing now. Even if arrested as an artifice burglar, or worse, as some sort of stalking sex pest of ladies' used underwear within the laundry washbasket, at least he could bear his suspended custodial sentence, job or no job, with the satisfaction that *he was onto something*. Perhaps the Palmers, knowing the game was up (he would tell the investigating Detective Sergeant to inform the Palmers that he had bumped into Katie the other day and that she had given them her love), would reason with the police. 'No no officer, Paul. Dear old friend. Just checking up on us: we realise that now. No need to press charges, really there isn't.'

He closed the door behind him and made his way to the side annexe where the Palmers had first presented them with the history of the house in Lounsley. The door was already open and even before entering it he could see the old photos laid out exactly as before. He thought that strange. It had to have been, what…three months now? Would they really have left them there in forgetfulness after their visit? Early and long-retired, would they not have had time to gather the photos and pack them up again? Or perhaps their photocopier had broken down, a regretful Bernie ruing the lost opportunity to contact the Fewings as promised. 'Patrick, we can't very well take up their kind offer of dinner in the old house without presenting them with the photocopies, now can we? Let's leave the photos in the annexe until it's repaired.'

Hmmm, he thought: rear wing closed to save on heating bills or not, three months was a long time to save up to repair a photocopier. And it was only 20p a colour page at

Brenham Library - the Fewings had already agreed to pay for them after all.

Paul walked past them, glancing to his right as a precaution again to the driveway beyond. He raised his hand briefly to the cedar tree once more in fealty, in mutual understanding that they were both there as guardians of good governance of the fine old building. He looked towards the north-east corner of the room and noticed a large draughtsman's desk that he had not noticed previously, set at a diagonally vertical plane as is their purpose; indeed so convinced was he that it had not been there at all during their first visit that he approached it. Upon it was the plan of a floor of the house, but which part of the house? There were two large bedrooms separated by a small corridor. A nice size but too small even for the rear wing itself surely, which was its obvious provenance: the part of the house excluded to their visit, almost certainly Patrick's retirement swansong, his and Bernie's final and extravagant grand design. What more beautiful way to spend each evening together than here in the annexe, with a glass of wine, discussing and cementing forever their hegemony of The Old Vicarage?

But it wasn't a part of the North Wing at all, Paul realised.

It was a plan of the second floor of Paul and Anne's house in Lounsley.

Chapter Ten

He stared at it. There was no mistaking it. Patrick Palmer had erected one of his old draughtsman's desks here in the annexe at some point since their visit and decided to remind himself of the layout of the top floor of his old house. Unnerved by the fact, Paul found himself instead involuntarily attempting to discern a quite normal explanation for it. It was after all, he noted, juxtaposed to a series of old photos of the same house upon a nearby table; here was context if nothing else. The house in Lounsley had been the Palmers' big dream, the founding expression of professional intent, the grand project of the late sixties which had eventually led to the magnificence of their life in The Old Vicarage. Which house, Paul rationalised, could have bequeathed the greater joy? The first poem you wrote, the hideously contrived one, as a teenager, expressing the woe of rejection of unrequited love perhaps. You kept that one did you not, forever? And Lounsley was hardly an early and embarrassing articulation of designer poetry was it?

Not sure whether he wished now to be reassured by the competing jurors' voices within, or rather disturbed by them, he tried to remain neutral and with his forefinger gently scraped at the bottom right corner of the plan to see if there was anything beneath. There was. He swept the topmost sheet upwards and over the back of the desk.

There before him was a plan of the first floor of his house.

It was clearly the iteration of the current Lounsley house, rather than the one that they had originally purchased in the late sixties because, to Paul's untrained eye, it was exactly the same layout. The geometrically true and straight lines of the various rooms, doors and hallways were testament to that. For some reason however a pencil line, in a shade of light brown, neat but clearly without recourse to the straight edge of a ruler, traced its way from the right edge of the first floor plan, where the stairway is, and stopped in the middle of the landing. Further differing colours continued the neatly hand-swept line into each of the four remaining rooms: master bedroom, study, bathroom and lavatory, the occasional arrow proving the line's direction. The blue line which traced itself towards the last of these rooms appeared to terminate with a small cross beside it. He pulled back the top sheet to view once more the second floor plan and realised that the same brown line swept from the rear bedroom towards the staircase which on this plan was over on the left. A fainter yellow line moved in a tiny arc from the centre of the room towards the south-facing window and, from the small landing, a light green line traced itself into the north-facing room right up to the window. He finally checked to see if there was a plan of the ground floor but there was not.

Taking his phone out of his pocket he hurriedly photographed both existing sheets. Again he glanced at the time: 1:35 p.m. His goal was to be out of the house and on to the hill by 1:50, to cater for additional risk such as, god forbid, Lech and Aaron suddenly realising after their second pint that the reason Aaron's father knew Lech's uncle was because he had murdered him or something, prompting a physical fight at the bar, being thrown out and Aaron desperately chasing Lech towards the house and remonstrating with him that it was all history now.

As he re-entered the cellar, Paul began to wonder why anyone would really want to tank it at all. It wasn't exactly dripping with water down there and for a couple obsessed with photocopying costs it was likely to invoke some considerable expense. There was so much down here and so little time remaining that he elected to concentrate on the pile of storage boxes that he noticed when he had first entered it. The uppermost box contained books, *old* books, the kind of books that Paul would readily peruse for hours in some crumbling, antique book shop. Not now, he said to himself. The box beneath contained paperwork, scribblings of sums of figures and presumably esoteric references to architectural matters of some kind.

Next.

The following box beneath, which rested on an old rug, contained photo albums. He seized upon the first few; they contained photos of Bernie and Patrick on various holidays, small annotations belying their location: Morocco, Paris, a small Greek Island port, Rhodes Town perhaps. Slightly smiley pictures, but always with a hint of melancholy he thought. Could it have been because their daughter had shunned their invitation to join them? Her decision to accompany her dad to Dublin notwithstanding, Ellie had already begun to moot that she might not be coming on this summer's holiday with them. Paul set the benchmark for such phenomena by his own - he had been fifteen when he and his older brother went on the last family holiday, to the Greek Island of Lesbos. His mother had sunbathed topless for the first time ever – well, that he knew about - in front of not just him, which was bad enough, but complete strangers, and he had wondered if it was her way of asking him to move on with his life.

The fourth box contained further photo albums and Paul instantly recognised some of them. They were the ones that had been ceremoniously presented to them over tea and cake, as if a provenance of their tales, of their unsolicited intrusion into the Fewings' lives. Paul glanced quickly through them, increasingly aware that time was running out for his unsavoury little adventure into amateur sleuth.

A photo was missing.

Which was it? He struggled to recall. He thought that it was important to remember because these were the sorts of photo album sleeves which had a sheet of protective cellophane over each page and he felt sure that the photograph in question could not merely accidentally have fallen from it. He put the lid back on. It was now 1:45 p.m. and time to retrace his steps. As he stood up he saw that there was an A4 envelope which had been tucked between the boxes and the wall and his curiosity overruled his innate sense of nervousness at leaving the conclusion of his project to such a tight deadline. He opened the envelope and gently shook it; three or four photographs slid out onto the rug. One was the photo of the *ghost boy* in the tree, the one that Ellie had insisted on defining and now Paul realised that it was this one that had been taken out of the photo album in the previous box; he remembered the sequence now.

But why?

Patrick had certainly been bemused by Ellie's insistence that it was not a simulacrum at all but an actual boy. Might Patrick's curiosity have led him to examine it further - but to what end? Two of the photographs he did not recognise: or rather he recognised the subject matter; various external shots of his house, but he did not recall having seen them at the time of the first visit. The final photo was nearly as large as the envelope itself and had fallen out upside down.

As he turned it over Paul's pulse surged as he instantly recognised the face of the woman in the restaurant, the face of the Palmers' supposed daughter Katie, the photograph so proudly displayed on the wall of the conservatory during their visit, but now consigned to a lonely troglodytic existence in the dungeons of the house.

How bad does a falling-out of parents and daughter have to be to deserve this? he wondered. But for the bizarre episode in the restaurant, that's where he might have left the thought, yet there again, wasn't it that singular episode that had prompted him to embark now upon the criminal act of trespass? But here alone was justification indeed for his criminality, surely the world would agree, dragging a reluctant Anne along with them?

It really was time to leave he thought and he did that thing that he did every time he went to exit the house each morning for work. Are you *sure* the back door is locked? Are you *sure* you switched the iron off? It was a kind of mental illness he was sure, but he quickly ran up the interior stairs and looked about the hallway to make sure he had not left behind some horribly incriminating item. For was not the worst crime of the dopey burglar who is habitually caught, as reported in the papers, not the criminal act itself but the ignominious infamy, as surely to be reported on this occasion in The Brenham Chronicle, of the *thief who left his driving license on the kitchen table.*

He patted his pockets: no it was fine. He'd only after all brought with him today his wallet and his iPhone and he could feel their outlines distinctly now. As he turned back round to descend the stairs once more he heard a voice. It was not a distinct voice, like that of a man beside him, in an adjacent room even. But a muffled voice. He held his breath. Nothing. He exhaled and breathed again, foot now on the top of the staircase, pulling the door to behind him. The voice again. Damn! What was he to do? He pulled out his phone. 1:50 p.m. He was now behind schedule and dangerously close to the possibility of discovery by the loosely appointed guardian of The Old Vicarage, a Polish tanker called Lech. But surely the possibility of humans in an officially empty house, not just any house, but a house in which a mystery of sorts was clearly evolving, was worthy, no *essential* to any terrible TV series involving an amateur sleuth? Rosemary and Thyme. Scooby Doo. The Famous Five. All had a bloody lot to answer for he mused. Right, one last time, he thought and re-opened the door at the top of the stairway.

This time there was no mistaking it and it was a lot clearer because it was now a female voice and its tonality seemed less muffled by the weight of molecules of masonry which he suspected concealed its fullness. It was coming from the left of the house somewhere. The north, he realised.

The North Wing.

Whoever she was, she was distressed and the man seemed to be offering some sort of authoritative, but diplomatic defence of some kind to some *thing*. He realised, with a sick sensation in his stomach, that he might well be intruding upon an argument of some kind between Patrick and Bernie Palmer. Who else could it be? The nearest neighbours were some fifty yards away: the Old Rectory or something it was called. Is everything on this side of town the *Old Something*, he wondered. Could it be house-sitting guests, curiously confined to the perennially closed-off North Wing? That made no sense to him and besides, why would Lech not have been informed?

The very possibility that Patrick and Bernie were still *there*, albeit not in the body of the main house, beneath a pretext of holidaying somewhere else completely, disturbed Paul in a way which he could not rationalise completely. A neutral observer might certainly objectify such an arrangement as little more than odd. 'Let's *pretend* to go to Cornwall for the week darling. But we'll stay in the North Wing which we haven't slept in since *that* night. When you pretended to be the wicked Count de Montfort and took me so brutally by the hearth.' That's the sort of sexual self-help therapy that you can read in the back of The Sun these days isn't it? he thought. Pretend this, fantasise about that. Why, hadn't he and Anne done precisely the same thing the other evening in a kind of way? And back to the theme of the seemingly proscriptive cost of the photocopying, Cornwall for a week could, he knew from experience, be a bit brutal upon the finances. Save it all, and use a massive part of your enormous house, as a *virtual holiday*.

But there was crying now; muffled female sobs. If it were a holiday, then it was going awfully wrong. But suddenly none of that mattered. Paul's all-invasive curiosity, all-encompassing investigative obsession, now became subordinate before he knew it, to something older still, something primordially English.

He felt ashamed.

If it was the Palmers he'd heard then what was it after all to do with him? If the daughter on the wall were not even theirs, cruelly invented from some inner turmoil, to impress visitors, what of it? What crime is committed here? None really, he considered honestly. And whose business was it to anyone that they had pretended to go away on holiday to Cornwall? Lech's? Paul could not imagine Lech's pained and wronged face in the Canterbury Small Claims Court. 'Sir, I have no money claim at all, they pay me well.'

'Mr Adamski, are you wasting the Court's time? What *exactly* is your grievance here today before the Defendants?'

'They lie to me sir. Say they go holiday. But all the time. They here in their house. My human's rights feels violated.'

No, that's not how those things work Paul. Their house. Their imaginary daughter. Their grief of some kind. Absolutely none of my business. And he rapidly wanted to remove himself from this terrible, terrible sense of intrusion and never have anything to do with any of this again. He looked at his phone. 2:05 p.m. He could not believe it. He could not understand what he was looking at, what the numbers could possibly mean. Had he not just four minutes ago noticed that it was 1:50?

He panicked. He pulled the door to and ran down the stairs, tripping over one of the boxes and landing on his right elbow, sending a sharp searing pain up into his arm. He yelled out, rubbing at it furiously and realised that this was a horrible mistake, to make any sound of any kind at all. A few photo albums now lay scattered on the rug of the floor of the cellar and, suppressing his strident need to groan with all his mental strength available, managed to pick them up with his left hand, his right quite useless for now. He stepped over to the door to the exterior stairs, flinching as he instinctively reached for the light switch with his right hand, the pain in his elbow excruciating, before flicking the switch with his left, plunging the cellar back into its familiar darkness.

He was alarmed to realise that he had not factored in the time he had somehow to fix the door, albeit now with only one effective hand. He pulled the door towards him and was astonished to find that the latch clicked into place; the unfolding catastrophe was not all going against him. The spring-bolt action he had forced himself against earlier had not broken, just been overcome and no-one could possibly now know that there had been an ugly forced entry.

He stumbled up the stairs to the garden, wishing beyond all hope to expunge the whole sorry episode from his life, forever. Anne would ask him how his day had been and he would innocently tell her how much *more* he always got done working from home and Patrick and Bernie would be some distant memory, whimsically dredged up from time to time with sneaky giggles over a lazy Sunday picnic in the garden with cheese and port. Please, gods of the world, please Cedar Tree, if you care anything of my well-meaning intentions today, no matter how ill-informed, I entreat you now to be guardians of my safe passage to the lane, the waiting world beyond the gates. And I will go to Dublin and I will secure a deal and I will be an upright, loving husband and father for the rest of my contributory days to this good Earth.

As he diligently lifted the horizontal wooden door-hatch a fraction to check that the path was clear, he realised that it wasn't.

Lech and Aaron were slowly and stumblingly walking directly towards his hideously temporary place of sanctuary. A Polish song of some kind was being sung joyfully between them. Paul tried to think. This was the stuff of nightmares. The thing you dreaded most of all in life, that only happened in very bad dreams. The moment of being *caught*. Money Paul thought. It was the only thing, he resigned himself to thinking, that could mitigate such awfulness. Not just the awfulness of trespass, but the now ghastly realisation that Aaron was immediately to be revealed as *accomplice*. The *Shame of Lublin*.

But money surely could buy anything, everything.

If you had it.

Which he didn't.

Well if it had not been for the darned EU he would be quite a rich man to Lech. But he wasn't. He was just a fellow European worker, in the economic sense. And keeping Lech quiet might require the sale of an asset so significant that it could surely not be kept from Anne. 'I thought I was doing the right thing darling. I'm so sorry. I know your grandparents' grandfather clock meant such a lot to you.' The very notion was so nauseating that Paul instinctively thought the unthinkable: to re-enter the cellar and make his way back into the house. He felt for his phone to create some light and then immediately underwent a different kind of illumination.

It's a phone, not a torch, you idiot.

How many times had he played the fool to Ellie when his employer reluctantly agreed to upgrade his iPhone to the next level. 'Does it still do phone calls?' he would seemingly, innocently ask her.

'Dad!'

It was another game they played. Like the one in Canterbury on Saturday lunchtimes. These were the games that he cherished most in life. Because soon she would be a woman and it would all end. A *game-changer*.

The crunching of Polish footsteps so close to his lair of shame were voluble now and he realised he had one chance, god forbid there was a signal in this place, the vastness of the Cedar Tree swamping all life below it.

I beseech you Cedar Tree.

He was now curiously aware that the capitalisation of the Cedar Tree in his psyche, its metamorphosis to proper noun, must become a permanence, and hoped that such a promotion would reward him in some abstract way. Fortunately Aaron's number was topmost in his *Recents* tab and he clicked on it desperately.

Footsteps approaching, slowing. The time had come.

Lech, surely after all that beer in pubs where you cannot smoke you must really, really need one now before you merrily recommence tanking for the day? Their song was coming to its Slavic crescendo; *rallentando, ritenuto…risoluto*.

Paul's phone connected.

But the singing immediately outside was too loud, even if Aaron's phone was not on *Silent*. No, no: a Polish window cleaner could never allow his mobile phone to be on *Silent*.

You don't migrate to the other end of Europe to miss *business* calls.

'*Wupu Zupu, Wupu Zupu. Niech po polsku zyje*!!!'

Their song was over. Paul now knew, ahead of the horrific frisson of the poker player with his entire stake on the table and his opponent's hand about to be revealed, that life could go either way.

Aaron's phone was ringing.

'Paul!'

'No, no, not Paul, listen Aaron!' he hissed into the phone as he traced his steps as far away to the bottom of the steps as he could, through fear of revealing his existence. 'Don't *say* anything. Just listen. I'm on the cellar steps. Lech cannot open the door, do you understand? My life would be over. You would lose my business.' He immediately regretted what seemed hideously like blackmail.

'Ah...OK.'

'Stand on the door, now, please so he can't open it. You pretend I am your other Polish mate calling you: Tomasz. Patrick has called him because he, stupidly, now realises that he ignored the window-cleaning leaflet. Why he would do that on holiday I have no fucking idea but it's all I have right now. The only reason he has not taken him up on his kind offer previously is because he was not sure whether to include the windows of the North Wing. It's not used and it faces a wooden copse. No need to clean it at all really but now, sitting on a beach in Cornwall, he...just...feels really bad about the North Wing and he wants an opinion. Are the frames even sound enough to warrant the windows being cleaned: would that be a false economy? Should he be thinking of renovation actually, wood preserving, a form of *tanking?*'

Paul heard Lech say something. He understood no Polish but it sounded horribly as if he were now suddenly impatient with Aaron. Impatient that he was preventing him from what: *working?* By the love of Jesus, Aaron has just bought you three pints, calm down you Polish fat fuck…

'He needs you to go around there right now and count the windows and consider the condition of the windows. Tell Lech that he *has* to help you arrive at an opinion here.'

Paul felt relieved as Aaron spoke in Polish into his phone, a sure indication that he realised the enormity of the situation. Aaron rang off before he knew it and continued in Polish this time, presumably to Lech. The tones of the conversation of the two men above him ranged between mild admonition and hearty endorsement, as the grand fiction seduced one of them into the thought of yet further future lucrative business.

A final series of Polish utterances of reassurance above him led the new-found pals to crunch themselves away from Paul's grotesque concealment and when he felt that their voices were sufficiently distant, he dared to lift the hatchway once more. The light pierced his eyes, belying the passage of even so brief a time upon the sealed-off, darkened cellar steps. Lech and Aaron had disappeared from sight, presumably feasting their eyes on imagined opportunities of wealth-creation upon the North Wing.

He hurriedly extricated himself from the steps and hatchway and dashed towards the Cedar Tree. He rounded it so that he was out of sight of the house completely and then looked up, doffing his imaginary cap one last time to the greatness of his Tree God. He was vaguely aware that a *returning* Patrick from Cornwall might cause a mild degree of confusion should Lech be so impertinent as to enquire about an additional impending business opportunity. But he dismissed it readily: the fine, hardworking economic migrants of Poland would never understand the casual, almost charming, duplicity of the English in covertly assessing the likelihood of employment opportunities, only to deny that they ever existed and it would be a foolhardy employee to take umbrage at it.

And so Paul thrust his hands into his pockets and enacted the air of a casual visitor to the house. Any suspicious Polish man returning from the North Wing to his tanking even now could not but be little interested in the casual proclamation, if challenged, of a slightly bored and nonchalant Englishman, that he was on a chance visit to his friends the Palmers, and who would try again when they came back from their holiday in Cornwall.

Chapter Eleven

'So let me get this straight,' began Anne later that evening, 'I understand why you didn't bring Ellie back from London this evening as you were working from home. So you're taking the train into Victoria tomorrow morning where her mum will be waiting with her and then you bring her straight back here. Then she's staying over on Sunday night so that you both drive off to Dublin on Monday?'

'Yes, is that OK?' replied Paul a little nervously, painfully aware that they were not to have *their Sunday evening* alone together. For Anne, that period on Sunday between 8:30 p.m. when an exhausted Paul would stoically smile at her upon his return from his gruelling round trip to London and back, and 11:30 p.m., when all pretence that it was still the weekend was dashed altogether, was inviolable. They were three hours that nuanced recklessly between heaven and purgatory. Tea was then taken to bed and half a chapter of a book read in the vain hope of delaying the inevitable yet further. It was something between a sumptuous finale, helped enormously by the earlier several glasses of wine, and the realisation that there was to be yet one further week at least in her tedious, corporate existence before her dreams of creative liberation bore fruition. 'I'll...I'll make sure she's up to her bedroom relatively early, even though it'll technically be the school hols,' he offered lamely.

'No, no, it's fine darling, really it is. It's just that I wondered if you'd have time this weekend before you go away to investigate that damp patch in the kitchen, just above the cooker. It's now a slow drip. The other day a drop actually fell into the pasta. I know you said it's almost certainly a slow leak from the mains but it's not worth risking if it's from somewhere else is it?' She inserted a modicum of diplomacy, realising that Paul might feel aggrieved that his perennial list of *to dos* in the old house might be perceived as *nags*.

'Ah, sorry love. Hadn't realised it had progressed,' he said, suspicious that she was exaggerating in order to present the request as a *fait accompli*. 'OK, that'll be my one thing to do this weekend then,' half-relieved now that fixing a pipe of some sort was a mild victory really considering that there were far more challenging tasks ahead: the rotting dormer window in the top front room for example, or his vague promise to construct a lean-to against the outside wall facing the back garden. No, no the pipe, if that's what it was, was indeed a salient win. Something you banked without revealing to the other party quite how easy a task it was going to be.

'Thanks, *would* you darling. I don't like things to get out of hand you see. And what we cannot allow, at any cost, is for that to spread to the hessian wallpaper. I only painted it last month with that expensive wood emulsion.'

'Yeah, no. That's fine. Just so long as you're aware that whatever it is, it's coming from the head end of the bath, where that built-in box is; you know the one that Patrick said he made for a laundry basket, where you keep all those bottles for cleaning.'

'You mean where *we* keep. You know there's no law to say that a man cannot clean the bath now and again—'

'I do, I do—'

'Yeah, right,' she said in mock, comical retribution, a mutually accepted reference to the suspicion that Paul's cleaning of the bath would rarely involve the contents of the built-in box at all. 'Oh, before I forget, how was today?'

'Fine, fine. It never ceases to amaze me...'

'How much more you get done when you're working from home!' they both finished in perfect unison.

Paul was desperate to tell her in what way he probably could have done far more, if he had not been sneaking around other people's houses and even now he was greatly tempted to reveal all. But he sensed that this would not have been a very good idea. He still could not be sure why he felt this way. Certainly finalising probate documentation in Galway next week played a large part in the decision for some reason. The fact of the matter is that he had not yet found the time in the last few hours since his return to the house to piece everything together and he wasn't sure that Anne was in the mood for playing mysteries. So he said nothing and they got on with the rest of the evening like they did every Thursday after work, only they kept stopping whatever they were doing and giving a little yelp as either or both of them realised once more that, hell it was Friday after all. Ellie's absence kept fooling them and Paul would say how guilty that made him feel, that he was actually somehow *enjoying* a Friday night with just the two of them.

'The weekend started yesterday really, if you think about it, as tonight feels like the night before the weekend. So cheers!' one would say to the other as they raised their glasses, and no matter how irrational, they both believed it in some small way.

The next day Anne found herself driving to Canterbury for her Yoga class, alone. She had mixed feelings about this.

She had missed out on the last lunch, the one that Paul and Ellie had had without her, the one which when she had asked them about it, Ellie had said nothing and then subsequently marched off to her bedroom, leaving Paul simply to shrug his shoulders as if to say, *Since when did a thirteen-year-old need a reason to be in a huff?* And now she would miss out on another, on account of Paul insisting that he would be all slumbery after a Canterbury lunch and Sunday was cutting it a bit fine for the dripping water repair. But there again, if it meant Paul fixing the damn thing...

She definitely needed the Yoga class today more than ever. Something uneasy nibbled at her insides at the thought of Paul alone winding up the affairs of her parents in a distant solicitor's office in Galway. She was undeniably grateful, but a kind of melancholy descended upon her that for this, the finality in a sense of her parents' formal existence upon the Earth, she should be absent. What would her parents think of that, if they existed somewhere spiritually, ghostly inhabitants no doubt of the Heaven taught to her at school from the Bible, where they must surely now reside? Her father would approve she felt sure. Her husband Paul, the man of the house, stoically instigating his role as concluder of matters important. Her mother she was less sure about.

But she also felt somewhere a little between cowardly and guilty. Cowardly that she was running away from something, but guilty because she knew that without Paul and Ellie in the house, she would have perfect peace, the backdrop for all manner of ideas that were floating around inside her head. Perhaps if Paul did manage to fix the leak and tidy all his tools away this weekend, why she could soak in the bath in the evenings, the bathroom suffused with scented candles, listening to meditation music or even a Radio 4 play perhaps as she sipped Prosecco, creative ideas condensing in the sultry, perfumed fog around her. She pictured herself wandering down to the living room soon after and lazily transferring to her laptop her bold new designs of some sort: tastefully refurbished ethnic rugs, ethically sourced from India or deliciously irreverent business plans which guaranteed the buyer a stake in regenerating the area where the rugs were made. She loved Paul with all her heart and Ellie really had become an instant teenage daughter of sorts, but the house to herself for a few days? Now even her parents in Heaven would not chastise her for that, she concluded.

A sudden squall descended from nowhere as she entered the city's ring road and she flipped the wipers on to double-speed, amazed that the sun in front of her still shone with ferocity through purple clouds; spectra of a feast of colours, dancing on the rain drops and gladdening her heart that something so beautiful and contradictory at the same time in some way sanctioned her inner dichotomy. She laughed a solitary laugh out loud and felt almost as if she were entering a yogic field of transcendence a little earlier than she had planned.

'Fuck.'
'Da-ad.'
'Sorry my innocent teenage daughter. "Bollox" should have sufficed. I'll work on that for next time.'

His initial reverence for Patrick's old hinges which he had affixed all those decades ago to the horizontal lid on the cupboard at the end of the bath, had metamorphosed into a brutal fight to remove them at all costs. The proprietary anti-rust lubricant had, as usual, turned out to be a sort of ritual observance, a doomed precursor to the macho inevitability of having to remove things by force and the hammer he was using to drive the relatively small chisel into the hinges' screws had slipped and bore its full force upon his left thumb.

'Aaarghh,' he continued which led to Ellie uncharacteristically taking control of the incident. She ordered him to sit down on the small embroidered chair that loitered awkwardly in whichever corner of the bathroom it needed to be, to allow access to whatever it was that normal people needed to do in the opposite corner. Rifling through the cupboard above she retrieved a bottle of something that vaguely offered relief to minor abrasions and a medium-sized plaster. 'Thanks Ellie. Very kind,' he said, 'but I must crack on.'

'Just not your knuckles Dad.'

A few more deft taps on the chisel and the hinges were off. It was potentially an unnecessary step in the grand scheme of things but he liked simplicity and the idea of gaining further access into the alcove without a damned door getting in the way of things. Ellie removed herself onto the landing to let him figure it out; she did not want to admit that she was worried about him injuring himself further and so actuated her default position of nonchalant interest in her iPad whilst slumped on the floor outside. 'Call me if you need me Dad.'

Paul realised he would have an even greater access to the alcove if he removed the entire side bath panel which he did very easily, much to his satisfaction, wondering in the process how many times previous occupants of the house had done just the same thing, to gain access to their own plumbing conundra of the time. The first thing he noticed was that the gap from the front to the back of the alcove was shorter than the gap from the side of the bath to the back wall. 'Ah,' he muttered to himself, 'mystery solved. He's somehow boxed in the pipes, just as I thought. Must be coming from in there.'

Availing himself with what he anticipated would be the necessary tools, Paul lay on his front and adjusted the position of his lamp, running its cable along the landing to the study. He pulled himself into the gap, as it now was, and gingerly tapped away at the wooden box at the back, fearful that if he did this too manfully he might pierce one of the hidden pipes. The front appeared to be a half inch-thick rectangle of soft-ish wood and he managed to lever a flat-head screwdriver into it and found that by gently moving it from side to side, the panel began to give way. A final tug and he was in. This time he used his phone's in-built torch and stared inside for a while. He was disappointed and confused. He had expected to discover an array of 15mm and 20mm pipes and joints, the epicentre of the aquatic highways which serviced blissfully ignorant visitors to the bathroom. Instead he found emptiness and was immediately struck with a sense of failure; that he could not now announce to a spiritually relaxed and returning Anne that the man of the house had delivered the modern-day equivalent of a skinned rabbit to the cooking pot.

He decided to mitigate his disappointment by tracing where the hell the surrounding pipes did all venture and conjoin, realising that their paths disappointingly but rather obviously simply diverted around this end-section by bearing down into the floorboards at a right angle, to continue their silent conduits, hidden inconspicuously between floor levels, to emerge in other obscure locations within the house. He sighed as he reversed himself backwards into the main body of the bathroom, sitting upright to contemplate his next options. His disappointment must have been palpable as a cheery Ellie rounded her face into the doorway. 'Cold beer Dad?'

'Oh darling, would you? It's thirsty work in there and I need time to think.'

As the dutiful Ellie pranced down the staircase to play the part of perfect daughter, Paul felt the need to glance in the gap again. Something didn't add up but he could not be sure what it was. So much so that he decided to postpone the guilty pleasure of a cold mouthful of beer, so richly undeserved in the wake of his impending failure, and ease himself into the gap on his front again. He decided to tap the rear wall of the box-within-a-box, convinced that the back wooden panel could be nothing more than a veneer to the unsightly brick of the partition wall to the two adjacent properties. But instead of the staccato tap of hammerhead against such a vast density of hidden masonry, he was amazed to hear the dull tones of reverberation that implied not a veneer upon brick, but the acoustics of a thin wooden panel across yet more space.

But how could that be?

'Da-ad. Here you go.'

'Oh OK Ellie, that's brill. Just pop it on the side there for now. Just. Have. To. Work. This. Out. Actually darling. Could you push the drill over to me? Oh and make sure it's plugged in, ta.'

Ellie duly slid the Black & Decker through to him and he was pleased to notice that a larger-sized wooden bit was already in place. With not a small degree of vexation, Paul gently pressed the bit up against the centre of the panel or dividing wall or whatever it was, and pressed the button. The wood was clearly hard but he was through in less than five seconds, his momentum driving the whirring bit into a void of some kind with no resistance at all. He shone his phone light into the hole but found it hard to discern anything which might explain what was happening; *had* happened in the past. His phone's torch seemed simply to shine back in his face somehow and he realised that he would need to make a few more exploratory holes to discover anything meaningful. This worried him as he felt that he was somehow encroaching on a space which in some vague way he supposed to be a mutual delineation of boundary between the houses. The word *trespass* reared itself once more into his thoughts, but he shrugged it off with a half-smile. A drill-bit is not a man, he mused whimsically. Several holes later, fashioned in the pattern of a rough circle, he decided to throw any lingering caution to the wind. After his loyal teenage assistant passed him his trusted jigsaw cutter, he quickly sliced through the wood joining the holes and found himself peering into the void, for there was no mistaking it now, between 71 and 73 High Street, Lounsley. He introduced the glow from his phone once more and a flash of light reflected back, blinding him for a few seconds. 'What the fuck.'

'Dad, what is it? You're scaring me now. Come out please. Your beer is getting warm.' If that didn't retrieve him from his strange little expedition, she thought, nothing would.

'Coming Ellie. Just let me. One sec.' Fearful of what he had discovered himself, rather like when he was waking from a nightmare and had to find out the identity of the terrible face shrouded in dankly dangling hair in front of him before it was too late, he ripped aside the entire dividing panel. He decided to reach for the mains lamp so he could illuminate everything. Perhaps he'd seen too many horror films in which the wily director would tease the audience by ambiguously hinting at what lay before them, with deliberately dappled and suffused studio lighting bearing down upon some ghastly wizened half-face of a lost and lonely half-child.

The lamp shone within and revealed to him some sort of curved metallic surface. Assured that there was no half-child's half-face within, he emboldened himself sufficiently to pull himself forwards and glance around this new-found space. He swivelled his head upwards to see what was above him but felt a dull clanging pain.

'Fu—. So-rrr-yyy Ellie. Great big bollocksters.'

'What Dad? What's going on in there?' an increasingly fretful Ellie ventured.

He reached his right hand upwards to rub the top of his head and *clang!* This time there was no mistaking it. There was some metal barrier above him. Increasingly frustrated with the developing proceedings, Paul rotated his torso 180 degrees and looked upwards. The metal curvature above him at least continued the theme at the back of the space.

'It's...umm...blimey...dunno really Ellie. You fancy taking a look yourself? I'm sort of a bit too big really to *map* the situation if you know what I mean.'

Paul stood once more in the bathroom proper and greedily gulped half his beer down in one go, relishing its still icy imprint on the back of his throat. No sooner had he placed his glass back down than Ellie had scuttled agilely into the space that he had just vacated. She was just showing off now.

'Easy now Ellie, one step at a time darling.' He suddenly felt anxious that he was allowing her to venture into the unknown.

'It's OK Dad, this is easy,' she replied clearly relishing her new-found value.

'Can you stretch your neck inside? Here, push the lamp up close if that helps.'

'No need Dad. I have my phone on me,' she retorted, 'and I can do more than that. Look, I'm in!'

Paul knelt down and peered in, expecting to do so over Ellie's outstretched legs, but there weren't any. Amazingly, he thought, she had squeezed her whole torso into the smaller space. 'What is it? Is that metal curving all round the back and the top? What can you see? Over!' he ended, fleetingly realising that his oblique reference to a walkie-talkie might be lost on a teenager.

'Yes it's all metal, like curved, sort of thing, but there's like a lip of some kind.'

'Right. I mean, can you tell if that's it? That's definitely the back of the whole thing, right?'

'Well I think so.'

'So look, push your back up against it very gradually and see if it gives a little.'

'Ah, OK, just wait a minute. I just need to stretch my legs like that and push...'

And then she was gone.

Paul blinked blankly at what was before him for a few seconds. Nothing. It took his faculties another two seconds to make sense of what he was, or rather was not, looking at.

And then terror gripped him.

'Ellie!!!' he roared. 'Ellie!!!'

He dived into the gap again as far as he could place himself, his feet desperately scrabbling against the tiles on the bathroom floor, forcing the soles of his shoes to make some sort of purchase so that he could gain a half a second, a second, anything, to propel himself into this emerging nightmare. He scraped his arms against the inner frames, forcing layers of skin away in the process, but he didn't feel a thing. He banged his head once more on the roof of the inner void and fleetingly observed that it was no longer metal, as before, but a hard wood of some sort.

'Ellie!!!'

He forced himself, as she had done just seconds before, into the rear wall of metal, his sides barely clearing the frame behind him above his waist. But the slight concave curve that he had noticed previously was now reversed and it bowed out convexly towards him.

Think, Paul, think, he said to himself frantically, experiencing the raw visceral fear of the parent that has lost their young child in a crowded shopping mall. As rationality creeps in, like the Big Bang plus one thousandth of a second, the sense of helplessness dawns too. Monstrous thoughts instead banged at the sides of his throbbing head. *She was always such a cheerful girl*, her father reported at the inquest.

'Ellieeee!!!'

Silence.

And then, a muffled retort.

'Dad?'

'Ellie, Ellie, is that you? Tell me, are you OK?'

'Yes, I think so...I sort of...' but he could not make out the rest of her sentence.

He tried to suppress a kind of primordial joy that was enticing him back to something like normality. And yet his daughter was still not there before him.

'Ellie, repeat that again. Do you know where you are?'

An unrecognisable sentence began before she cut in with words that he could make sense of. '...'nother room.' Further distortion. '...room...just like ours...' She didn't *seem* distressed, wherever she was. '...just a second Dad...be long...'

'Ellie, if you are next door, please just find an adult. OK?' He immediately regretted the remark. What if the adult in question had long since despatched Mrs Carmichael? He could not recall when he had last seen her. Was the fiend now waiting for his prey to run innocently towards him? He involuntarily found himself pushing backwards as before, with the sole aim of rushing next door and banging, demanding his way in. Or should he go straight to the back and if there were no answer, stave in the rear door window glass? If a few days ago he was willing to solve a mystery by risking a prosecution for trespass, then a stretch for *Breaking and Entering* would be as nothing to hold his daughter in his arms once more.

In light of the fear that must have gripped you Mr Fewings in pursuit of a felicitous reunion with your daughter, the court has decided that it be appropriate to suspend the sentence for two years herewith.

This time the pain on the back of his arms as he squeezed himself backwards was palpable, as was the faint odour of freshly drawn blood. His body had presumably decided that his stay of pain in order to survive, his allotted fleeting period of grace, was over. He was sitting upright again, the various recent contortions of his body making his head swirl, faint with giddiness. Not now. No no. Fight it, he pleaded with himself.

Just at that moment Graham the cat appeared in the doorway. 'Graham, not now, out!' he shouted at the hapless feline. But Graham refused the command and instead did that stalking thing that cats do, as if instinctively detecting the movement of a small vole inside a bush. The only time that any of the cats stood up to him with the threat of do-or-die violence, it seemed, was when he tried to remove a still half-alive bird or mouse from their fangs. In those situations, he seemed no longer to appear to them to be five hundred-times their size, rather a lumbering, ruminating herbivore, his jugular now for the taking. He wondered in the moment if this was the right time to call Graham out on who had the killing rights. And yet some instinct in him elected to do nothing, in this most desperate minute of his life, for surely that was still what it was, a minute frozen in time as if a never-ending eternity. Mesmerised and curiously unable to move, Paul watched as Graham, oblivious it seemed even to his catatonic presence, issued a low growl.

And then everything seemed to happen at once.

The bright, late morning sun, ponderously clawing its way towards a saphirey southern sky, all fizzing with miniscule spots of wispy cloud, suddenly broke free from a branch of the sycamore tree that framed the garden's eastern perimeter and a ray of razor-phosphorescence speared itself like a dagger into the heart of the boxed-in arena of the unfolding drama. As if a cue for its impending *tour de force*, Graham hurled himself at the apex of this phalanx of tightly knitted strings of light where it struck the rear wall within the void, emitting a battle-cry against some hidden invader.

'...that you...Graham?' the half sentence of concealed daughter snapping him out of his trance. 'Ah well, got, ...go...'

Paul closed his eyes, mustering the will to act, to strain his molecules into a being, a being of supreme and purposeful action.

He opened his eyes in order to flee to some muster station of prosecution.

But stopped himself.

For Ellie was there again.

'Silly Graham,' said Ellie. But Graham had already left, his grand stage-entrance now a footnote in theatrical history, the staccato thrum of his paws upon the stair carpet a diminishing fade-out on the prematurely closing curtain of his grand cameo, so deftly unannounced to a still-bemused audience.

Paul had a thousand questions right now. A wish to write a complex thousand-page book on the science of disappearance in walls between houses and the art of reappearance. A thousand blogs on the mystery and strangeness of life. A thousand self-flagellations, to know of the reappearing corpulence of it. A thousand incantations to dead relatives everywhere to know of the clarity of their purpose to him. A thousand refusals to drink, to have sex, to dare to take pleasure in anything that might even momentarily rid him of the sureness of this daughter before him. Leaning into the void once more, without the slightest shadow of emotion upon his sociopathic face, he calmly gripped his daughter's wrist with the inviolable vice of his right hand. He knew there was pain, this very second, a result of the prang in The Old Vicarage cellar and he laughed at its futility of purpose now, its uselessness to pretend that it could alter the path of human existence.

'Dad, that hurts,' Ellie squealed, but to no avail as Paul did not let the screws of the vice unwind by the tiniest fraction. Until finally she was brought unto him standing, the truculent and pressingly luxuriant strands of her teenage hair upon his lowered cheek as he breathed all of her in: an act so long denied him by the awkward assertiveness of the march of time beyond the fragile bond between helpless, gurgling infant babe and all-encompassing protection of the blissfully naive infant father.

'Da-a-ad,' her tone less urgent now; the pure and beautiful currents of the perfectly annoyed teenager swirling around this presence before her, this necessary but pitiful basilisk of *Being* that was her father.

And Paul somehow knew that this was the last time that it could be thus, probably ever. Perhaps it would return in some other form, some other Ellie-yet-to-come. The one bearing him a grandchild upon the lonely cottage garden path in a distant shire. *Sorry, stuck in traffic, Dad. Izzie, say hi Grandad! Garden's looking great. Where's Anne?* But never like this. Not the child before him, her youthful spirit departing his life for good. And as he held her to him closely this last time, he rejoiced at having known her and breathed the essence of all that she was into him. A sort of goodbye at the train station, a carriage taking her away to a new life without him. There would still be lunches in Canterbury and trips to Dublin, he knew all that. But never would he feel that they were as one again, she part of him. And instead of the fear of her loss, so minusculely recently upon him, he felt the strength of the purpose and very meaning of life.

He looked leftwards and out of the window. Graham jumped up onto the garden wall and as he brushed himself against one of the sycamore branches, the great beam of light followed him and rent itself upon it, scattering soft fronds of ochred light onto sleepy nearby flora. Like the moment you are blinded by the setting sun, low ahead as you walk the street and it darts behind a cloud: all is suddenly clear before you; the underlying morphology of objects stationary and moving, colours all alive beneath the fleeting eclipse. Paul felt that clarity now. Not the thing of it, but the sense of it. The sense that a clarity was descending upon him. It lapped at his viscera and gently stroked the cortices of his brain wherein was previously caged his dormant intuition. It was on the way, this clarity, whatever it was and as he temporarily allowed it to recede, he gently released his grip on his daughter. She glanced at him with curiosity all aglow in her eyes for the briefest of moments and then she was away, through the bathroom door and into the house, their house.

Chapter Twelve

Later that evening Paul sat with Anne in the garden summerhouse, a hastily erected construction of late last autumn, as the embers of its dying warmth fought vainly against the coming winter frosts. They'd just managed to tack in the roofing felt and hang a ridiculously spurious woodpecker-themed bell over its front door, before a great storm erupted and they ran inside the main house for good. No-one could remember actually revisiting it at all since that day and now Paul felt school-boyishly proud to be enjoying the delayed fruits of their long-forgotten toil.

'So, well done you for fixing the damp,' said Anne, 'An extra treat for good boys,' and giggling she refilled their wine glasses from the bottle.

'Ah it was nothing,' his perceived modesty belying the fact that he was, unknown to Anne, telling the truth. After Graham and Ellie had left him alone in the bathroom earlier that day, he thought things through as rationally as he could, as he reconstructed the various panels around the void. Any temptation to investigate the physics of what actually had caused Ellie to disappear were subjugated below a burgeoning awareness that a cover-up, in both senses, was necessary for a purpose that he had yet to fathom. He felt it had something to do with the clarity that had licked within him so fleetingly after Ellie had strolled away from him. Something unknowingly profound warned him that the strange event should stay for now between Ellie and him. And Graham of course, he added as a technicality to himself, Anne's book *How to speak Cat* worryingly kept from the *throw-away* pile they'd taken to the farm shop a fortnight ago. As he nailed the remaining panel pins into the outside of the inner of the two dividing walls, he'd felt a drop of water on the back of his left hand and, looking up, saw that a half-hidden rusty old isolation valve was the source of it. He remembered that he had a pair of miniature mole-grips in the side pocket of his portable tool kit, which looked like they had fallen out of a deluxe Christmas cracker. But to his surprise and relief they not only just managed to squeeze behind the rear woodwork that framed the back of the bath, but with every ounce of effort from his fatigued and throbbing wrists, he sensed the tiniest of turns to the clockwise. He waited a minute, two minutes and finally, content that he had miraculously fixed the damn thing, quickly rebuilt the rest of the wood panelling.

'And modest to boot,' she replied.

'I'll miss you Anne.'

'And I'll miss you very much too my darling.'

'No, I'll *really* miss you,' and he threw his arms around her waist as he dramatically fell to his knees before her.

'Hmm, I think I know where this is going. Hold on, where's Ellie?'

'She just ran a bath. You know what that means right? Two hours at least.'

Smiling, she held his head in her hands and gently pressed his face into her skirt. And she thought to herself that she probably shouldn't tell him quite so often how much she would really miss him too. She closed her eyes and they were now secret lovers in a beach hut somewhere on an unknown, hidden island northwards off the shores of Kent, as waves, so many waves on a spring tide, lapped at their nestling sides.

*   *   *

On Monday morning, Paul was shaken awake by a familiar perfumed Anne, leaving the house for her morning commute. 'Yes, yes, Lech...I know...I can explain...'

'What are you talking about, you daft bugger,' she laughed, amused at his waking, mangled memory of some fast-disappearing dream. 'Well at least Lech is a man. I hope that's a good thing, right?'

It took him a few seconds to leap between the parallel universes of night and day and to realise that he was talking nonsense, only rather dangerous nonsense. In his dream he was in the metal pannier between adjacent dwellings and tumbling into the other house. Only in the dream it wasn't next door's house but the cellar of The Old Vicarage and he landed on a box of old photos and Lech was staring down at him menacingly.

So you followed the arrows?

Paul tried to answer but words would not come.

You followed the arrows and look where it's got you. There'll be consequences, you know that don't you?

He forced the waking words out of his mouth with his very greatest effort, just as Aaron appeared behind Lech. But it was and then wasn't Aaron. It became a boyish, blurry face that petrified him as with fixed staring eyes it swung its axe in an arc towards the Polish man's neck.

And then Anne was there: the characters in the dream had vanished and the cellar was his bedroom. He'd forced the words out so vociferously that they'd tumbled, ragged and feeble, into the adjacent cosmos of his woken self.

'What?' he said to Anne, yawning over-dramatically. 'Who the hell is Lech indeed? Why do some dreams just vanish completely? Annoying!'

'Darling, have a *lovely* time in Ireland. I love you. I'll miss you. Good luck in Galway too. I am so grateful to you, my beautiful man.'

'I love you too...'

Then she kissed him gently on his lips, arose upwards from the bed, smiling lovingly at him as she backed herself towards the door and disappeared through it.

'So tell me in your own words: what *exactly* happened on Saturday?' asked Paul glancing only briefly to his left to address Ellie as the car lurched onto the M2 heading west. Several times on Sunday he had nearly given in to the temptation of interrogating her, against his better judgement, but Anne was clearly intent on remaining home-bound for the remainder of the weekend. He'd toyed with the idea of contriving a spurious trip to the supermarket with Ellie alone, as was often the case, but it felt too furtive; the very idea of bringing the car to rest in a distant corner of the car park to collude in verifying all the details, somehow conspiratorial. He'd managed to survive this hugely unnatural procrastination of imminent *reportage* by reassuring himself that four days with Ellie, with mostly just the two of them, would afford a delightfully long period of reflection. An interlude of contemplation within which he could attempt fully to understand all the implications of her brief *inter muros* disappearance. 'And Ellie?'

'Yes?'

'For once I'm going to allow you to utilise as many *likes* in a sentence as you need to. I *swear* I will not complain one iota if you *litter* each sentence with them. My lips are sealed. It's very important that you go with the flow here. If your brain is *like, literally, like* buying time to find the right descriptive narrative, then I will be very happy.'

'Rude.'

'Not intended, apologies. Proceed, please.'

'Well...it's hard to explain...the metal thing. The only way I can describe it is, like, you know when we were recycling those books in the farm shop car park?'

'Go on.'

'It kind of felt like I was the books and I was suddenly swung into the bin. Only it wasn't a bin. It was, like, this dark space. I put my phone on. I mean I pressed the light. I heard your voice, but I was too scared to shout back to you so I thought I'd better work out where I was. The space was about the same size as the other space. Well it *was* the other space but on the other side. It didn't sink in at first but then I remembered you saying that the house next door, the one on the right as you look from the road, Mrs Carmichael's house, was a mirror image. And then I realised. I *was* in the same space but the mirror-image version next door. We're doing it in maths. Symmetry. I was, like, in the symmetry you see. And then I wasn't scared because, I thought, it was only Mrs Carmichael's house and I know she's a bit scary, but I didn't think I was in any danger. I didn't realise that the metal compartment could swing back the other way at that point, I just thought, like, I have to get out of here. Get downstairs or something.'

'Pannier.'

'What?'

'The swing door. It's like some sort of pannier. A metal swinging basket. You're right Ellie - just like the one outside of the farm shop. When you went through, you couldn't have realised that, I mean you're not a book are you? The books can't decide to come back the other way into the farm shop—'

'That's what I'm saying Dad. I can see what it was, I mean *is* now, but I didn't figure it out when I was on the other side. So I pushed the panel on the other side of the er, other side…and it flung out and…I was looking at a cat. Mrs Carmichael's cat, Bobby; the one she thinks is a boy but we think it's a girl because of the neat and lady-like way she sits on the wall. It was sitting in the bathroom, *her* bathroom. She started purring, she loves me you see, and I crawled out and she sat on my lap.'

Ellie paused. Only to Paul's dismay it wasn't a pause at all but she appeared to have ended her narrative, for as he glanced left again she was looking out of her window, the magenta early-morning sun astern, striking her wistfully smiling features as it reflected from the outside mirror beside her.

'*And?*'

'Oh and well, nothing. I was stroking her and she was dribbling on my lap and purring and then I was just about to, I swear Dad I was, just about to let you know that I was OK, as you did sound a bit stressed.'

'Stressed. Ha ha. Yes stressed. How very perceptive of you.'

'When I heard Graham hissing on your side and I suddenly felt, like, *really* bad, as he won't let Bobby come into our house to play and here I was in Bobby's house, like, *playing with her?* So I said goodbye to the cat, I mean Bobby, and pulled the panel back towards me and it kind of clicked in place and I went to tap on the metal to let Graham know that I still loved him very much and he was still hissing, so I pressed my ear to the metal and went to say that, when suddenly I *swung* like literally back on to your side. And then you like went all *weird* on me. Come on Dad, you were like really weird and hugging—'

'But,' he cut her off, 'what else, what else?'

'Er…what do you mean?' her faux thirteen-year-old mock exasperation redolent upon her face.

'Oh I don't know. Something. Anything. Right, right, I mean, what did the bathroom look like?'

'Oh I see…um...well about the same size as ours I suppose. But like an old person's house. You know, like *carpety*. I think there were some old bottles of stuff, like old shampoo and jars of stuff, but, like, sort of dusty. Sorry, it was all over quite quickly. And I really just wanted Bobby to know that it was me and I was her friend, which I am, I mean she knows I am.'

Paul thought for a moment. A small bird-of-prey hovered above the field of rape beside him as a tractor flung sprays of some liquid all about it in the distance, liquescent drops of some frighteningly efficient growth hormone, all shimmering with lonely incandescence as they danced upon yellow flowers, enjoying their swansong of purpose before being crushed into cheap oil.

'Tell me Ellie. When you say the panel on the other side *clicked* into place, did you get the sense that it would just have been like it was before you kicked it out? I mean on our side it was all panel pins. It's difficult to reverse them into the same holes. You know what I mean?'

'Yes Da-ad. I know what you mean. This was like when you click something back to what it was.'

'Like clips?'

'Yes, like clips. Like that clip on the lawnmower handle, the one that keeps the cable tidy.'

'Yes, like clips, I see.' Only he didn't really see. Didn't see anything at all really rather than a foreboding sense that anyone undertaking any kind of work in next door's bathroom could easily have prised the panel off without a second thought, only to be confronted by a very odd metallic gateway to another world completely. But what of Mrs Carmichael? It seemed improbable that this admittedly rather eccentric, but otherwise harmless old lady, could have any knowledge of what lurked in the hidden recesses of walls behind bath panels. And was she not a lady of ancient disposition and frugality he supposed, who would balk at the idea of opportunistic plumbers mucking around with her pipes? Had she even lived there when the strange hidden gateway was constructed? Was the provenance yet older still and entirely innocent?

Her front ground-floor window, ostentatiously and marvellously convex in construction, spoke conclusively of it once having been a shop of some kind. Though it was not featured in any of the local library archives, either by reference or photographically, it *had been* a shop. Paul's house was demonstrably not, its front windows being the original Georgian frames: beautiful but indicative of an aspirational middle-class family in the early reign of George IV. But, windows apart, the two properties *were* mirror-images of each other, with their ruddy brickwork and identical parapets shielding the world from the hidden roomy living-lofts behind them. What was to say that the pannier that they had discovered was not the old-forgotten remnant of both a way of living and a conducting of commerce long-forgotten?

Anne often fantasised that their house had been the abode of the local doctor. What could have been more convenient than the shop next door being his dedicated pharmacy and part of the ground floor of his house, his surgery? It would certainly explain the old photos that the Palmers had shown them: the unnecessarily roomy corridor that allowed the ground floor to have separate access doors to each of its functioning chambers. He imagined the satisfaction of the doctor as he twitched a wire that led through a small hole between the two houses by his surgery desk. All sorts of different codes; Morse Code why not? And then the reassuring thud as a small tube of Godfrey's Improved

Harmless Arsenic Wafers or a bottle of J. Collis Browne's Laudanum (Opium, Alcohol and Stomach Bitters – Keystone to Health!) gently rolled from the pharmacy into his office, an ingeniously horizontal dumb-waiter for the aspirational but cautious physician. What a glorious theory, he thought, picturing himself guiding a Channel 5 film crew up the stairs and excitedly explaining to camera how delighted he was that they had uncovered one of only three surviving examples in Britain of the short-lived late-Georgian phenomenon of *tied surgeries*. Young, aspirational General Practitioners, who cared passionately about the working communities of which they were a part and part-funded by the profits of the dominant emerging pharmaceutical companies. Profits from the sale of stock so magnificently and ingeniously, yet wonderfully discreetly, transferred via the patent-established, swing-door-industrious and entrepreneurial wile of a London inventor.

Morgan & Slattery's Patent inter-connecting stock communications device for the discerning physician's discreet management of everyday pharmaceutical necessities.

Now that would be something to tell Anne when I'm back, he thought.

And something else inside him, something unsettling, wanted him to say it more than anything.

'Yes, hi darling, no sorry, I didn't catch that...driving ...here's Ellie.' Paul handed his mobile from the hands-free stand to his half-snoozing passenger. 'Sorry Ells, didn't know you were asleep, can you talk to Anne?'

'I was *not* asleep,' Ellie retorted, for some reason unfathomable to Paul, an accusation seemingly as severe as insinuating that she fancied boys.

'OK, OK, so-rry.'

'Anne, yeah, hi,' continued Ellie, 'No, no, I've been staring out the window for ages. Not sleepy at all actually.' She stared sideways at her dad with annoyance in her eyes. 'We ah yeah, we're nearly in Wales. Right Dad?'

'In Wales darling,' Paul said brightly and diplomatically, daring not once more to imply that she had slept like a child as they crossed the River Severn.

'Yeah, sorry that's what I meant, in Wales now. Oh, OK, will do. Yeah love, bye, bye, bye…' her familiar telecommunicated sign-off to either Anne or Paul, the correct admixture, Ellie thought, of suitable respect and glorious indifference. 'She says to call her once we're on the ferry.' She yawned which made Paul do so too and he now regretted not having broken the journey - he kept meaning to but he was thinking too much about everything and kept ignoring the slip roads. They might as well arrive at the port a bit early and have a lovely *very* late, beery lunch in the last proper inn available, before they reached that curious margin of mass commercial travel, where everything was formulaic, transitory, and full of gormless fellow travellers with their boring agendas. Then they would sleep throughout the crossing and when they awoke, the cerulean tides awash the lowering fires of sun would lead them softly but relentlessly unto the port of old Dublin town, the beginning of the end of the Earth, and its Emerald Isle.

Chapter Thirteen

It was late when they arrived at the Queen's Hotel in central Dublin; by the time they had showered and Paul nervously surveyed the minibar for signs of extortionate prices, it was clear that it was too late to dine formally. This secretly rather pleased Ellie, as there seemed at that moment nothing more delightful than an exorbitant room menu, a sort of posh take-away to be delivered by a smiling, smart and suited young man, a far cry from the crash-helmeted delivery riders that, silent and expressionless, brought their Indian takeaways occasionally to the house in Lounsley.

'What, can I, like, order *anything* from this?' asked Ellie.

Paul was torn between showing off his grand status in life by declaring in the affirmative and weighing up the wisdom of putting in additional hotel expenses, clearly for more than one person in the room. Plagued by the remotest possibility that the company might consider that he was doubling-up the business trip to entertain some young Irish harridan, he found an uncharacteristic surge of assertion well up inside himself. 'Yes you damn well can Ellie. I have absolutely bloody well brought my daughter with me on a business trip to Dublin. Because...erm...that's what real people do. Good people that close big deals and love their family first. Order away!'

So she did. She had no idea what a club sandwich was but it sounded vaguely worldly, anachronistic even, in that nostalgic way that made her yearn to be in one of those old seventies films that Paul and Anne would occasionally watch on bank holidays. The ones in which besuited, handsome, confident men would tap a cigarette on the restaurant table, before bequeathing some knowing adult look upon the glamorous lady across from them. That's why the couple on the front-cover of the old canal guide, the one Dad rescued from the book throwaway box, were smiling. It went with the cigarette that came after the bottle of wine that they had shared *with their club sandwich*.

And she made sure that her club sandwich came with a side plate of a *delicate assortment of plain and sweet, thinly sliced, crushed and sautéed potatoes*.

They drank and ate in silence whilst Paul searched the TV stations. They settled for an old British film with actors speaking in ancient, clipped English accents with lots of knowing looks between them and, she wondered, with the frisson of an off-camera shared club sandwich nestling somewhere between them.

She very slowly awoke the next morning in a different bed in a different room. Her dad's phone-alarm was beeping and she couldn't figure out why he had transferred to the other room as well. But as she surveyed the room and saw the gentle dance of yellow dots on the wall beside her, she recognised them as the pattern of the curtains in the first hotel room; the sun was pouring in through them, thick and luxurious though they were. It *was* the first hotel room and she was no longer lying on her front on the main bed next to her dad. She'd fallen asleep before the film had even got to the inevitable car chase and her dad must have carried her like a sleeping babe over to the single bed on the very far side of the room. Suddenly embarrassed, she checked to see what she was wearing and was relieved to find that they were the very same clothes she had climbed into after her shower last night; she momentarily forgot her role of general indignation and defiance in life and, still dreamy, didn't seem to mind one bit that her dad still thought of her as a child.

The thought was, she realised slowly, doomed to an ephemeral state of existence and she rather reluctantly brought her main stage role in life back to the fore. 'Aarrgghh...Daa-aa-ad.'

'*You* have nothing to *aargghh* about my darling daughter, as *you* can go back to sleep. Enjoy your childhood...I mean teenage years and do procrastinate the inevitability of having to have *meetings* with people you don't care for, about subjects that you have no real passion about, so that the people you love can order room service in posh hotels.'

She had no idea what he was talking about but she sensed a levity in his railing and, having finally promoted her brain into the new day, thought that nothing could be more delicious than sinking back into the old ancient morning again with dancing yellow dots gate-crashing her previous dreams, whatever they had been. Something possibly involving, she blushed, the young man who had brought them room service. In the dream he knowingly tapped a cigarette on the table beside her as he winked and gently pressed the ace of clubs into her flickering palm.

'But before you do, please listen Ellie.'

God no, he had *lecture* written all over his face and voice, she thought.

'I'll be gone most of the day. Might be back for lunch, but there again I might not be. All depends on the client. I *order* you just completely to have fun, relax, use any of the hotel facilities you like, right? That's your key card on the side. So that's the pool, the spa, the gym. Order whatever you like: as many club sandwiches as you like, go wherever you like, but...' he paused for dramatic effect, 'under no circumstances, other than imminent death by fire or terrorist incursion—'

'Da-ad.'

'Must you ever, ever leave this hotel. Do. You. Un. Der. Stand?'

She pulled the very best *whatever* face she could muster, but realising that what was on offer was spectacularly, quite possibly, the backdrop to the best day of her life, ever, she cut her dramatic-rebellious-indignation mode from a hyper *ten* to a pliant *one*. Without the slightest loss of teenage face, she marvelled at her, on any other occasion, pathetic and subserviently fawning reply: 'Oh yes Daddy, I can manage all of that!'

'Good girl. I love you. Have fun. See you later.'

She still managed to smile sweetly as he kissed her forehead, gathered up his man-bag, ruffled his hair one last time in the hallway mirror, barked a final farewell, and confidently closed the door behind him.

Ellie's day ahead just *might* have been her best day, ever, but something lurked menacingly at the very edge of her thoughts. She checked the time on her phone, all the better to gauge the glorious trade-off between further time curled up in bed and the awaiting decadence of life alone in a top hotel *without the slightest burden of adult supervision*. And that's when she saw it, the worst thing, ever, in her life. The reminder on the front screen of her phone.

Remember to do one of your homeworks today.

She'd plain forgotten that the school was trialling a new summer holiday homework initiative. Because so many parents had complained at the beginning of the school year about pupils being bogged-down with academia for the six weeks that they should be forgetting about school altogether, the PTA had brokered a deal whereby far less homework was set, on the condition that it should be completed during the first week. The teachers had pushed for this so they could assess the darn things and get on with their own holidays without having a plethora of marking to undertake when the new school-year arrived.

It was cruel beyond belief.

It was like the dream with the liquid chocolate lake and the new-born baby ducklings all around her floating body, and waking up to find herself on her back in her bed in Hammersmith, the chirping of the chicks her morning alarm and the dawning of the truth of the school-day to come. She now prayed, more than anything in her life, that things would not go *too* smoothly for Dad and his boring but important meetings. And whoever these important people were, they would make him sweat and drive a hard bargain.

I think we should all sleep on that. Reconvene in the morning and see if we can't still find a mutually-agreeable solution.

Just one extra day in Ireland, oh please everyone. You can manage that, surely you can, all of you fine people? Just one day so that my reminder can be delayed by twenty-four hours. I would actually consider dropping into a lower stream, just for that. And Dad, I love you very much, I know that sounds strange, and to me very much so, but do you know what, it's true, oh yes so very surely. You see, I want you to be a very successful, lovely Daddy, but you have been on the face of this planet quite a while haven't you, like, nearly half a century, and do you know what, all I'm asking is please to delay your inevitable brilliance as my greatest Daddy in the world and, basically, just, all I ask, is *let us stay an extra day*.

So she made a plan. She couldn't possibly know until Dad came back, worst case scenario, this evening, just how well or badly the big meeting had gone. Early signs would be evident. Cursing, prolific use of the F-word, mitigated with a yet-greater frequency of apology, reaching for one of the larger bottles in the mini-bar without recourse to checking the cost and the associated shaking of his head. Yes there would be early indications alright and she would even dare to seek advantage, surreptitiously, innocently, teenage-savvy. *Play it cool Dad. Let them sweat. You know like that old actor in the film the other day. The one who whenever he's in a movie you go all funny and start saying 'You lookin' at me?'*

The thought gave her the succour to start one of her homeworks anyway. If she worked really hard she could get it done before lunchtime and then, the thought was overwhelming, she could sit at a table in the restaurant all on her own and look important, a touch of make-up, her short black dress, without Dad there to scrutinise her face disapprovingly, to all the world a genius teenage Start-Up geek, with a touch of glamour, still struggling to cope with her brilliance at such a young age. Or if that proved too daunting and she lost her nerve, more room service. *Oh just over there if you don't mind.* Dad had left a small bowl of one-Euro coins by the room's phone and she would distractedly, nonchalantly hand one, no *two* over to the smart young man, her eyes on the bogus magazine before her, for any eye contact with him would immediately give her away for the sham that she was, her blood rushing inevitably to her innocent cheeks.

No time for breakfast. The mini-bar had small bags of dainty snacks and salubrious bottles of soft drinks of some kind. The sparkling water alone looked like it would go well with a club sandwich. No, this was breakfast; she would get her head down and then she could tick a homework off. The afternoon would be hers. *But could you imagine a whole day like that,* she wondered; and she prayed that Dad would still fuck things up, just a very tiny, tiny bit.

* * *

When Paul came back that evening she was disheartened to discover that his day had '…gone very well indeed all considered.

'So much so my little flowerpot, that I think tomorrow all I really need to concentrate on is taking the Riverview folk …um…Jim and Sarah, they are the important people I have to do the deal with…out to lunch and then go in for an internal sort of wind-up meeting and then, basically I think we're done.'

Ellie said nothing and forced an unimpressive smile from her crestfallen face.

'Thought actually sweetheart I could take *you* into the office for that last meeting, if you don't mind sitting around and then I could show you off to everyone. That would be amazing.'

This was not even bad. This was a heinous infringement of her human rights.

'But Dad…that would be cool but you cannot believe how much homework I have.' She had to think quickly. 'As it is I'm going to have to do a good hour tonight before we go down to dinner. What time is dinner anyway?'

'Oh, whenever you like. Remember. Hotel. No rules really.'

'Oh OK, let me get started anyway…I mean, I don't mean started. I mean: start to finish.'

'So no fun today Ellie? Ah that's a shame, but I'm very proud of you, setting your priorities like this. Maybe you might have some time tomorrow? Oh and don't forget I'm driving to Galway on Thursday. I'll be out all day. Might not get back till late. You OK with that?'

He was out all day Thursday? This was unexpected. This was beautiful. It was surely unprecedented in the history of humankind that someone, anyone, it happened to be her, could be so cataclysmically inept to think that they were travelling back on Thursday when clearly it was going to be Friday. Why, if his lunch went really badly tomorrow, might she even dream of returning on Saturday?

She would retain the knowledge for now that she had earlier enjoyed a refined restaurant lunch, which she survived intact by repeatedly pretending to look at something important on her iPhone whenever another diner glanced amusedly at her. She then had a positively wonderful spa and swim - she skipped the gym, life in a hotel could be exhausting on its own - before sipping a frappé gracefully through a straw in a most divinely elegant ground floor lounge. She'd effected a withering sense of haughtiness, she imagined, with a broadsheet newspaper before her which bafflingly contained hardly any news, certainly anything that she considered news, but rather column upon column of financial crises and forecasts.

Chapter Fourteen

On Thursday morning Paul headed west on the motorway with rather a lot on his mind. When he had returned to the hotel room the previous evening, Ellie had been positively radiant and animated. Her vivacity was that of a talk-show guest, excitedly telling the studio audience and the watching millions, all about her adventurous day, only it was Paul alone dutifully who took the full and ardent force of this beaming, juvenile raconteuse before him. The truth was that, whatever the trials of his own far from plain-sailing day, she had represented a burst of welcome brilliance within, he deemed, his current path of professional and commercial uncertainty.

He felt wretchedly guilty that he had not yet even spoken with Anne on the phone at any point since leaving her, both parties seemingly content with the inane certainty of the mandatory three kisses that completed their texts to each other, the electronic proclamations of undying love which made everything just fine between them. Did they unwittingly both fear the uncertainty of the human voice, with its remorseless tendency to betray everything real within its multifarious tones? Why was he even thinking like this? Everything had never been better between them and here he was, stoically motoring towards his engineering a conclusion to her past, that could only make her feel yet more dependent upon him, a thing in itself for which he craved more than anything, to be *required* by someone. Someone he coveted both physically and emotionally, spiritually even he often wondered, marvelling at how his scientific background could be so hopelessly seduced and subsumed within such a primitive belief system.

As for his own situation, he had it seemed, committed the cardinal and commercial sin, right there and then at head office yesterday, in front of potentially their biggest client, not to mention the senior decision-makers within his own company, of conjuring up what he'd considered at the time, their best commercial offer within a sea of counter-offers. A brilliant *coup de grace* with all manner of attractive add-ons that he privately knew could not be bettered anywhere else. And so it came as an almost mortal and brutal blow when the potential client's lawyer, initially waxing lyrical about how his client was hugely minded to select the offer before him, and who was indeed deeply attracted to the idea of a relationship of longevity between the two companies, proclaimed that he could close it today, tomorrow, this week. If only he could return to his client with a single compromise, *anything* really on the tendered offer, which indicated that Paul's company wanted the business, that they respected his client enough to close it right here, right now.

What the lawyer meant of course, was that he had to justify his own existence, his own fee. That was how lawyers operated and the plain truth of the matter was that Paul was too commercially stupid to know how the great game of business-life operated. Too honest, too naive, too trustful, too logical, too scientific. Too *anything* really than the single thing that mattered: to play the system that pays the man that tells the other man what to do.

And he'd fucked it up.

Having gone in with his best offer, and marvelled vaingloriously at his performance in the boardroom yesterday, the stark truth was that he still had to close the deal by offering a compromise, a compromise which he had no mandate whatsoever to sanction. Whether or not the senior partners, who had all turned to him in synchronised harmony as the potential client's lawyer delivered his diabolical, and yet he now realised perfectly sensible, denouement, had any clue whatsoever of his impotence before them, he wasn't sure. But he was brutally certain of one thing: if he failed to find the required compromise, his ascendancy within the company was destined to be dramatically reversed, annihilated even.

Anne stared out of the bathroom window to the garden below and wished that the rain would ease up; just for a single day that week would be nice. One of the reasons she had decided not to take any time off from work whilst Paul was away was because she would still be arriving home with at least a glorious hour of evening sunlight before her. She could still avail herself of the peace of the house. There were so many long soaks in a bath surrounded by scented candles a lady could sensibly contemplate and she longed for the serene pleasure of wandering around the garden with a glass of something in hand, vaguely planning some new feature or other that would benefit from her leftfield vision of landscape innovation. She realised there was a degree of self-deception in some ways. The gently intermingling stems of different flower species, once discrete and resplendent in their mechanical rows of some ancient formal *Par Terre*, now leaking their colours into those of their neighbours, an orgy of osmoses, hues running amok on a withering, ageing canvas. *The Wild Garden* she had declared it to their infrequent visitors, artfully contriving the notion that she had designed it that way, rather than describing the phenomenon itself; the relentless entropy of plant life, ignoring the often pointless efforts of scurrying humans across generations to control its wanton fecundity of purposelessness.

Even the cats had boycotted the garden this week, often joining her in her vacuously meditative contemplation of the sodden things outside, no doubt frustrated by the dearth of simple small rodent and fledgling kills to their name, which she found comforting for two reasons. She enjoyed their company, the sense that they thought the same things as her about the great continuity of the grand external scheme, but also because she dreaded burying dead things herself when Paul wasn't around. It was not so much that she was squeamish of mangled remains, rather that she always had to say a prayer, a prayer gratefully given, but heavy with melancholy and the relentless pointlessness of creatures going to the trouble of being born, only to be despatched by domestic carnivores who would eschew their meat for cleverly marketed, slender packets of cat food products with names like *Feed Me Mummy, Miaow!*

And yet she marvelled that Mrs Carmichael was herself outside in the adjacent garden, rain dripping from her headscarf onto the sort of old shiny, *patently shiny,* mackintosh that you only ever really saw these days in vintage bijou clothes shops. She carried in her hands a dead bird - even Anne could discern it at this distance - and silently shook her head as she lay it in a small hole that she must already have dug in the soil of a small garden border by the opposite wall. Anne continued to watch, fascinated, as the old lady paused momentarily before filling earth into the hole and, with much effort, patted it down with the back of an old decaying garden spade.

Then Mrs Carmichael was gone.

It had been in some ways a beautiful and reassuring sight for Anne and yet…something was slightly odd about it and she could not think what it could be. Whatever it was would come to her, as it so often did when she was thinking of something else entirely. Her left hand involuntarily moved to the crucifix around her neck and its contours brought comfort to her at that moment. But it did something else.

It made Anne realise what it was that had seemed slightly incongruous.

The old Irish lady had not at any moment during the interment of the bird, made the sign of the cross upon her chest.

Ellie counted. The fifty-five seconds still to go of the sixty most definitely required would in all probability be impossible to achieve and she would die. She would die here drowned in an opulent swimming pool in one of the grandest hotels in Ireland, which end could be worse she supposed. Death was but a passing luxury compared with the alternative she felt.

Fifty seconds.

This morning after her dad had left, she'd taken breakfast in bed as she was far more confident now as to how to behave in hotels. The trick was just that: to be far more confident than your personality would ever normally be allowed to be. She supposed that, if you spent most of your life acting in this absurd way, you would at some point simply fool yourself into believing that you *were* actually a confident person after all and if you rallied the deceit at the drop of a hat and regularly, such a stupidity of purpose would become you. She knew she was far away from this dramatic junction in life but thought she might as well get some *hotel miles* under her belt for now. Her confidence earlier that day, if anything, was in considering that she might undertake her self-imposed mandatory morning of homework far sooner if she dispensed with the arduous formality of choosing clothes from the wardrobe, brushing her hair, anointing her face with makeup and all the other preparations that a young lady might be tasked to consider whilst staying in a nice hotel. And have breakfast brought up.

Her confidence was checked however when there was a knock at the door and she nonchalantly opened it. It was *him*. She froze.

'You ordered breakfast Madame?' he'd said and she had meekly nodded and uttered a pathetic child's voice of acknowledgement. Was it the lengthening of the word *Madam* by adding an 'e' to the end, impregnating it with something French and risqué, which unsettled her and made her face turn into a lump of throbbing beetroot? Or was it his mildly bemused grace of purpose before her? She could not tell, but very slowly backed away from him and jumped through the adjacent en suite bathroom door. She'd stammered something vacuous and remorselessly ridiculous like the fact that she'd left the water running or something. As long as he could no longer *see* her, then the terribleness of it all would be reduced by a few percentage points and life might, just might, go on, without immediate life-threatening self-harm.

'Just leave it on the side please!' she forced from her trembling lips, realising that *on the side* could mean anything really.

'Right you are Madame,' was his reply, his vicious refusal to relinquish his Francophilic distortion of her title, mocking her yet further.

But then steps, the door closing. It could be a trick. 'Oh and one other thing...' she tested the silence before her.

Sure now that even the most depraved of hotel staff could not refuse to communicate in this way with a guest, she darted her head around and into the corridor to make sure of its emptiness. She proceeded to do the same with the rest of the suite, even looking under the beds, feeling ridiculous but relieved that she was perfectly all on her own. She decided that venturing out in future for any remaining meals, fraught though it might be with the possibility of unrequited encounters, could never be as saturatingly demeaning as being alone in a room with *him*.

Forty Seconds.

After breakfast she'd completed her remaining maths homework and calculated that if Dad would not be back from Galway until late, she would have time for a leisurely lunch *and* a swim, perhaps a nap even, before tackling what would surely be one of her most formidable homeworks of the week: history. Not just any old history, like the Evacuation of Dunkirk or the Battle of The Somme; no this was *your* history, not you yourself, that would be boring, but the history of the house where you lived. She was still not sure whether to choose London W6 or Lounsley, Kent, but increasingly felt that the ease of accessing content on the Internet would decide it for her.

Thirty Seconds.

She felt she was starting to slip away. The water began to feel like air and she wondered if drowning was like in her dreams. The dreams where you breathed in the water and it *was* like air and the sensation was unimaginably beautiful, second only to dreams of flying. But the game would be up as cognitive acceptance of the paradox of breathing like a fish would alert the dreaming brain to its status and the dream would soon be over: how annoying she thought. Only sixty seconds earlier it had all been so wonderful. She'd rearranged the order of everything and after a sumptuous lunch of some sort of exotic seafood salad, she'd snoozed a little in her room and upon awaking thought that nothing would be quite so delightful and refresh her for the afternoon's academic toil quite so much as a gentle swim in the hotel pool. And there she was, standing with her toes curled over the edge of the deep-end and her arms aloft, ready to dive in, when she heard a familiar voice behind her.

'Tis warmer than it looks Madame.'

It was *him* again. Only this time she was virtually stripped bare but for her swim costume. How had she been so obtuse as to assume that he only did room service? Surely you had to be a life-guard to be in here or something? Perhaps he *was* and he just tricked his way into doing room service for the tips, to complement his meagre life-saving salary. Would he now be staring at her every aquatic move, her far-from-graceful front crawl technique, god forbid the murderous awkwardness of her flapping around on her back, all hideously exposed to his prying eyes.

Twenty seconds.

So she'd dived in and swam to the bottom, hooking her fingers into a grill there, and here she was. The end. Farewell Daddy. I didn't mean for you to return from Galway after a hard day's work and be quietly guided by a senior member of the hotel staff to the hotel morgue (Level Minus Two in the lift - accredited key holders only), to be confronted by a watery, anaemic cadaver. I hope my maths homework was correct though - you would have liked that and it might have aided your grief even. Mum, I never meant the things I shouted at you, you must know that. You gave me my brief life upon this Earth and I will be forever grateful for that. And all the cats, please come and play with me in Heaven.

Ten seconds.

She was being lifted upwards. Is this how it goes? How lovely. But suddenly she was gasping for air and her lungs hurt and worried faces were staring down upon her. One of them was *him* again, alongside others, but he was no longer mocking her, no longer teasing her and he was dripping with water as he held her to him, lips hovering above hers, ready to breathe life into her shuddering body.

'I'm sorry,' he said, 'I'm really sorry,' and his eyes meant it, she could tell. And then he was no longer there and she was engulfed in towels and hot drinks pressed to her lips by a kindly lady with a reassuring Irish brogue.

'It'll be alright now. You put the heart in me crossways but we'll soon have you dry. No more swimming like a fish for you today.'

Chapter Fifteen

The offices of Blake, Harvey and de Burgo are tiered upon three separate floors of a fine historic building in the heart of Galway, not far from the junction of St Francis Street and Eyre Street. In fact so unlike a conventional office did it appear, that Paul initially walked straight past it. He was about to reach for his mobile phone to report to his waiting hosts his inability to find where he thought it was according to his print-out from Google maps. He knew there was an app on his phone that would effortlessly and without destroying the planet, do the same thing - Ellie had shown him the previous evening - but he'd forgotten what it was or where it was on the phone and he had an intuitive fear of being late for meetings through failures of any kind of portable hardware connecting to something called the *Cloud*, whatever that was. He wasn't even sure where the Internet was kept, if it physically existed anywhere, and supposed that the World Wide Web was in some way coating whatever this Cloud was with filaments of tiny strings of information. No, a piece of paper was far more dependable. And yet.

And then he saw the sign, swinging in the late afternoon breeze that slinked between the old stone walls around him. He realised this really was how he'd imagined it. A trusted old firm of solicitors, partners replacing partners, in the grand cycle of learned prognostications over hundreds of years, the Latin never changing, only the ever-aggrandising sums of writs and court orders that overflowed the old teak drawers that surely lined wall-upon-wall of these hallowed rooms.

There had been no pre-agreed meeting or deadline or anything really other than the swapping of emails with one of the legal secretaries in order to assent to his collecting the several boxes which comprised the sum total of the estate, now wound up in perpetuity. He was even at this stage mildly apprehensive as to the size of the boxes. Their car was a mid-sized 4WD vehicle and the rear seats could be lowered, surely enough to contain the boxes, but he was more worried about how he might have to carry them to the car which he finally had to park in an expensive underground carpark to the south-east of this part of the city. This was not after all official company business and he needed to be a little careful in what he claimed today.

The woman at the reception desk was very young he thought and quite informally dressed. He'd assumed that all the staff there would be positively Dickensian in their attire for some irrational reason. 'Oh hello there, it's Paul Fewings: I believe Mr De Burgo is expecting me?'

'Just one second there if you will, Mr Fewings,' she replied, 'Oh, yes and do take a seat just there for a while.'

All very casual. Perhaps she'd change her tune when one of the senior partners arrived, he wondered. He stared out of the window into the street. An old man, clearly drunk on his afternoon beer stopped right outside and frowned at him menacingly. Surely he's not going to come into the reception area of a solicitors' office and confront me? Paul found himself fretting. He can tell I'm English. They've never really forgiven us have they? Oh Lord, no. But the man broke out into the broadest smile, doffed his cap and might as well have mouthed *top of the morning to you*, before staggering off, singing some old Irish sea shanty no doubt.

The breeze outside freshened just as a young woman walked past him, her skirt rearing upwards to reveal a glimpse of a grey-patterned stocking top. He blushed and willed her not to look at him, to notice his inadvertently prying eyes but she was oblivious to him and fell into the arms of the young man suddenly beside her, all kisses and laughter and abandonment of sensibility. And Paul realised how lonely he was. He loved being with Ellie of course, but this mild and involuntary act of voyeurism had made him yearn for the first time that week ardently for Anne, her warm and brilliant smile, her coyness whenever he showed signs of physical longing for her. Sharing the family room with Ellie meant that he had not allowed himself the faintest morsel of physical reminiscences and he wondered now if it had been quite so healthy a policy to deny himself such sensual thoughts.

'Paul Fewings.'

It was both a statement and a request he thought and turned to face whom he imagined would be a reedy-voiced senior partner, Mr De Burgo himself perhaps, a gentleman of great standing in the community who had decided to attend the office today for the most solemn and important transferring of probate documentation to this equally grand visitor from England. But it was the receptionist, smiling at him holding out a pen, the same pen she had just used to sign something on a clipboard given to her briefly by a stooped middle-aged man in a brown tunic and sporting slightly unkempt thinning hair: a porter clearly, he resigned himself to thinking. A pair of unremarkable-looking boxes no bigger than a sheet of A4 paper in dimension and about five inches in depth were stacked on the desk before him.

'Oh sorry and this,' said the receptionist and passed him a much older-looking manila package of some sort, tightly bound with a myriad of elastic bands of various colours, not much smaller in size than the boxes themselves.

'Oh so that's it?' Paul ventured, a part of him relieved that he would not need to hail a taxi to ferry an enormous load of large heavy boxes to the car. What did he think the remnants of an estate would resemble? Large pieces of old furniture that the executors were unable to liquidate at the time, because of a history of doubtful provenance? Silver antique candlesticks which were not to be bequeathed to a single soul under any circumstance? He felt foolish, a foolishness no less awkward when he realised that he was expecting one of them to say something. The smiling receptionist did not seem inclined to say a single word as Paul dutifully scribbled his signature on a piece of official-looking paper and so he broke the silence himself for a second time. Clearly his last utterance she had considered to be rhetorical. 'I mean that's it...ah...in terms of...uh...the necessary...well what I mean to say...*finalisation of the probate process?*'

'Not quite,' she replied and Paul felt a glimmer of hope that there might be something vaguely *ceremonial* to come.

'Some ID please, preferably passport. That'll be grand.'

Still slightly numb with the banality of it all, Paul reached for his wallet and presented it to her, her cursory glance and nod of approval outrageously short of any due diligence, surely, in such a grave matter. His sudden pique propelled him momentarily from his absurdly effete English deportment and he found the words rushed from his mouth. 'Surely I am to be meeting Mr De Burgo at the very least?'

The receptionist looked up at him with an uncertain look, mild astonishment perhaps. 'Oh that's a fret; forgive me Mr Fewings. I hadn't realised that you had booked an appointment with him, only it's not...' she tapped on her keyboard and glanced at her screen '…it's not in his diary or any of the meeting rooms.'

'No, no, I'm not saying that I booked a separate meeting or anything quite like that...'

The receptionist's uncertainty now began to give way to the appearance of bemusement and Paul could contain a brewing sense of injustice no more. 'Look, do you know whose estate these documents relate to?' He might as well have uttered the age-worn desperate words of a C-list celebrity pleading entrance to an exclusive night club in Piccadilly for all that the impact of his words achieved, as if the receptionist, having dealt with some of the greatest deceased celebrities that Ireland had ever harboured, really had heard it all before.

'We meant to cause no distress Mr Fewings. Had I realised that you wished an audience with Mr De Burgo, we certainly could have factored that in to agreeing a diary date. If you wish to write your thoughts in to him via letter, I'm sure your feedback would be greatly appreciated.'

'I...do you know what? I'm going now. Is there any other...*formality*...that I need to observe or may I take the finalised probate documents of *The late Dean of Tuam* with me now?'

'Sure look it, Mr Fewings. Mind how you go now.'

He could bear his presence in the hallowed offices of Blake, Harvey and De Burgo no longer and swept up the boxes and package from the desk, smiled distastefully at the receptionist, and bore his way out of the main door into the welcome swirling coolness of the air outside. The drunk waved at him from the other side of the street, his raucous rendition of something vaguely maritime having edged up a key and Paul felt a sudden urge to join him in his railings, buy them both a double Jameson in the bar opposite and raise toasts to the destruction of faceless corporate people everywhere. It was only the prospect of the long drive ahead that willed him to wave briefly back and march along his side of the road back to the car.

As he turned to be on his way the old drunk started pointing purposefully up at the sky, shaking his head.

Paul's disillusionment with the way in which he'd been treated in Galway with its hint of inane Euro-homogenous corporatism, had made him balk at the idea of returning to Dublin on the quintessentially Euro-homogenous M6. The Satnav suggested it was an hour longer by the so-called scenic route along the R446, and with no more official business to attend to that day, he thought he'd treat himself to driving through the *real Ireland,* the one which seemed hitherto to have eluded him this week.

As he drove, he mulled over the possibility of going through the paperwork tonight back at the hotel. Would it distract him from preparing for the grand finale of securing the largest ever contract for the company that he had known, possibly securing an even safer future for the three of them? Or would it work better the other way and in a positive sense *distract* him from the next day's business?

He flipped the wipers on as a sudden squall descended. He hadn't even recalled passing much in the way of traffic in either direction for a while, but he had after all been in deep thought: maybe it was time to concentrate a bit more keenly. He didn't like the thought of breaking down around here. Would there be a phone signal even? The weather soon worsened yet further and he twisted the wiper knob to maximum speed, placing the rear one on full also as he couldn't see more than a few yards behind him. Time to slow down, he thought. Ellie will be perfectly fine on her own if he was to be a bit late returning. He relaxed his foot on the accelerator, nervously assessing the likelihood of being tailgated and rammed. But nothing. It was the car and he alone in a gathering maelstrom of alarming proportions. He brought the car to a halt. This was Ireland for heaven's sake, a small island really in the grand scheme of things, notorious surely for the startling ephemerality of its wandering air pressures and cocktails of gung-ho gusts of wind and fizzing blasts of rain. Knowing locals would not have stopped. They would have shaken their heads imperceptibly and muttered to themselves, nonchalantly turning the radio tuner to the shipping forecast perhaps. He suddenly felt hungry and glanced at his watch. Four o'clock? He thought it was nearer two; no wonder he felt sick and light-headed: he'd had nothing to eat all day. No, he had to press on; this ridiculous deluge could not continue. He indicated right to pull back onto the road and continue his journey, a mildly futile gesture to the empty road behind him. He was soon convinced that the wind and rain had demoted itself kindly to a mild gale and thought that 30mph would not constitute a heinous affront to following traffic more used to these conditions. His caution felt vindicated as a dark shape reared abruptly up into his view. Initially unsure as to what he was actually looking at, he instinctively slammed on the brakes and skidded, aquaplaning across the steady stream of water on the road ahead and finally, with a jolt, the car was brought to rest...rammed up against a huge tree that had fallen across the road.

Paul jumped out of the car, initially impervious to the lashings of rain that thrashed at his hopelessly inadequate attire. His sole involuntary reaction was, he self-congratulatorily later reflected, to warn others of the impending danger they must surely face. He ran to the rear of the car frantically flailing his arms to vehicles that clearly didn't exist and then rather dutifully repeated the gesture as if to satisfy a symmetry of purpose by scrambling over the tree trunk and manufacturing the same futile gesticulation to equally non-existent traffic from the east. 'Bastards,' he exclaimed. 'You Irish bastards all knew this was coming didn't you,' he cried impotently into the unimpressed winds that tore into him. 'You all watched as the stupid Englishman headed east out of the city, with his stupid English number plates.'

He thought of the old drunk pointing to the sky as he had walked away from him, a drunken madman perhaps, but a benevolent seer all the same.

His fit of pique was interrupted by the realisation that the rain was actually hurting his face and hands and he quickly rolled himself back over the tree trunk and eased himself into the car. His sodden clothes slipped easily over the shiny leather seat and he was relieved to find the engine still running, the wipers whirring away and all the lights dutifully peering into the darkening squall around him. He put the car into reverse and felt a wave of relief as the car obeyed him and he drove backwards and onto the verge. No clunks, no strange sounds. Good, he thought. This was a 4WD after all. It may be a cheap Japanese version of the British stalwart on which it was modelled but it could hardly fail the *gently ram into a tree test* could it?

He drove a hundred yards back in the direction he had travelled from and, deciding that the only Irish in Galway who might have attempted the same journey as him in his wake could not be bastards after all, parked the car with its full beams on, to warn any oncoming traffic of their imminent danger. He pumped his horn a few times to boot, embarrassed by its honky campness, an emasculated ringtone against the baying roar of the gale outside. But nothing. The bastards. He reached for his phone, but there was no signal. There was really no choice left to him now he realised. He would have to drive back the other way and find a landline at the very least.

Ten minutes later he had still not found any sort of service station but a sign pointing to the right instead with the words *Glafarnach Inn*. He glanced at the Satnav. He *wasn't* on the R446 at all it seemed but had somehow forked slightly obliquely left just North of Clostoken. The words *Meadow Court* hovered on the screen. What did it mean?

The rain was still driving ferociously into his windscreen and he decided that the most important consideration of all was to make contact with Ellie so that she would not fret too much. Another two hundred yards to the right along a turning more like a mud track, he pulled into a space outside what he now realised was the Glafarnach Inn. He instantly yearned for something strong and amber that would warm his sodden limbs through.

It can be the *Slaughtered Lamb* for all I care, he muttered to himself as he strolled across the gravel path towards the front door. Please let it be open, he thought to himself, vaguely aware that it might be, as in England, that worst of periods: the evil two hours that separates pub lunch and evening opening times. He was relieved when the handle turned and he could push the door inwards. The inn was empty but for a stout middle-aged lady wearing an unseemly medley of clothing of different colours and patterns that made her appear like a comic character in a not very funny seventies TV sketch.

'Oh hi there,' began Paul. 'Is the inn open?'

She looked up, a semblance of suspicion illuminating her features. 'Go way outta that; what a most curious question to be asking,' she replied and carried on mopping the floor area by the bar.

'Only I really just need to borrow your phone if I may...I mean I'd pay for the call of course.'

This time the cleaning lady, if that was really her main role in life, spoke without looking up at him: 'Paying customers only, if you please.'

'Well yes like I said, I'll pay you of course,' but he knew before he'd even started that this was not an economic transaction that would win the business this hour. 'I mean, please, a double Jameson.'

'Finbarr!' she shrieked over her shoulder, 'Customer.'

A few seconds later and a man appeared as if from nowhere behind the bar.

Paul held a hidden guilty predilection for national stereotypes but wondered if he would be considered racist by ever reflecting on them publicly, so he didn't. Thus he was measurably enthused by the appearance of the man that was before him. Tall, slightly stooped with that type of black and grey hair, thickly lustred and swept back from the forehead, a green waistcoat upon a crisp white shirt, topped-off with a loose red neckerchief. Have I finally found the real Ireland? he thought to himself mischievously.

'Can I help you with today sir?' said the man, his Galway accent as thick and creamy as his hair.

'A double of your finest whiskey, sir!'

The Innkeeper, for this is surely who he must be, began to reach for a bottle of Jameson on the shelf behind him.

'Haven't you something…more local?' asked Paul.

'Tis but a small island here. It's all local. Now if you preferred a Bushmills Original, I have a bottle of that right here. And if you really want me to push the boat out, I'll go below for a Paddy or an Irishman, I might even have us a Connemara.'

Slightly disappointed that his escape from the storm was not quite like the movies and frankly worn-out and ragged at the edges, Paul shook his head. 'No, no, Jameson would be fine,' and the shots were poured. 'Please, one for yourself,' he quickly added, a growing sense of appeasement collecting within him that the words *customers only* might be something to be won rather than be gained by transactional logic.

'Very kind of you sir. I might take you up on that a bit later,' he paused, '...I assume you'll be wanting a room for the night?'

Paul took a large sip from the glass, the liquid quickly imparting succour to his frazzled senses. 'Oh no, no. Just passing really, filthy storm and all that. Did you know about the fallen tree?'

'Why no sir I did not. Fierce weather: that do be bringing you here today so it does?'

Paul was not entirely sure if the quaint final three words constituted a return question, or a subtle localised colloquial subjunctive. Anne spoke to him with a thoroughly received English pronunciation and therefore the nuances of Irish-speak were mostly lost on him – they were things said in films which required no social interaction. Paul instead looked feverishly for body language of some sort, some clue as to whether he was being asked a question. The use of a phone had now aggrandized into something almost desperate and he sensed a creeping feeling that normal, simple solutions, such as throwing large amounts of cash onto the counter might not be the way to go.

He waited a few nervous seconds and, sure that the Innkeeper was no longer particularly interested in the greater logistics of the fallen tree and its importance in Paul's decision to drive to the inn, he offered a rather tame but situationally homogenous 'Aye…' It seemed to work, for the man just grunted and began to attend to the cleaning of some glasses, presumably that of the previous lunchtime trade. This whiskey is working he thought. 'Another of those please if you don't mind,' and another double shot was poured.

Paul was now confident in two ways. Confident generally because of the relaxing influence of the Jameson and confident that the purchasing of four shots of liquor and one in the wood for the Innkeeper must needs constitute, by the assessment of the most pessimistic of observers, the basis of his being considered a *customer*.

'I say, do you have a phone that I could use? Only I have to get an urgent message to my daughter in our hotel in Dublin. There's no mobile signal you see. I mean I'll pay for the call and everything.'

The Innkeeper was clearly not inclined to look up from his vital work of preparing clean glasses for his evening customers. 'Aye you could sir…' Paul did not like this word *could*. Did he mean *may* or was he about to impart a terrible condition of some kind? The answer came soon enough. '…if the line do be working. These storms you see.' A large clunking old plastic telephone was suddenly slammed on the bar in front of him. 'Be my guest, if you will.'

'Oh terribly kind of you, thank you so much.' Paul quickly brought the hotel's number up on his mobile phone and carefully went to dial, literally, the numbers onto the inn's phone, amazed that such ancient technology still existed in anywhere but local museums. *Evolving Telecommunications In The Twentieth Century Home.*

There was no ring tone.

A sense of unease crept into Paul's stomach and he realised that it was not a dissimilar sensation to that which he experienced when Ellie had disappeared into the house next door. Logically everything was different. The situation here was that his smart, confident thirteen-year-old daughter was confined to a luxury hotel in one of the safest cities in the world with access to virtually anything she wanted.

But his articulating the matter cognitively within succeeded only to reduce a sense of panic to one of his abandonment and neglect of his own daughter. He winced at the thought of her mother finding all this out and lecturing him viciously on parental responsibility. She had only ever used the word *authorities* once before, during a diabolic exchange of emails when they had first separated, but the word frightened him more than any other in the English language. The thought of having to don a Spiderman costume and wail from the roofs of the Houses of Parliament about fathers' rights appalled him, his fear of heights more so than the embarrassment of his work colleagues seeing him nationally shamed on TV as he was led away by the police.

'There's no ring tone,' he declared bluntly, not much caring now if he sounded in the least bit rude.

'Is there not now?'

'No there is not now!'

The Innkeeper paused, perhaps assessing, thought Paul, if there had been an intentional sleight of his colloquial, lyrical pattern of speech.

'Look, I'm sorry to sound short, really I am but, I absolutely must contact my daughter somewhat urgently.'

'Sure look it, sir.' Another pause, which Paul decided to leave unsullied in the hope that space to think might inject a modicum of empathy into the man's cognitive deliberations. 'I think the storm must have brought the line down. Or just interfered with a junction box somewhere. That'll probably be it, I dare say.'

'Could you, do you, I mean, when that happens do you sometimes try your mobile phones?' It was desperate stuff now, wondered Paul, but he had to try everything.

'Meteor you might.' It was the cleaner. She had listened to everything and now it was her turn. 'The main networks are hit and miss, especially when you get the weather like this.'

'Aye,' said the Innkeeper, 'you'll not be wrong their Mrs Connolly.'

'I don't. Suppose. Either of you. Would have your mobiles. On that. Network?' asked Paul slowly.

The Innkeeper scratched his head. 'That was last year's contract, if I remember rightly.'

'Aye, same with me. GoYoFone now; wish I hadn't bothered,' said Mrs Connolly, slowly shaking her head as she stood away from her mop and bucket temporarily, as if the matter were serious enough.

'Well look, I'll have to be off in that case,' announced Paul abruptly, his annoyance with everything to do with the inn superseded by the practicalities ahead in driving somewhere, *anywhere*, where he might reconnect with the world, the world in which existed his only daughter. 'What do I owe you?'

'I wouldn't be recommending that on a night like this sir.'

Was there a hint of menace in his voice? thought Paul.

As if reading his thoughts the Innkeeper continued. 'If you leave the road again in this storm, the Guards'll likely notice your number plates and breathalyse you. EU regulations now, so there are. And that network you're on. The same beyont. Once this lot has died down, you've every chance of reconnecting. That right Mrs Connolly?'

'Every chance Mr Connolly, every chance. The landline too I shouldn't doubt it. Every chance.'

At that point Paul could not be sure that the insinuation that they were either brother and sister or husband and wife, on surname terms whatever their relationship might be, was in any way a little macabre, but it had the effect of focussing him greatly.

'Well if you're sure…of the chances…' He paused, perhaps foolishly anticipating a mathematical formula of some kind. The probability of telecommunications signal versus the storm force number. But the Connollys simply carried on with their early evening tasks. '...I will take you up on your kind offer of a room for the night.'

'Mrs Connolly!' Finbarr Connolly raised his voice. 'If you will.'

Chapter Sixteen

Before Paul knew it, he was following Mrs Connolly up a very narrow set of stairs to a room that overlooked the front of the inn, his car outside forlornly swaying in the winds that still battered the building and all around it. He felt alone and defeated and willed Ellie to be strong for him. She was a creature, as all teenagers are, of the Internet and she would be sensible and run weather reports and road reports and she would not panic. She would not call her mother; she would know that that way lay trouble and besides, her mother would likely call the police and there would be some ridiculous EU regulation barring the abandonment of thirteen-year-olds in hotel rooms by parents away on business meetings. And Ellie would be taken away to some god-awful temporary Safe House whilst cables between Irish and British diplomats were relayed across the Irish Sea. No, she was cleverer than that. She would call Anne. Yes Anne of course. Anne would be freaked, she would be worried. She would be lots of things, but what she wouldn't be was, is…a person that panics. She would reassure Ellie, ask her if she had everything that she needed. She would be sensible and soothing all at once. The stultifying rigidity that Paul experienced in his shoulders right up to his ears began to ease. He was alive and so must be Ellie. And even the grand closing of his greatest of deals tomorrow was but a pittance of importance in the list of importances in his life. Life itself *was* the most important thing in his life: it all seemed so simple. And the vagaries of day-to-day existence, the hapless toil of his everyday contributions to that existence seemed utterly absurd to him.

He suddenly longed for England and a place within it that eschewed his being a part of anyone else's existence, outside of that of Anne's, Ellie's and his own. How very beautiful, he thought. He pushed the room's net curtain to one side to peer outside. As if to acknowledge his accession to new dimensions all around and within, this burst of unsolicited mania, so swiftly risen from despair, a blade of the greyest of celestial light smote his forearm and like an ember catching on newly-found kindling, pulsed like a blotch of yellow-pink on his still-wet skin.

'Ellie. Hello,' he said out loud and he smiled as he felt her close. He felt her close because she was that light, she always had been. And wherever he was, and whenever he would no longer be, she would burn brightly.

For Ellie, the afternoon's progression, as disquieted as she had initially been when her father failed to return at around the time she had expected, had been very much less fraught with emotion. She had flirted with the idea of calling Anne but she could not imagine what the benefits of that action might be. For her: the more sensible road of calm reflection and deduction. It was clear from the local news, or rather the national news – there seemed little difference frankly – on the TV, that the weather slowly rolling in eastwards from the Atlantic Ocean was worthy of being elevated to a news item and as soon as the word *Galway* was added to one of the commentaries, she relaxed a good deal. For Ellie, what was exponentially more terrifying than loss of phone signal was loss of Wi-Fi signal. The thought of yet *another* night in the hotel, she realised guiltily, was but another catalyst in her calm contemplation of where the hell her dad might actually be.

Armed with the knowledge that she only had two homeworks left to do, history and English, and realising that they would surely not be leaving Ireland now until at least Saturday, she decided that there was no shame in wanting to know that Dad was fine, or at the very least *likely* to be fine and so she decided to dig further into possible scenarios.

It didn't take her long to find a website which offered real-time updates on network coverage for AgilCom, Dad's network provider. It didn't look good. But hold on. What about the tracker? Family SafeSpy! Dad had insisted on it being downloaded to her phone if she wanted to go into the town with a friend. It was a bargaining position to which she readily conceded. In turn she had, half-jokingly, insisted on familial reciprocity and Dad had bafflingly agreed to add it to his so that he could be tracked in turn. Perhaps he'd read one of those wishy-washy books about how to be your child's equal. She clicked on the app straightaway and the screen honed in immediately to a position on a map, his last known position before the 3G network collapsed. The nearest town was Clostoken...in County Galway.

To Google Maps: the nearest inn, Glafarnach.

She closed her eyes and imagined it. She imagined sweeping down from the sky now like the large flapping Arakuth of her daydreams, looking for signs of melancholic fatherhood, so she could shine the tiniest of lights upon him and let him know that she was OK and that she knew he was OK. A head, she was quite sure, turned in a window towards her and she felt a small surge of static in her heart.

Hello Dad. Good night Dad. See you in the morning.

And then she began to plot the evening ahead.

She was from a generation that didn't even stop to think that he could call her by landline. In the world of the thirteen-year-old it might as well have been something you saw in a museum. And as for Wi-Fi, she mused as she slowly shook her head, Dad's success at logging into whatever local facility there might be, was about as likely as his naming Justin Bieber's latest hit.

Paul winced as he drank from the glass of red wine – it tasted like slightly astringent, corked sherry. During the course of the evening he had gradually come to the conclusion that the aspiring novelty of lodging in a quintessentially authentic Galway Inn was no match for the awkward reality of its peculiar regimes and people-challenges. It should really not have surprised him one little bit that ordering supper, so bereft of a proper lunch as he had been, would be the greatest challenge of all. He had asked to see the dinner menu and, politely enough, checked for the time within which a selection of its contents might be ordered. The response was for Mr Connolly, going straight to character it seemed, to be mildly incredulous at the effrontery of the suggestion that there might be a choice in the matter. 'Mrs Connolly makes a quare hearty supper. Plenty to warm your insides on a night like this Mr Few Tings.' Paul had quickly discarded any attempt to press for further details of Mrs Connolly's culinary magnificence alongside his even swifter decision not to correct the rather amusing malapropism of his surname.

As it turned out he had failed lamentably to understand the sequence of the cause-and-effect in the matter and was politely informed that *Mrs Connolly do be fetchin' ya* when the meal was to be served. Retiring to his room he had decided to relax as best he could and not even the peeling paintwork and yellowing shower screen in the en-suite bathroom fazed him in the slightest – there was hot water, a courtesy soap and what looked evidently like clean towels. Things were looking up he had thought ruefully. And when the appointed hour came and he was seated at a lovely old oak table by one of the windows that stared out onto the mists, the last feeble remnants of the earlier tempest, delicately daubed by the setting sun, it mattered not in the slightest that he was served with ham, potatoes and cabbage. For what else could he have expected, moreover its size and simplicity were just what his mind and body needed, harassed as it had been and slapped around all afternoon by the heavens and presumably the gods therein.

As he sat in his room, having mastered an ingenious technique to nullify the mild rankness of the wine by holding each sip in his mouth and sluicing it around his gums for a while, he thought that he might as well busy himself in examining some of the contents of the boxes he'd collected earlier. He switched the TV on for company and was vaguely aware of a bombastic talk show host, whose every sentence seemed to stir his audience into ever-greater cacophonies of laughter. The reception pulsed in phases but he had a sense that it was gradually improving – the aftermath of the storm was already here and he dared to hope that phone signals would abruptly and miraculously materialise.

The first box contained receipts of various kinds, statements, ancillary schedules to several legal grants and a plethora of letters which did not seem to contain much more than citations to assorted enclosures. He raised an eyebrow and then theatrically his glass, when a recently signed and dated cheque materialised, Paul avidly scrutinising the numbers for zeros that might indicate unforeseen wealth. A week in Spain; could be worse, he thought.

The second box was more of the same but with references to funeral arrangements, for both of her parents as it happened, gratuitous lists of inventory items and their current status - most stamped almost industrially with the word *sold* in red ink, its lingering finality somehow brutal and irreversible, like the lives it had come to describe and supersede.

There was a smaller musty grey envelope which contained a dozen or so photographs. A couple were of Anne's parents on their wedding day and one in which her father was shaking hands with what appeared to be a visiting clerical dignitary of some sort, her father's smiling expression one of awkward deference. Now there were several with the three of them, with Anne as a young girl of maybe five through to her mid-teens. He was fascinated as, when asked about early family photos, Anne would often shrug and say that she always hated her unphotogenic appearance and it didn't bother her. It was such a shame that there were no photos of her at an even younger age, a baby photo perhaps. But what saddened him most was that there were no family photos with the four of them. He was embarrassed to admit to himself that he could not recall the age of her brother when he died. Perhaps she had told him once or twice but he'd forgotten and was loathe to bring the matter up again as she clearly found it painful to talk about.

There was a second sealed envelope and he opened it. In it was a single photograph: that of a boy, a boy of about seven years of age. Paul furrowed his eyebrows as he momentarily considered that he had seen him before. Could *this* be her brother? He felt truly awful that he didn't really know. Had Anne once shown him a photograph of him when they'd first met perhaps? No, he simply could not remember, but the vaguely familiar face suggested that this could be the only explanation. But if that were true, why did he not appear in the other family photos? For some families perhaps the pain of loss was so awful to bear, the enormity so dispiriting, that previous examples of group cheerfulness were expunged from the records. For a religious family that didn't make sense to him however and, in as much as the original personal effects were all bequeathed to Anne after her father had died, he now seriously wondered if Anne had them hidden somewhere else; in an old suitcase or locked in the vaults of some other solicitor's firm through fear of her revisiting her family demons on a spontaneous, drunken whim.

Was this it? Was this desperately gratuitous paperwork and some old photos without which they had been bubbling along with their lives in absolute ignorance of their existence, really worth a trip across Ireland and in so doing abandoning his precious daughter to the bright lights of old Dublin town? He felt almost cheated, the novelty of the *game* of swirling the rank volatile esters of the wine around his gums, fast receding, like the ageing tissue around it.

He walked to the window. Why? To see if the car was still there? To push his mobile phone to the edge of some miraculous post-tempest signal? The evening felt meaningless.

He looked over at the large packet at the end of the bed. Surely there would be more of the same. And yet what else was there to do? Carry on moping about what Ellie might be thinking whilst searching for local news items on the TV? He flopped himself at the foot of the bed and began to open the packaging, or rather tried to open the packaging - it had been taped up so long ago it seemed, and so keenly, that his fingernails alone proved impractical for the purpose. He remembered his nail scissors, the ones he kept in the side pocket of his jacket, alongside his retractable comb and chewable diarrhoea tablets – emergency items - what a middle-aged git he had become.

The blade tore into the wrapping tape and then proved quite satisfactory in slicing aside a line of old powdery staples to reveal inside yet another manila envelope, with the words *Highly Confidential - Senior Partners only*. Paul's attention turned now from a state of nonchalance to one of bemused interest and very carefully and delicately he cut through the outer flap to find yet further inside a sheaf of papers. He spread them out and deliberately gulped some more wine, for now he felt a nervousness within himself – was it again that same feeling of foreboding when Ellie disappeared briefly in Lounsley? Or was it something deeper - something that had always niggled him about the strange world of Anne's Irish past, that other country that seemed so incongruous with the woman that he had come to love?

And there it was before him.

Adoption papers.

The words tumbled all around him as he quickly and urgently scanned each of the documents that he carefully laid in rows on the bed. Words stabbed meaninglessly, initially without context. *Child - Source - Orphanage -Saint*. But no matter how illogical and unscientific, how unprofessionally hurried his current and immediate thirst for knowledge had become, there could be no doubt about what it was that he had discovered.

Anne was an adopted child.

Her parents who had given her everything, the more so after the tragic death of her brother, were not her blood parents at all.

Paul's mobile rang.

He jumped towards the window where it rested.

'Ellie?!' he shouted into the phone, realising his mistake almost immediately, for what father would be so irresponsible as to exasperate an already worried daughter through any sense of desperation in his voice?

'Dad?!'

'Yes, yes Ellie.' Time to take control; the signal could go again at any moment. 'I am safe and in a hotel.'

'Da -a -ad...' Her voice was intermittent, weak; but there was no mistaking the fact that it contained an element of disquiet.

'Yes, Ellie. Are. You. OK.?'

'...Sense of...OK...suppose...' Silence.

'Ellie, take your time. Explain.'

'But...scared Daddy....' Silence. She used the word *Daddy* and therefore something was incorrect here. Something was wrong. He had a vision of himself driving like a maniac, too much alcohol in his blood for driving now an absurd consideration, a year's suspended prison sentence and a withheld driving license a pathetic sacrifice for somehow alerting the Garda to some sort of emerging crisis in Dublin. The words *golden hour* formed menacingly in his head: *authorities* yesterday's word, the result of a silly altercation between squabbling parents.

'Where. Are. You?'

'...OK Daddy...in the hotel...'

'Are. You. Alone?'

'...I...alone...scared...you never told me.'

This was horrid whatever it was, Paul thought, but the sense of there being an unfolding atrocity abated. Was she having some sort of teenage meltdown? 'Ellie. I don't know what you are talking about but I will be with you in the morning. Do you understand? Repeat, do you understand?'

'Yes...Dad.'

'You don't leave the hotel room, do you hear me? Just eat and drink whatever there is in the mini bar.'

'...K...'

And then her voice was no longer there.

Paul ran to the bathroom and splashed cold water on his face; his heart was beating fast. He then dashed down to the bar area which was now deserted. He didn't care. If Mr Connolly so much as barked any telecommunications protocol at him right now he would feel close to murder. He picked up the landline receiver. But it was still dead.

He returned to his room.

Paul threw open the window and gulped in the still faintly electric air; between gasps he allowed himself to think. Ellie was clearly safe, he surmised. Something quite bad had affected her, but seemingly not anything criminally physical - like an assault of any kind. And besides she had a mobile phone. She surely knew that, if she didn't know the number of Ireland's emergency services, she could call Anne - the hell she could call the hotel's reception, assuming that terrorists had not taken it over. *You don't fuck with the Irish,* he found himself thinking almost manically. *Take those fuckers on at your peril.* He turned the TV back on, dreading the words *Mumbai-style massacre*. But there was no breaking news of terrorists taking over a hotel in Dublin in a particularly stylised atrocity of any description.

No, his thirteen-year-old daughter had suffered some sort of psychological episode. He had not been there for her and there was shame in that. There was shame in his clearly absurd decision to drive to Galway for the day before having checked the weather forecast: there may even have been shame in his having agreed to taking her to Dublin at all, with the full knowledge that each day he would be leaving her there in the hotel on her own. He would live with all that, learn from it; he would even contemplate an *authorities*-laden rant from his ex and take it all in silently and stoically like a man. He would do all that because Ellie was, he was very certain, safe from catastrophe of any meaningfully permanent kind. He threw himself backwards on to the bed and laughed the laughter of relief.

His phone rang.

The celerity of his response was becoming second-nature.

'Ellie!' the nuance of interrogative now lost in his voice.

'Paul?'

It was Anne.

'Darling! How...how are you?'

Paul wasn't at this point entirely sure if the intermittence of her voice was as a result of the treacherous signal or some other emotional basis.

'For Anne to be...Girl...She is...Needeth...Hand...Sweet Jesus...'

Was she drunk? That would be a novel turn-around to the usual dynamics of the relationship, he smiled sardonically to himself. 'You alright love?' he chanced an ethereal, almost dismissive tone, partly so as not to exacerbate some conceivable state of psychological capitulation on the other end of the line, but also to hide within his own voice the unpalatable consequences of the unfolding drama at his end of it.

'*Needeth* for heaven's sake Paul...what can she mean?' There was no mistaking it now. Anne was crying.

'Darling. Look. I am stuck in a storm in an inn in Galway and your reception is bad. Do you understand?'

'Yes...think so...'

'I will be back in Dublin in the morning and I will call you from there. Whatever is happening. Do not leave the house. Do not go to work tomorrow. If you need help call the police, no matter how trivial you think it is. Do you understand Anne?'

'But...cross...darling...'

'No, no look I'm not cross. Hold on, are you cross with me Anne? Please explain.'

'No...sign...cross...'

'No, ahm, no darling. No sign whatsoever. Because, you see I'm not cross with you, why would I ever be? I love you more than anything Anne. You must know that.'

'Love...you...too...'

And her voice vanished.

At that moment Paul felt that if he had to cut through the fallen tree with his nail scissors in the morning he would do so and he would, through some shared mechanism of mutual trust with the middle-ranking rodents of the West of Ireland, some totemic understanding of the enormity of good and evil that abounded between the separate species of God's shared earth and all that had survived the Ark, enlist the greater animal Politik and gloriously slice asunder the one thing that had led to his having been so preposterously removed from the two most important humans in his life.

A fallen tree in the middle of a minor road, North of the R446 near Clostoken, between Galway and Dublin.

Chapter Seventeen

Ellie's history homework had simply been set as the *History of your House*. Safe in the knowledge that she had just this and her English assignment left to do, she knew that she had time to research whatever this history might be. The ghastly incident of yesterday had contrived to keep her mostly confined to her room, safe in the knowledge that *he* had been so visually shaken by the turn of events in the pool, so evidently contrite in his demeanour, that even if he were to bring her anything to the room, his teasing predisposition would be palpably absent. And besides, even if it were not, where was her latent embarrassment left to go? How bad could it be? She slowly bit into her last slice of room-delivered pizza and started some Internet searches on the house in Hammersmith. A slightly famous early 20th Century painter had lived about five doors down from them. It was where he first sketched and later completed his seminal *Girl With Paint, Paints Girl* apparently. A vision flashed into her head of a canvass within a canvass, and in that canvass were an infinite shrinking number of smaller canvasses until the human eye could detect none further. She made a note of this intriguing and contrived statement of something abstract, the sort of thing her art teacher Mr Tumbler would gloat over and give her a chance of getting more than a C Plus for a change. But there was nothing about *her* house. She could lie of course, pretend that in the corner of a bedroom wall, she once came upon the unmistakable brush strokes of the Artist, the masonry providing a temporary surface for the mixing of paint, as the second, slightly smaller girl took form. *It was fascinating to behold the more suffused greys take shape upon my bedroom wall, as if the Artist had been there himself only yesterday.* Mr Tumbler would love that shit. But he was also the sort of scheming man who would check her home address in the school records and she would be undone.

Frustrated, she began searches on the house in Lounsley. But it was a similar situation. Speculation from local historians about the growth of the village around its founding buildings, rest-houses for weary travellers, associated poor-houses, the old Norman church itself. There was a fascinating listing of the local lunatics and where they had lodged. Gosh, she thought, how many mad people could there be back then? She privately hoped that none of them had lived in their house, through fear of unwelcome ghosts, much as it would have written her homework for her. *Stephene Parsones - a Ne'er-do-well and harmer of chickens.*

But at the bottom of the list hovered a link. *For access to the full archive, click here.* She did. A page popped up inviting the visitor to a discounted first month's subscription to the Brenham Chronicle full historical archive. *Or why not choose 3 months' half price - this week only?* No, one month should do it, she imagined and clicked on the hyperlink. £6.99. She paused. Now what is £6.99 compared with a club sandwich in this place? she chuckled to herself and found herself reaching for her dad's credit card, still untouched upon the side table, for everything else she had simply charged to the room. There was one thing you could guarantee about parents, she reassured herself, when it came to *Education* they became all silly and doe-eyed, perplexing really when you analysed what their own priorities seemed to be in life:

making money, procreation, ranting about the relevance of unaccountable chambers, whatever that meant, hidden cellars full of stolen junk no doubt.

No, £6.99 was a devilishly handsome investment for everyone. She had the chance of finding out something, *anything*, that might have happened in the row of fifty or so houses that lined the main high street and *were* the village of Lounsley. Surely in two hundred years something must have happened at the house, the row of houses even. Not even Mr Tumbler would pay £6.99 to catch her out on that front.

Stolen charabanc left abandoned outside butcher's.

And she would undoubtedly receive untold praise from Anne herself, the purveyor of all things house-historical and permanent domestic fantasist. She wondered if Anne's birthday was any time soon and whether she should upgrade to the three months option.

I just wanted to get you something different this year. You have all the bath salts in the world.

So £20.97 it was. She would pay her dad back when she could, which was likely never, she thought guiltily, consoling herself with the fact that she never *asked* to be born.

She was in.

She typed the street name in the search box. Nothing. She had a sinking feeling that over a hundred years ago Lounsley was so distant to Brenham that residents of the latter had no interest in what happened there. Either that or they were at war: *knowledge costs lives*. A vision hovered within her of a Victorian insurgent, a Lounsleyan man later hanged for treason, stealing out into the night and clandestinely bending the *One mile to Brenham* sign the other way. Had she really just wasted all that money on nothing? Then with incredulity of the fiercest proportions it slowly dawned on her that this archive, this hidden library, was not like the

Internet at all. Supporting a sort of rustic technology that seeped from the very tales of history themselves with which it interfaced, it absurdly, risibly appeared to work on the basis of clicks leading you to a *.pdf* of an actual *edition* of each newspaper, the countless iterations of print that filled the epochs backwards to the dawn of time.

Oh. My. God. She thought. The old things *before* her existence she got. Horses and carts, gas lamps, kings in tights - she understood all that. But the idea that someone would photo and scan and then convert to free downloadable software, formats which could not be character-searched, rendered her aghast. She shuddered; not just at the draconian effrontery of the idea but also the realisation that she could be there all night. Paul would not be too long now surely and she longed to be his daughter again, dress up in a sensible frock and be accompanied down to the restaurant, protected absolutely from the terrorist threat of awkward human social interaction.

She had better get moving quickly. She started from the beginning. The first available editions started in the 1890s, at least seventy years after the house had been built, even she knew that. There were fascinating articles she conceded, though the print was invariably small and she had to keep zooming in on things.

HYTHE

SUICIDE OF A YOUNG FRENCH LADY – On Thursday an inquest was held at Hythe, before Mr. G. S. Wilks, Borough Coroner, on the body of Juliette Lorieoux, a Parisian lady, aged 29, who has been residing with her mother at Sutherland House, Hythe, since August last. The deceased shot herself in the brain with a revolver she had purchased from Folkestone, under the pretext that she was afraid of thieves. Some time ago she was brought before the

Dover magistrates, charged with attempting to commit suicide by filling her room at a local hotel with charcoal fumes, but was dismissed upon the promise of the mother that she should be well looked after. It was believed that the cause of her strange conduct was her sweetheart's death in Paris. The jury returned a verdict that she had taken her life while temporary insane.

She began to realise that most of the more interesting articles weren't even in Brenham, let alone Lounsley. She knew where Hythe was because they'd driven there recently for Anne to pick up some pottery she'd painted weeks earlier – it was miles away!

Time was running out. Where was anything to do with Lounsley, Brenham even? But that's the whole point, she thought. Once you had motor cars and trains then you had the expansion of commuter-belt towns in the home counties; they'd learnt that in geography. As those towns grew with all that new housing then you got *conurbation* and villages joined their nearby towns, exactly what had happened to Lounsley. There was a gratuitous 100 yard gap between the last house in Brenham and the first in Lounsley, as if the town planners couldn't quite bring themselves to annexe their neighbours completely.

The Victorian news had not been particularly sensational: it occurred to Ellie that the more recently you ventured, the more likely there would be more interesting news, and more factually reported. What would be the most recent decade which you could think of as the *Olden Days*? The 1970s!

1975 would be a good start she decided and worked backwards from there. As she clicked on each Wednesday edition, for the paper was weekly, there began to appear more references to Lounsley, but most of the specified locations were all the shops and businesses. She had had no idea how thriving the village had once been. *Four* pubs, a bakery, a butcher's, a general store, a haberdashery, whatever that might be, a green grocers and a doctor's surgery. Ah, she thought, didn't Dad or Anne have a theory about how the house might have been just that once upon a time? But the accompanying photo to the article, *New Brenham Medical Centre Closes Lounsley GP Surgery*, showed an angry crowd of locals with placards outside an old building: but it wasn't their house.

Pensioner Tom Whittle: 'My family have been coming to the surgery for generations and now my wife is expected to walk the mile to Brenham just to have her pills, it's a disgrace.'

Three hours later and she'd somehow quickly scanned all the editions back to 1970, realising as she went that most of the remotely interesting news was confined to the first three pages generally, such was the genteel existence of people in the *Olden Days*. A numbness descended upon her. This was utterly ridiculous. Her eyes were hurting so she walked to the bathroom and splashed cold water over her face before raiding the mini-bar and pouring herself a *real lemonade* which was disgustingly flat. Where was Dad? If he had been there he would have been on the phone to Reception immediately. *Please note that we won't be paying for the gone-off lemonade, thank you.*

Come on Ellie, she willed herself. We have to get lucky soon. She returned to the laptop and was about to scroll upwards to the rest of the seventies when she noticed 1969 temptingly adjacent to the last batch of links. *The Swinging Sixties* she thought to herself. That's what the adults say don't they when they go all doe-eyed about it. They would say nonsensical things that meant nothing to her like *If you remembered the Sixties then you weren't there*. A statement of the most heinous paradox imaginable. *Does a falling tree on an uninhabited island make a sound?* was at least a debate they could all occasionally enjoy, but the notion of some parallel universe where you either existed but somehow simultaneously non-existed was just a bit silly really, even by the standards of the most arcane of Religious Study discussions.

The articles were not that very different from the ones she had just read in the early seventies. Except that most of the men had shorter, if not totally weirder hair with ridiculous sideburns and curiously fashionable spectacles. Even the most civic of female stalwarts of the community however seemed obsessed with showing off their legs in an unnecessary but hugely hilarious way. Some of the articles were quite funny and she kept getting distracted.

I met Cassius Clay at Garden Centre.

And even some set in the village.

Lounsley GP Surgery Admits Supplying Drugs. Mrs Margaret Whittle: 'I went to get my green pills but later I came over all queer.' A spokesman for the surgery told our reporter that a prescription for Mrs Whittle and her son Dylan were accidentally mixed-up. 'The surgery is profoundly sorry for the error but would like to go on record as reassuring Mrs Whittle that the stimulant she took is not life-threatening.'

She was becoming tired now and quite hungry. The effects of the pizza had long-dissipated and she realised that she was close to defeat. She wanted nothing more than a hot shower and decided that she would then order up some proper food. She looked at the clock by her bed: 20:45. Where had the evening gone, let alone the day? And where the hell was Dad? I'll give it one more go, she thought to herself.

She returned to the list of weekly editions and was curious to notice that one of them stood out. It was the only edition of the weekly paper that had been published on a Tuesday. She clicked on the link. *Tuesday July 1st 1969.*

At first she stared at the screen not really taking it in for several seconds.

For there in the middle of the front page was a large photo of their house.

It looked almost completely as it was today. It might have been the photo that the estate agents had sent them when Dad and Anne were thinking of buying it, except for a solitary police officer standing gravely by the front door, his helmet and deportment more similar to the photos of police constables a century earlier, rather than those of today's smiling, dancing officers whose community-friendly antics invariably went viral.

Above the photo loomed a large headline.

Village Vigil Continues For Missing Child.

Ellie found that her arms had grown suddenly cold and her face clammy.

She wished it all away. Whatever it was, this was not some clever homework before her. This was some hideous history that should never have come to light. But there was now no escaping it.

She read on.

Kent police officers have this week been searching for Francesca John-Bangoray who disappeared from the family's house in Lounsley High Street while her parents Patrick and Bernadette dined with guests on the ground floor. She was last seen asleep in her bed at about 9 o'clock on Saturday evening, but when her parents checked on her as guests left from the dinner party at around midnight she was no longer in the house.

As the Chronicle goes to press in the early hours of this unprecedented early Tuesday edition, Det. Supt. Bill Dane spoke to reporters near his mobile radio unit which has been set up in the rear garden of The Crown, Lounsley, courtesy of the landlord, and issued the following update.

We regret to report that we have no new leads on the missing child Francesca Kathleen John-Bangoray, who went missing from her home in Lounsley High Street sometime in the late evening of last Saturday, 28th June. We ask the local community, including those residents of the wider Brenham area, to be particularly vigilant in the coming days. We ask residents to check their gardens as extensively as possible and those of absent neighbours. Her parents have asked the public to call out to her in the name of 'Fran', which is how she is addressed at home.

'Her disappearance is very difficult to explain given the circumstances of Saturday evening. There have been no sightings of her which adds to the seriousness of the situation.

'We are flooding the area with specialist officers and dogs. Every resource that we have that is not being deployed on 999 calls is being used to search for the little girl. The worry is that she may be lying hurt somewhere. We are combing local gardens, parks and woodland which her house is close to, as well as outbuildings in the area and the nearby stream and flooded gravel pit.

'Any information that members of the public possess, no matter how irrelevant it may seem, such persons are urged to contact the police as soon as possible. We have issued to the press the most recent photograph of the girl, who is 3-years-old.'

Local resident Eddie Epps told our reporter that a large majority of the village was out looking for the three-year-old.

'There is not a man in Lounsley that I know that has clocked into work this week. Some will lose wages that's for sure and we've set up a collection. We won't leave a stone unturned until the little girl is found.'

Arthur Wraight, who runs The Crown on Lounsley High Street, and from which premises Kent Police is organising the searches, said that the pub was completely empty during the day on Monday as locals joined the hunt but that it was exceptionally busy in the evening.

'We've drafted extra staff in this week and the local brewery has kindly sent over extra barrels without an invoice. Any man who comes

to the Crown after sundown this week as part of the searches will have free beer. But there are no celebrations in Lounsley this week.'

Officers of the C.I.D., who are increasingly concerned about the girl's whereabouts, are speaking to 'all family members and dinner party guests' about the disappearance.

One thing is clear, at this gravest hour: the good people of the village of Lounsley and the town of Brenham have become but as one in their vigil for this much-loved, local missing girl.

As she came to the end of the article the sense of creeping dread that had built up inside her was primitively interrupted by a precipitous burst of rain against the hotel window. The street lamp outside, previously so reassuring in its quietly brooding luminescence, now as it bulged its way into the heavily aqua-planed window, took on a sinister quality, like a voyeuristic demon feasting upon her fresh and nascent fear.

She felt very alone and wanted her dad with her right now - this wasn't funny anymore.

She reached for her phone and tapped the icon that said *Dad*. It had not rung more than once when suddenly he was there, her father's voice.

'Ellie?!'

'Dad?!'

'Yes, y...llie'. The line was wretched but just knowing that he was there, *somewhere*, partially eased the cloud of fear that had taken her since the awful discovery.

'Dad, where are you? Are you OK?' Her voice felt weak; she tried desperately to hide any panic within it. She knew that that would make her dad's predicament, whatever and wherever it was, just worse.

'Y...llie. Are...K?'

'Well in the sense of "Am I OK?" yes I suppose I am. Yes, yes I'm OK Daddy. Just need to tell you something but it can wait.'

'Ellie, take...time...plain.'

'I'm not scared Daddy...' She was conscious of the fact that she had used the word *Daddy* twice in a row now and that this was unlikely to be construed as slip of the tongue. But it was too late. Too late to be the cool teenager.

'Where...you?'

'I'm OK Daddy. I'm in the hotel.'

'Are. You...lone?'

'Yes I'm alone. It's OK. I won't be scared, it's OK, OK, just, just,' she suddenly felt angry, 'you never told me.'

'Ellie...talking about but...with you...orning. Do... derstand? Repeat...derstand?'

'Yes, I'll be fine Dad.'

'You...leave the...room...hear me? Just...rink ...there...ni bar.'

'OK Dad. Are you in a hotel somewhere? And you're coming back in the morning right?'

But his voice was no longer there.

And she was left with the dread, the dread of being alone with the dead.

Anne floated upwards, and upwards. What a curiously delicious sensation, she half-thought. The bath was barely large enough for her to float at all and yet here she was being sensuously dragged up to the ceiling by a swirl of sodden, scented mists that danced lightly on the cooling stream of air emanating from the bathroom window. Her favourite meditation CD was throbbing gently somewhere in the background. *Special Bonus Track...Well-Being (Chakra Balancing)*...Her eyelids barely registered the delicate flicker of half a dozen candles that lined the side of the bath and daubed the faintest of heat upon her right cheek and arm. The swirling eddies that seemed to meet together in her mind in this rapture of the bathroom ceiling were almost tangible in the sense that she felt she could control their direction, their colours even. What can they be, right here, right now - what should I allow them to be? A swaying room of sniffing rutting Centaurs, all bowing to me, their Queen? Or chocolate in the sky, all innocent and there for the taking as I survey the fickle treats of my watery-sky kingdom? I'm tip-toeing through corridors with no sides, gliding aloft waves of heavenly scented bubbles, swimming through vortices of undulating flames that tease and tickle but never burn.

And then something was wrong.

Something was waiting and watching her every gentle move. It had a voice. An unkind voice. A voice she had heard so many times and yet...never before. She would rather it would be so many times because then she would know what it was that was waiting for her, calling her and she would not feel the inching terror that oozed into her gradually ebbing state of ecstasy. 'For Ann...' It had words now, a structure. And this meant that she could no longer stay in her ceiling kingdom. She was being lowered into the bath again by the vaporising molecules around her, the tendrils of reality that would have her floating again in a simple, mundane bath.

And now the Chakra was a part of some cheap meditation loop coming from a speaker in the corner of the bathroom and the warm water, relaxing though it was sloshing around her body, was what it was: bathwater infused with mid-range toiletries and surrounded by the sort of scented candles you get every year at Christmas from someone else's children. But the voice still came. It came from somewhere behind her, slightly to the right as if from the wall itself.

For Ann to be the girl she is, needeth the hand of sweet Jesus.

It sounded both familiar and yet alien and she realised that she was utterly paralysed. If her head had gone under the water at that moment she would drown she was sure and though there was no reason that this might happen in a bath in which she could not technically float free from the sides at all, she felt desperate. Desperate for the voice to stop. Was it inside her head? Was she finally going mad? But no, the voice was that of the old lady next door, surely. Was she in the adjacent room to hers, presumably next door's bathroom itself? That could explain it. The old lady, Mrs Carmichael, she was eccentric to say the least: well there was no point beating around the bush they decided after they had first moved in; utterly bonkers they had all thought, but harmless enough.

The paralysis began to wane and Anne felt her knees jactitate reassuringly, like when she was suddenly awake again after nodding off in the summerhouse chair. She moved her eyes and lifted her head. Now would be a good time to get out of the bath completely, to calm herself.

For Ann to be the girl she is, needeth the hand of sweet Jesus.

And why *wouldn't* the old lady use her name? Yes it was a bit creepy that she was ululating something strange from the bathroom next door, presumably without the knowledge that Anne was there just a few feet beside her, albeit partitioned by a bloody great Regency wall. But you can't pick and choose the lyrics with daft old mad people; she might as well be chanting something about Graham the cat. And yet, thought Anne, as she stood upright on the bath mat, reaching for a large towel, it *was* a bit *creepy*. She glanced in the mirror and it gripped her. She wasn't sure what it was that gripped her, something shadowy and all-knowing and utterly repugnant, like something inside you that doesn't belong, not like putrid bile backing up in your throat, but something intangible and quietly, insidiously enormous, something that could own you if you didn't flee it, smite it, *understand* it.

For Ann to be the girl she is, needeth the hand of sweet Jesus.

She continued to stare at the mirror. Why did the Ann in the voice not have an 'e' at the end, or rather did her brain choose to truncate it this way? Why would her mind cogitate the old lady saying Ann and not Anne? Why, it wasn't her at all then was it? It was her defence-mechanism reassuring her that the old lady was barking on about something to do with…what? Ann Miller? Ann Rutherford? Ann Widdecombe? It was a pretty common name really wasn't it…Ann…You could stick an 'e' on the end and ennoble it, or in her case *Dutchify* it, but she was just another Ann really wasn't she at the end of the day?

And then the voice stopped and she could tear her gaze from its mirror image before her; she suddenly felt exhausted and alone. She would do anything right now to have the familiarity of the voices of the people she loved around her: Paul, Ellie, yes Ellie even. Yes Paul and Ellie. They could bicker and storm off from each other all they liked, for hours on end. She wanted normality and strife and the banality of family life to erupt around her.

She would go downstairs and pour herself something akin to a cocktail if the drinks cupboard would allow it and call in Eric or Graham and play silly games with them. She needed to think and yet not think. She went to the window and looked outside to see if she could discern any hint of a scruffy tabby cat tail waving around in the gloaming. It was becoming quite dark now, even for late July; it must be past nine o'clock even: a drink was definitely in order. Was that Eric by the fence? She strained her eyes.

She was suddenly aware that she was peering at the aged, malevolent grin of Mrs Carmichael, who stared straight back at her from beside the fig tree that spanned the fence between the two gardens. She jumped back from the window, her sense of embarrassment contorted by fear. Was it a trick of the darkening after all? She gingerly moved her head back to the window.

But the old lady was no longer there.

Anne padded down the stairs, swaddled in her towel and bathrobe. Telephone? Drink?

Both, but the drink first. She went straight for a neat gin and threw a couple of ice cubes in from the little freezer draw. She slammed it back, refilled her glass and tottered over to the large sliding French windows, the ones into the garden, the garden she decided that she was absolutely not going to enter this evening. The dread from the chanting voice was all around but in the garden it might find mathematically peculiar ways of killing her.

The coroner concluded that the lack of physical injury to the body meant that she had no choice but to declare an Open Verdict.

She slammed the lock into place and without looking out of the window once, for fear of meeting the menacing face of the old lady, she pulled both sets of string down so that the Venetian blinds severed her existence from the outside world completely. Another gulp of gin and she was by the house phone and carefully, but urgently, tapped in the digits for Paul's phone. Please be there, she begged.

Paul's voice *was* there, all crackling and cutting out, but he was there all the same and she felt safe again from whatever the terror was, for it could not be something physical in the house and the voice of the man she loved in Dublin was all that she needed right now. That he answered the phone by declaring rather manically that he thought she might be his daughter, a subtlety which might usually rankle, seemed now an irrelevance beyond anything worth anything in the world.

'Paul?'

'Dar...ng! How...you?'

'I'm, I'm fine...no really I am.' As soon as she said the words she realised that only a fool could believe her and that for all his naivety, Paul would be alarmed, so she waited patiently for his reply. But the line was a crackly near-silence of white noise which held her mesmerised except for the words that she could not stop from tumbling from her mouth, as if to deny them would be to banish her existence in some unfathomable way.

'For Anne to be the girl she is, needeth the hand of sweet Jesus.'

She must sound like a woman demented she realised and hoped that the line was still a temporary lost thing. But his next words suggested otherwise.

'You...right love?'

She tried to find words of reassurance but they could not come and so silence, deafening, prevailed within her.

'Darl... ...ook... ...tuck...torm in...Always and your... ...bad...ooh understand?'

'Yes...I think so.'

'...back...Ublining...call you from there...happening... not leave the house...go to work...orrow...help call the police, no matter how trivial you think it is. Do you understand Anne?'

He was all strong for her, dominant like he rarely was and her vulnerability felt cocooned and safe and it made her seek answers from him involuntarily.

'But she does not do the cross darling.'

'No...not cross...on...you cross with me Anne? -plain.'

'No no I meant the sign of the cross. She doesn't make the sign of the cross.'

'No...arling. No sign...ever. Cause, you see not cross with you...ever be? I love you more than anything Anne...that.'

'I really really love you, all of you so much, all of you too.'
And then there was silence.

Chapter Eighteen

If Paul's inner physiology portrayed embryonic signs of exhaustion by ten o'clock the next morning, he was certainly unaware of it as he entered the Queen's Hotel. He'd sent a text to both senior partners before he finally bedded down for the night in the Glafarnach Inn and no sooner had his alarm sounded at six o'clock than he was aware of several successfully received texts. Three were from Ellie, he quickly ascertained, before their brief and ambiguous telephone conversation yesterday evening and they were suitably of the teen-brief variety, one simply asking, 'Omg, y r u ignoring me?' One was from Anne saying, 'Sorry about earlier, I hope you are OK, I cannot wait to see you; all my love, Anne,' but if he was completely honest the one that pacified him the most was that from Eanna Clery, one of the senior partners: 'OK, we'll push it back to two-thirty. We'll take Jim and Sarah to lunch first. Good luck with the tree!'

Ah, yes the tree, Paul had thought as he took his shower. Well I had to mention it to them didn't I? He'd deliberately set his alarm not ridiculously early in order to give the authorities time to clear it. He'd figured that if the beast were still there, he would have time to U-turn and circumnavigate everything via the R446, allowing him to arrive at the hotel by midday latest and his text of last night factored all of that in. He'd made the decision to text Ellie rather than speak with her, not least because teenagers were never grateful for sleep interruption (irrespective of any worry she must surely have experienced last night). As it happened half the tree was cleared by the time he'd reached it and a simple hand-held stop/go operation was in place, which rather amused him as it was really a go/go sign that could be flipped either way upon the excitement of the occasional approaching car in this seemingly permanent vehicle-less backwater. That had allowed him to continue north to join the M6 and ensure that he arrived at the hotel as quickly as possible. He had had enough of the *real Ireland* for now.

He positively skipped into the lift, relishing the sight and sound of even the grumpiest teenager that the world could throw at him. Reaching their floor, his lifted spirits condensed and sank abruptly when he saw that the room's door was ajar. He dashed in to find one of the cleaners, clearly startled by his sudden presence. 'My daughter, is she, was she, *did you see a girl?*'

'Eengleesh no much. Girl, yes. She no leave room. So when I see no sign on door, I think ha, she leave, she must breakfast. I clean. Room must need cleans.'

Paul ran back to the lift and waited impatiently behind a large American couple with too many bags, he testily reflected. The lift stopped and he said, 'Terribly sorry, late for the speech, I'll send a porter,' which incoherent English-centric babble seemed to do the trick and he pushed inside, turned and lightly bowed to them as they stared at him, the doors closing.

She was there in the breakfast room and a million rigid molecules were swept aside from his neck muscles and he didn't think he'd ever been more ecstatic in his life at that moment.

For Ellie, receiving her dad's text early that morning was a huge relief and she sensed she might cry. She managed not to, but worse was the inescapable *possibility* that she might blubber like a tiny girl if her dad came back to her in the room and even worse still was the inescapable *certainty* that her dad would blubber and say things that she sort of wanted to hear, but didn't want to hear. Words like *love* and *so* and *much*. Her mind represented the perfect storm of ambiguity, confusion and reassurance and she concluded that a thoroughly more public-setting for the reunion was clearly demanded, for both her sanity and her father's dignity.

It worked: they could not help but beam at each other and it was enough.

She knew a really rather huge hug was coming and she was not only prepared for it, but needed it very badly and the lines she read from her actor's script might or might not have been believed by any innocent bystander let alone her dad, but they made her feel suitably in control of her own poise. 'Da-aa-d…Get *off* me. I'm eating my breakfast.'

Paul was now too full of nervous energy to order anything, even if they were still serving breakfast, which he doubted and so he sortied to the area where there were still piles of toast by a machine and packets of butter and jam and still-fresh coffee. He returned to the table and realised before long that he was rambling and barely ate anything, just gulped the coffee until it made him yet more excitable. *What had she made of his absence? His phone call? What had she tried to tell him yesterday? Had he told her yet about the tree?* Her replies were polite but monosyllabic and a great weariness descended upon him. He yawned. 'I think I'll have to lie down darling. You OK? Important meeting this afternoon. Let's have a proper chat later, right? We're staying tonight, you do know that?'

Yes she did and Dad, you really need to sleep. Everything is fine.

As he lay on his back on the hotel bed, shoes cast off onto the floor beside him, he really did begin to think that everything would be fine after all. Sleep would cure everything. Ellie was OK and Anne, whilst a terrible sadness lay in store for her there was no doubt, well she was flesh and blood, and she was his, and if a bad telephone line last night had exaggerated some upset that she had tried to communicate to him then that was one thing, but their love for each other would reign supreme. His mind descended into some sort of holding area and he felt undulating waves of softness engulf him. The last thing his conscious mind remembered as the currents took him down, was the face of a boy in a tree, in the photograph, but it was smiling and then it was Ellie and she was smiling too.

'Da-aa-aa-dd.'

Paul started. Ellie shook him awake. 'Time, what time is it?' There was panic in his voice.

'OK Dad. Half one. It's OK.'

'How did you know? How could you know?' he gasped, altogether relieved by the revelation that he now had time to jump up, have a wash and put on a pressed shirt from the wardrobe.

'You had a text. I thought it might be important. It *was* important. It was that Eanna bloke. The one you once said you were going to do that terrible thing to, something to do with his eyes. The time I realised there is something seriously *wrong* with you. He asked if you were still OK for two-thirty. Otherwise it is *with some reluctance* that we shall have to try to close without you.'

'Ah, yes that Eanna. Well the truth is darling that sometimes you have to suspend terrible thoughts about other people. It's called *opportunism*. Stick that in your English homework tonight why don't you? Er…it is English left isn't it you said?'

'Yeah. Though I still haven't done history because…' She paused. She didn't want to frighten her dad just yet; she wanted him to *close* whatever that meant, though she suspected that his whole trip was based on *closing* something. '…I mean. I'll tell you later.'

'Brill, you do that darling. I'll help you don't you worry. And if the worst comes to the worst, we'll get Anne to get stuck in. She knows her history that woman.'

The next thing Ellie knew was that he appeared to be brushing his teeth about ten thousand times and making strange snarling noises in the bathroom and she felt that she finally had her completely bonkers dad back and she didn't care a jot.

Paul went to straighten his tie before entering the boardroom and then realised that he didn't wear ties, ever; it wasn't that sort of industry. A quick ruffling of his hair would have to suffice: something self-consciously liberating and becalming in order to sublimate the hint of the slightest discord within, the frazzled fading of the near-nightmare of the last twenty-four hours. He checked his phone one last time and scrolled down. There was an unread message timed at half past ten that morning which had not been there fifteen minutes ago as he left the hotel foyer. A text that had suffered late delivery. From Eanna.

He froze.

But a reminder that the 3 of us meet privately first at 2pm just so we are all clear of the strategy.

Never particularly *au fait* with any prevailing technology, least of all the latest smartphone that his work had provided him, he now saw numbers appearing at the bottom of the screen. Five missed calls in the last half hour. His phone had been on silent whilst he slept.

But it wasn't 2 p.m., it was 2:30 p.m. He turned the handle as if in a trance and entered the boardroom.

Jim and Sarah sat at the far end of the table and smiled serenely. Perhaps they had already discerned the silent wave of anxiety that emanated from the other two individuals opposite them, Eanna and Seamus, the company's senior partners, who stared at Paul now with a mixture of apprehension and barely containable loathing.

The sense of simmering hostility from his own employers caused Paul involuntarily to sit as far away from them as possible, at the nearest end of the table, a decision he now realised which only served to demarcate a brooding internal division.

Eanna spoke. 'Well, as we are finally all here…' Sarah raised an eyebrow slightly as if to reflect the fact that everyone had arrived completely on schedule for the pre-arranged meeting. '… I just wanted to thank you both, Jim and Sarah, for all of your time over the last three days. It's certainly been a pleasure to be able to discuss potential new business with you and we very much look forward to finalising a deal with you this afternoon.'

'No, look, it's been really great,' began Jim, 'tough but a real pleasure also. Thanks for having us.' He glanced at his watch and then turned to Sarah deliberately just above *sotto voce*, Paul was quite sure, as he spoke gently into her ear. '…Do we need to be at the airport?'

'Leave in say twenty minutes?' she barely whispered back, again thought Paul unnecessarily at a level which might just be interpreted as a ploy.

'Gentlemen,' resumed Jim, 'alas our plane to New York is unusually on time and we really don't have more than twenty minutes before our car arrives to take us to the airport.' Silence, other than a nervous cough to Paul's left. 'I think we are nearly there and I shall say this: Good Stride is the company we most want to work with. You have demonstrated a commercial regime which entirely fits with our business model and your passion, your transparency in particular, are qualities we seek in a long-term partner.'

'However,' continued Sarah, as if the double-act had been practised a thousand times, 'the market place is contracting. Too many players. But it can't last. We are here for the long-term as Jim rightly says, but when the hangers-on are cleared out we can't afford to be thrown in the trash can with them, because we made the fatal error of putting intangible assets, mutual goodwill and all the rest, before the bottom line.' Paul was sure he heard a swallow to his right.

'And therefore gentlemen,' Jim cut in with predatory aplomb, 'much as we really want this deal to work with you, the numbers are not quite there for us and that is something I say to you with a very heavy heart indeed.'

Paul waited for the next baton change of sound bites.

But it never came.

All eyes turned to him. He was on his own, utterly. Whatever Seamus and Eanna had wanted to discuss internally with him, he might never know; all he knew now was that the entire deal, let's face it, his career, would be decided in the next ten minutes or so and he drew in a final breath before he began.

Began what? He had no real beginning to anything really. Just a vague set of niceties which he had presumed over the previous couple of days would suffice. But the brief, creeping barrage of unmistakable certainty of purpose which had edged towards his trench-like loneliness so bluntly since he had entered the room, now scuppered all that and the rallying whistle of the final push was nowhere to be heard.

Paul cleared his throat and, without having any real clue what would come out of his mouth, began.

'Jim, Sarah. Thank you for your frankness in the matter. You cannot have made your position any clearer.' He paused, searching frantically for some purpose, some angle, some pioneering quality of business acumen which he knew deep inside was not there. Could never be there. Seamus poured himself a glass of water from the jug before him. It was the action of a man taking his last ever drink before the final, awful denouement. If not that of his own final hour on this Earth, the final hour of one of the biggest lost deals, by association, of his senior professional career.

'I have a daughter,' the words slipped coolly from Paul's mouth, in a tone of perfect, untroubled detachment from his professional self.

Eanna's eyes now betrayed the look of a man who had put his entire fortune into the hands of a lunatic, a crumbling mind whose final engagement with society would unravel here, live, as if before the cameras of the nation.

'Yes, I have a daughter. She's thirteen, *was* thirteen. Her name is Ellie. She's here with me in Dublin. Has been all week. Did I tell you that Eanna, Seamus? I can't remember if I did. But there you have it. It goes without saying that she is the love of my life.'

If either partner had a hidden button beneath the table to summon security guards then it would probably be by now that they would be pressing it. But the grand silence that pervaded the room suggested that they had decided to go down with the ship in a final demonstration of company unity.

'So why is she here, I hear you wondering? School holiday. Teenager. Surely she should be hanging around in

London with her mates, doing all sorts of teenage stuff? I'll tell you why she's here, Jim, Sarah. She's here because - today is her birthday. This may well be the last of those birthdays you know. You both look too young to have children yourselves, or at least those of the teenage variety, but you may just understand what I mean when I. Say. That. To be fourteen. What an age shall we all agree! *Am I still a child? Or am I, actually virtually an adult, in all but height?*

'And what of Ellie? Well she may be one or she may be the other but folks...you have all this to come...let me now tell you why my daughter came to Ireland with me. She came to Ireland, not to support me in closing some peculiar deal, not to be her father's daughter. But because she is still in the Wardrobe. Still thinks she can go *through* it. Yes the Wardrobe. She still thinks there might be a sort of Narnia and she is *so* close to stepping out of the Wardrobe and then turning to face it again, now realising it's just a functional big box of hanging dresses and coats. And what keeps her from that? From abandoning the *other side*?

'A. Dolly.

'Yes can you believe it, a doll. All that time a bloody doll. What's in a doll? What's in an Irish doll? Turns out there's a whole world out there that I haven't a clue about. There's this virtual doll, this online virtual doll called Dolores. She kills people, apparently. Bad people. And Doll Dolores is everything that Ellie aspires to be. She will *click* into the head of anyone who doesn't aspire to be Dolores and in her own head, she will exact some awful revenge. The games company that created Dolores is in Galway. If you want to apparently, you can visit the head office showroom and *buy* Dolores, or like a marketing version of her, a limited version if you will. So that was to be my birthday present and Ellie surely knew it when I said that I had to go to Galway on some other business. And that's why she wanted to be as immediately close to Dolores upon my return and the reason, I'm certain of it, why she wanted to come to Dublin with me in the first place.

'You see, once you buy the physical Dolores, the exclusivity of it apparently, and please understand that I haven't the slightest clue of the functionality here, you can then go out into the outside world, the real world that you, yes you, I think we can all agree James and Sarah, inhabit, and in some strange video-gaming world find *pockets* of intelligence, curious areas of Wi-Fi, that hurtle you, the game-player, to the front of the queue and make you the *Queen Supreme of Everything.*

'You know what? I got that. No, that's a lie. I didn't have a clue what she was banging on about. But I tell you what I did get. She may not have her dad's car and house and tedious little savings accounts, but Ellie believes she has vision. Doll vision. *Doll virtual vision.* And do you know what I did next everyone?'

The room was not just silent but metamorphosed into meaninglessness for Paul right now as he surfed the wave of some truth that was either peculiar to his own pathetic existence or a demise of inner hopelessness.

'I hit a...tree. Driving back from Galway, I hit a tree. What of it?'

Sarah stared at him now with either, and he really couldn't tell, a look of incredulity or awe.

'That tree changed it all. And here's how. The storm that brought it down last night, it brought down the entire mobile telecommunications network in that area and I was forced to spend the night in an ancient inn, in the middle of nowhere without any means of letting Ellie know that I would not be coming home that night. She's an industrious kid and she figured it out in her own noble, understated way; searched the Internet for intelligence of what might have happened to me. I realise now that she was very scared but, faced with fear, she didn't crumble and chose the route of hope and practicality of purpose. She could, for example, have rung an adult, her mother maybe, or her stepmum, but she rationalised that this might cause unnecessary anxiety in others and decided to shoulder it on her own.

'When I finally returned to her this morning, we hugged, without word, without histrionics. She was largely silent in fact and when I handed her her birthday present she smiled meekly at me and said, *Dad I know what it is and I accept it now*. But she didn't open the packaging and placed it instead within what appeared to be a pre-prepared box with a handwritten label upon it. The label said, "To Dolores's New Friend, Wherever You May Be." And as she sealed the box with sellotape she said simply, "Sorry Dolores, but I have to let you go now. Though I never really knew you, I think we know each other in some small way, and we both realise it's for the best. You have to know Dolores that I made a prayer with God last night that He had to bring my daddy back to me and, if He did, then I have to let you go to someone else, someone who needs you even more than me."'

Paul stared at every other person in the boardroom for a full three seconds each in turn and he was entirely conscious now that he had them. In some way that he didn't understand. He had them.

'And then I got it. Everything struck home. Ellie had left the Wardrobe. For good.'

Jim's face remained cool but that of Sarah was visibly disturbed, for the good or otherwise he could not entirely be sure, but neither now did he strangely care. As for the senior partners, their earlier recalcitrance was no longer manifest.

'The Wardrobe of what exactly? And in which direction exactly lies the certainty? Some would say that Snow Queens and Fauns and Centaurs are where the Certainties lie. Much more so than the Earth side, of interest rates and the Uncertainty of Globalisation.'

Jim's eyebrow flickered almost imperceptibly, Paul thought.

'So Sarah, Jim. Where is your Certainty right now? Where are your Centaurs? Your Mythological Beasts? Do they sit astride the Gods of Mammon? Do they play with the Faun of Fickle Chocolate Treats? Ha ha, no doubt you will go with your prevailing Grand Certainty right now and I commend you and will not complain of it.'

Seamus turned to him and smiled the smile of a man who seemed happy now to raise his glass not just to the condemned man but the condemned ice-struck ship in which they all now chose to founder.

'All I know right now, Jim, Sarah, thank you both so much for your time today, you cannot begin to understand how we, at Good Stride, have appreciated your time this week. It's just that I have a little girl, not so little now if I'm honest, who will steer her own little ship away from me, away from this big old buggered world, and create a New Future. And. God bless. All. Who. Sail. With her.'

Paul collapsed into his chair and, abeam the watery swell of his dying wave crests, was aware of two things. Senior partners pouring water into glasses and whispers among potential investors. His day, possibly his career, was done.

The next thing he was aware of was a sudden, frantic closing of heads around the table. Of senior partners and their balanced, nuanced tones. Of Sarah and Jim, checking watches and scrolling their iPhones. A secretary rushed into the room and whispered something into Sarah's ear. Or was it Eanna's? He really no longer knew nor cared.

And then there was silence again amid the five of them. Jim turned to Eanna and Seamus and...Paul in turn and said, 'Gentlemen, a second if you will.' There was no dramatic, audience-pleasing *sotto voce* now, just a quick flurry of genuinely furtive whispering stage-aside, before:

'Sarah and I have decided that we would like us all to go into the weekend with, ha ha...'

Paul felt it coming...he felt it stage left...he felt it stage right...

'...the *Certainty* of our wish to finalise what, I hope both parties will feel to be, a truly momentous deal.'

Paul was vaguely aware of handshakes and goodbyes and realised that he probably ought to join in, or had he already, as if in a trance? But when he looked up Jim and Sarah were gone.

The boardroom now contained three very silent men. And one of them said, and Paul could not at that point remember entirely who it was, other than he was quite sure, though he could conceivably have been mistaken, that it was not him:

'You absolute fucking bastard.'

And Champagne appeared miraculously before him.

Paul returned to the hotel room a changed man in many ways. Concocting a fantastic fabrication in order to help himself become more successful in life was something he had never before countenanced. But he was a man that lent towards empiricism rather than theory, on the basis that the great mysteries of life can never really be understood by upright apes in designer clothes. Apes whose cultural ambitions rarely stretched further than to walk aimlessly around shopping malls buying useless goods with tokens earned from endless hours of heavy toil for a select few more important apes whose clothing was even more designed and whose tokens were overflowing. And yet here he was; an ape returning to his temporary luxurious residence for one last night, all paid for by a few of those more important apes who were likely to want to make him more like them in the future. He was, he smiled to himself, an ape climbing up a tree. And if that meant there was another ape on the other side of the world, staring at a bunch of smaller bananas, with a rather forlorn look upon its face, then he was not much minded anymore particularly to give a damn.

'Hiya,' Ellie called over to him as he entered the room.

Should he tell her? Tell her anything? Would she be interested? And did he have the self-control and patience to send a non-committal text to Anne and then make her squeal with delight as he popped the Champagne cork from behind his back when they returned tomorrow?

'Well helloo Ellie.'

Ellie knew immediately from Paul's infantile vowel elongation to his greeting that he had good news. 'So good news then Dad?'

'Witch! How did you know? Is it that obvious?'

'Da-ad. You are like so predictable. You are such an embarrassment.'

'Yes an embarrassing dad, but also a clever dad. Now I have a story for you my girl that is so gut-wrenchingly awful in *its* embarrassment of riches that if I tell you, you will *like literally* die. And because I don't want you to die, I cannot really tell you as a responsible father exactly what it is that I said to close the business: all I'm prepared to tell you is that *you, yes you*, darling daughter of mine, helped me close the deal. But sorry that's all I can say.'

A pillow from Ellie's bed took him full in his midriff as she threw it furiously at him.

'Daa-aad!!!'

'Ellie, gosh, wow. Great shot,' he huffed as he recovered his breath.

'If you do not tell me immediately what the story is. I. Am. Going. To tell. Mum. You. *Abandoned me.*'

He'd lost the battle already as he knew that he would and so he told her the whole story of what happened in the boardroom. He was not entirely sure if she took it all in because for most of its narration she lay on her back, remaining pillow pressed over her face, making strange beast-like baying noises, her body writhing in perceived agony as the true awfulness of her fictional role in the unfolding drama materialised.

'My. Life. Is. Over.'

And the look of hopelessness on her face when she surfaced from the pillow, presumably to breathe, made Paul wonder if she did not finally mean it.

'But Ellie. Just think. More money for me in my job. I can take you to another hotel somewhere else, even better than this. Just think. You may even one day *thank* me for it.'

She had one round of ammunition left and she used it flawlessly, the remaining pillow this time taking on the more deadly momentum of the rifled bullet, angular momentum astride straight-line velocity and the revolving hurtled mass took Paul straight in the side of his head, toppling him superbly, completely and he lay writhing in *faux* agony on the hotel room's floor.

'Defeated, utterly defeated. Ellie Fewings, in the Queen's Hotel room 349, with a...pillow.'

And for the first time since she saw the terrible thing, Ellie was momentarily, illusorily or otherwise, happy and Paul, since he found out about the other terrible thing, was momentarily, illusorily or otherwise, happy. And for the first time since either of them could remember, Ellie went in for the final kill and jumped upon his smitten, flailing torso, bashing him repeatedly with the flat of her hand until they both roared with the laughter of simpletons. Simpletons lurching uncontrollably upon a grander canvass, bedecked within a gilt frame of an enormous truth which neither of them, at that particular juncture in time, really or fully had the slightest wish to comprehend.

Chapter Nineteen

'Love you too darling. No, no cry all you must. It's good to cry sometimes. And I will *completely* look after you tomorrow my sweetest, sweetest darlingest creature.' Paul glanced at his daughter to feign self-disgust at this most self-conscious of romantic superlatives which was met with a collusive, bombastic smile of repugnance. 'Can't tell you everything right now, but it's really good…I mean work …it's really good news and everything is going to be fine.' As he hung-up he convinced himself that not mentioning the other thing was correct under the circumstances. Why inflame her vulnerability with an ambiguous, faltering voice?

Her dad's demeanour was so upbeat when he rang off from his call to Anne, that Ellie wondered if she could bring herself to tell him anything at all about the awful thing; perhaps she could delay its impact in some small way, but she was still too angry that she had had to weather the storm of discovery on her own last night, to contemplate any such degree of altruism in the matter and she began. 'I found out something last night Dad. You might want to pour yourself a drink actually.'

'Like I need an excuse Ellie. I hope you didn't drink all the beers today,' he laughed.

Ellie drew a deep breath. She had to keep it together she thought.

'Bloody size of the thing. Look at it. Tell you what my girl, if your pa hadn't worked his magic earlier, I would refuse to pay for just a few gulps from such a stubby little thing.'

Ellie went for the blurt: 'Dad, a little girl was abducted from our...your...house in 1969. She was never seen again. It was the Palmers' daughter, only they must have changed their surname.'

Paul was on such a high from his earlier exploits, so full of adrenalin, that it took him a few seconds to register what she was saying. 'Eh, what's that? Hold on. Ah, this is English, not history, or both: you have to make things up about the past right?'

'That's it. I'm a liar now. A fantasist. Why have you and Mum never taken me *seriously?* Yeah, yeah, you're right, I just made it up. Funny, had you going there didn't I.'

'Well it was a bit close to the edge darling. Who's your English teacher? I might have to have a word.'

'Oh and Dad, the lies I'm telling you. They come at a price. There's like this *liar's* website that you actually pay for. Yeah. I used your credit card to access *lies*. Am I naughty?'

'Give me that laptop Ellie! What kind of stuff have you been accessing? I mean there has to be a bit of trust here between us. I don't want to be one of those dads that is checking up on his children's Internet activity all the time. I mean surely it's going to work better if we just have some *trust* here?'

Her fear of the terrible thing distinctly lurched to smugness now as she contemplated the joy, the *Schadenfreude*, of the dawning realisation to come.

'Hnnnh? What is this? Is this an actual website? It's a pdf isn't it? Oh yeah, like on a webpage. *Brenham Chronicle. July 1st 1969.*'

Paul's face dropped and his viscera churned as the photo of his house stared back at him with its dreadful headline.

'What the fff…'

Ellie stared out of the window enjoying the ephemerality of a new emotion supplanting the one she had lived with all night. Righteousness.

'Christ Ellie. I'm. I'm really sorry. Are you alright?'

'Hm. Well I'm not used. To being called a liar.'

Paul sat next to her on the bed and put his arm around her. 'It. It's. Look whatever it is, was, it happened a long time ago. We are going to have to deal with it. You know that?'

'Ye…pp.' She felt her voice catching and she feared the inevitable. 'You knew this, already?'

'No, no Ellie. God no. There's no way Anne and I would have bought the house and kept it from you. Yes we were pleasantly surprised by the price of the house but, look, it's on a main road. The village isn't exactly a thriving community any more is it? We just thought we got lucky. To be honest with you I doubt even an estate agent would have known about…about…'

Words failed him. It all seemed surreal. Do terrible things that happen in houses taint those houses for generations to come? Is it all in the mind? Do walls become impregnated with fear? He certainly was not going to start a late night debate about it with his vulnerable teenage daughter. 'Come here, you.' He put his arms yet more tightly around her and, though her face was turned away from him, he felt her crying; the gentle sobs and warm tear-drops upon his bare arms constituting a distant memory of slashed knees and spinning bike wheels upon a dusty, wet pavement.

Everything's going to be alright Ellie.

'Darling darling. Do you know how proud I am of you? Of what you went through last night? Of how you stayed strong for me? Sshhh now. Sshhh my little girl. My *big* girl.'

Suddenly she was up and away from him and into the bathroom, the door gently locked and he felt that he heard the sound of taps being turned and water cascading. 'You OK in there?' he asked through the door.

'It's fine Dad. Like you said, it's fine. I just wanted to freshen up before we go down to dinner.'

Paul was relieved. It was of course too early for dinner but he understood the invention. His moment of intimacy had dissolved but he knew it was for the best. He vowed to stay strong for her. But he had to be strong for Anne too. He would return to Lounsley tomorrow he realised with not one but two devastating revelations and he hoped that his boardroom performance earlier might serve to add a last-gasp positive turn to the unfolding dramas that awaited her. He swigged the last of the beer and lay back on his bed trying to make sense of the myriad of conflicting recollections of recent events, emotions and meanings. The high of the boardroom was competing for space with the sadness of Anne's past and the disturbing revelation of the history of the house. His mind wandered further and he thought of the brown pencil lines on the plan of the house that he had discovered during his trespass upon The Old Vicarage; the sadness he now felt for their awful possible meaning vying with the nauseating reality of the Palmers' brief flirtation with them in their lives. But was it pathos or sorrow, this emotion? Did it fit into the great sense of a darker truth that he had felt momentarily in the bathroom the day that Ellie briefly disappeared?

Disappeared.

But Ellie was there again, sitting by one of the hotel suite's desks, wrapped in towels, drying her hair and humming a tune as if she suddenly didn't have a care in the world. It was time for Paul to be normal once more.

It would be a welcome respite from the countless theories that swam around his addled brain. 'Drink Ellie?'

'Sorry? Hello? Hairdryer!' she seemed back to her delightfully cantankerous teenage self and he loved her for it.

'Oh-kay, I just wanted to know if you wanted me to get you a drink.'

'Ah. The mini-bar. Daddy's little mini-bar. No I'll get you a drink Dad. What can I get you?'

'Oh how awfully kind my dear,' he replied in a fake clipped 1920s society accent. 'Now let me see. Hmm yes. A vodka and orange my dear, if you really didn't mind, don't you know.'

'*Vodka y narancia, muy bien, señor*,' she retorted in a suitably daft attempt at feigning a Spanish waitress. Their new-found silliness, so clearly a joint attempt to gain vacuous sanctuary from the terrible discoveries of yesterday, was cheering them both up immensely and their glee was mutual and necessary, if not the manifest mirth of the temporarily broken.

'Ellie, yeah what was that thing you told me about the word *narancia*? We were in that restaurant in Canterbury.' His heart lurched now as he inadvertently recalled the sighting, the false sighting surely he now realised, of the Palmer's daughter. He had an awful feeling that he had addressed her as *Katie* but the thought was so gruesome right now and so contrary to their new-found levity that he buried it forcibly into the back of his mind. It would come back soon enough but he was not ready for it right now: he had to be strong for his daughter. Whether he had forced her to realise the same he could not be sure but if she had, she hid it well.

'Oh yeah. We learned it in Spanish. *Narancia* is Spanish for an orange. But then you see when they brought them back to England people would like say "A narancia please."

And the more people said it over time, you see not many people wrote things down in those days, then people began to think they were saying "An arancia please." So then when books started coming out, some writers started calling it *arancia* and it became England-size, no I mean *Anglicised*, and that got mixed up with the French and so before you knew it, it became *orange.*'

Paul felt something give inside himself. Something subtly desperate was afoot here. A dread.

Narancia. A narancia. An arancia. An orange. Orange.

Ellie found a gap for his drink on the table beside him next to an old brown package with papers spilling out from one end. She accidentally nudged the package slightly. 'Oh sorry Dad.'

A piece of paper of some kind slid to the floor. But it wasn't a piece of paper. It was the photo of the boy, the photo that he had seen at the inn yesterday.

Paul felt the dread again, tighter inside.

'Reversimulacrum,' said Ellie.

'Sorry?' said Paul.

'Re-verse-simulacrum.'

'Reversimulacrum,' he repeated. 'Why did you say that?'

'It just popped into my head. I don't know why. That's so weird. I have to invent a word for English homework and say what it is and why - and I think the two things combined in my head, and I just sort of said it.'

'That's amazing. I love that word. But, but, what. I mean what is it? Why did that form in your head. Do you even know?'

'Mmm...not sure really. Oh hold on, yes I think I've got it. You remember that photo of the boy in the tree that your like...weird new mates showed you that time? And you said that I was imagining it, because it was clearly, like, a *simulacrum*. So like I thought it was ghost-boy but actually the tree trunk had all these knots in it and my imagination created a boy that didn't exist?'

'Yes, yes, I remember.'

'Well that's it really. My new word. The boy in the photo. Not *that* photo. I mean this photo, the one that just fell on the floor. His face reminds me of the simulacrum. But he's real right? I mean it's a photo of a boy so he has to be real; it's not like it's a tree trunk that looks like a boy, like the other one. So in a sense he's the opposite of a simulacrum. I mean you could say that he *reverses* it. He's a *reversimulacrum*.'

Paul's fascination now drifted to something else. Something that gnawed at his solar plexus and he realised that he might be physically sick, something that he never really was and this in its own way frightened him, but worst of all he had absolutely no idea other than that certain words were jumbling around his inner mind, phrases he now recognised but contrived to make his insides convulse.

For Ann to be the girl she is, needeth the hand of sweet Jesus.

Chapter Twenty

Anne awoke to find him not beside her and felt a heave of sadness momentarily, and then realised in that strange transient state between sleep and the real world, the one that can only be but a few seconds in time, that the next morning he really would be lying here with her. And the dawn of the realisation that they really were together again would make their half-witted awakening from slumber metamorphose in that lovely sleepy way into something gradually carnal and warm, like slowly thickening, lumpy custard.

She blinked her eyes. Rays of sunlight strafed the curtains from the ardent east. It was still early, all excited-early, and she wondered if she should try to coax sleep back into her slightly befuddled mind, the previous night having been so stressful; it was the weekend after all. But something about the light fascinated her and she could not close her eyes completely. Yes that was it – the light was all ruddy and buzzing and gave the room a frisson of electricity. Intrigued, she climbed out of bed and went to the window. As she pulled back the curtain a brilliant red sky appeared before her. *Red sky in the morning: shepherds' warning.* Great she thought, no wine on the patio this evening. We'll all be holed up inside, watching the rain outside and giggling. I don't really care! She declared it to the room, the sky outside, and a bemused Graham and Eric on the bed beside her. All her strange thoughts and troubles would be swept away once Paul and Ellie were back.

How funny, she thought: the idea of having Paul all to myself, luxuriously, wickedly all to myself, has been replaced by us all being together again. Like a proper family.

The normality, banality even, of something akin to nuclear family no longer filled her with a sense of *compromise*. Now the very thought of a slightly morose teenager in their midst made her feel all warm and safe inside. How odd.

She turned again to feel the glow of the sun upon her cheek before it disappeared completely behind the east of the house, her eyes half-closed. A man was looking up at her from the corner of the junction between the main road and the side road which led to the modern housing estate. It was a turning into which they rarely ventured, leading as it did a quarter of a mile away to a small and frightening parade of shops which seemed to provide everything the socially- and economically-challenged enclave needed: a Chinese takeaway twinned with an Indian restaurant (was it the same business?) beside a convenience store called *Lounsley Liquor, Sweets and News*. She thought it so ghastly that if anyone ever asked her in passing where she lived she would invariably say: 'Lounsley, but the southern side, you know by the main road.' If that made her a snob, she didn't much care.

She darted her head back into the room involuntarily before a rush of anger made her realise that, bloody hell, this was *her* house and she was not for ducking her head anywhere. Like in those dreams of hers where she manically confronted the danger at all costs as she had nothing else to lose, and maybe part of her knew it was a dream, and that explained her uncharacteristic courage, she defiantly shoved her face to the window to stare back at the watcher.

But he was gone.

She had a knawing feeling that she knew who it had been, but could not be sure of his identity. She screwed her eyes shut and opened them again. And then it dawned on her. Shit.

Patrick Palmer.

'Darling!'

'Hi Anne. It's Ellie. Dad's driving so it's me.'

'Well if you're not too offended by being my darling. I've always liked you, you know,' laughed Anne.

'Yes well...ha ha. Dad says...Dad, what...I mean where are we again?' Anne could hear Paul's muffled, clipped voice as he barked something at Ellie. 'Oh yeah right; Dad says we're approaching the ferry terminal in, oh yeah, Dublin. And we'll be back...sorry Dad when will we be back?' Another slightly more antagonised growl from Paul, indistinguishable. 'Oh yeah, like, around eight o'clock. Dad wants to know whether you want us to stop off at the supermarket to get anything for dinner?'

'Oh crikey. Business as usual right?' She thought quickly. She really hadn't planned any kind of grand home-coming at all really. Perhaps she'd thought they would all go out for dinner. Hell yes, why not? 'Why don't you forget about the supermarket. We've got stuff for breakfast. Tell Dad we can go to The Crown for supper!'

'Oh my god. Are you like serious? The pub in Lounsley; will they let me in?'

'Well you'll soon be fourteen and then you can *look* at the optics without being thrown in the local jail, did you know that? Ha. Yes of course you can Ellie. They have that area at the back; it's more like a restaurant; all the sweary blokes, you know the old boys, sit out at the front.'

'OK that's cool, I'll tell Dad. See you later.'

'Yeah great, love to you both, bye.'

Blimey, Anne thought to herself. Had she ever, even glancingly, declared her love for Ellie, albeit alongside her dad? All the dread of earlier, of last night, began to recede into a flame of eager anticipation at the thought of them descending upon The Crown on a Saturday night. It was revolutionary. It was a plan to thwart the doubts of the past and, she thought, embrace new beginnings in some indefinable way.

But what to do now, thought Anne. It wasn't even lunchtime. What could she possibly do for eight hours? The house was unusually, spotlessly clean. Would this be her life if she were single again? A spotless house and no-one to moan to about discarded socks and tea towels not hung correctly upon the kitchen rail? No, she would go for a walk.

As she left the house she realised that she didn't have any sort of route worked out. There were only two real choices: left along the High Street and then left again along a public bridleway which wended itself up to some farm land that overlooked the village church. That would be nice on a day like this she thought, as the hidden sun sliced obliquely down through wispy cloud striking the windows of the houses opposite. But she felt a mild tremor of unsettlement at the thought of strolling alone, along a quiet bridleway surrounded by hop fields. Why was she so jumpy? It had been a nervy last few days for various reasons: the old lady next door, the man that surely had to be Patrick staring up at her window this morning. Was there anything after all particularly disturbing about a man nostalgically peering up at his old house during an early Saturday morning walk down from the town to the village?

And yet...she shuddered.

She didn't even rationalise it any further and turned right instead, past the corner where earlier so-called Patrick had stood. Perhaps Paul was right, she unexpectedly giggled to herself. His pretend fantasies about her in the big Old Vicarage. Perhaps Patrick did fancy her after all, knew somehow that Paul was in Ireland, and was plucking up courage to give Anne his own take on a tour of the house. *Ah so you have the bed this way round do you? Back in the day I would be lying here, like this.* Or the more straightforward: *Bernie and I, we have an open relationship you know. Your pulchritude is disarming. If ever you're lonely.*

By the time she had concluded her various conspiracy theories explaining why Patrick had been there this morning, she was already halfway up the main hill and nearing the first left-hand turning, north along one of the Edwardian, tree-lined streets that led down to the railway line. She took the footbridge and walked along the long straight road that led downwards into Brenham, occasionally surreptitiously peeking into net curtain-less living-room windows, some empty, some with young families preparing for their busy Saturday ahead. An old man was patching up his low front wall with small bricks and mortar, laughing along with his next door neighbour. 'At least it gets me out the house. And on a day like this.'

Eventually she arrived at the duck pond, which separates the Edwardian and new-build houses of the south of the town from the ones further north to the coast, where the really old history of Brenham lay, with its mixture of early Tudor, Jacobean and Georgian townhouses intermingled in a patchwork of fragmented history; the history of the expansion of a market town and creek barges trading with London and the world beyond.

She felt a frisson of daring as she contemplated a glass of cold, cheap pub wine in one of the two inns by the creek itself. She could sip it and watch the tide rising over the mud banks, watch the people, the jumble of locals and tourists that would stroll past her, half-admiring the boats and turning maybe to wonder at the demure yet Bohemian English lady all alone with her wine and thoughts.

She giggled slightly to herself at the very indulgence of the idea - she could even order a starter-sized Ploughman's or a plate of lightly battered squid. Seduced into the immoderate extravagance of her banal fantasy, she turned up the hill that circumnavigated the pond and cut to her right. How funny, she thought to herself; this will take me past The Old Vicarage. What if Patrick sees me? He'll think I'm responding in type, reciprocating his daring foray this morning to test the waters of our mutual ardour. Oh god no, this is not funny. Please don't see me. She put her head down and pressed on past the large gate and driveway to her left; well if he *did* see me from one of the upstairs windows, the garden even, he wouldn't find this body language exactly seductive would he?

'Mrs Fewings!'

She froze.

Started walking again.

Realising the futility, the utter rudeness of ignoring anyone calling her name so clearly, let alone Patrick, she stopped.

'Hey Mrs Fewings. Lovely morning for it.'

What? So blatant? But the voice was all wrong. It was surely too familiar, even for a demonically sexualised, predatory Patrick Palmer. She recognised the voice though. She looked up and instantly made the connection. It was Aaron, their window cleaner, halfway up a ladder at the...at the east wall of the North Wing of the grand old house.

'Oh, Aaron, hi!' she tried her best to sound casual, relaxed, but her voice seemed to come out all squealish and manic.

'It's OK Mrs Fewings. Come in say hi - see what for my job is here.'

She gingerly strode up toward the partially opened gates and walked a few paces along the gravel drive. 'I can't really stop Aaron. I'm on my way to...to town!' she shouted a little more confidently now. But Aaron was already down from his ladder and walking towards her and she realised that turning her back on him now would constitute an unedifying rebuff, the sort of thing a proud Polish man would take very seriously indeed, not least one that she occasionally, casually employed.

'No Mr Fewings today, Mrs Fewings?'

'*Anne*, Aaron. I told you, you can call me Anne. You're very sweet. I know you learned in English to be polite and use a lady's surname but you see...once they give you permission, you don't need it again. Please call me Anne.'

'Ahnn-ah,' he exaggerated from within his beaming smile, 'and…er...no...*Paul*...today?'

'He's driving back from Ireland. I mean from the ferry that arrives in Wales this morning. Back tonight.'

'Ah, he is international businessman. Like me!'

'Well yes you are really in a funny sort of way aren't you.' Anne felt a curious battle engage within her inner self at this point. The thought of a predatory Patrick confidently marching out of the main porchway, descending upon her, as if she were a stranded, injured, fluttering bird beneath the cedar tree was ghastly...and yet...The temptation of asking her window cleaner what on earth he was doing here at The Old Vicarage of all places, bane of her recent existence in some indefinable way, and the more so because of his evident *intimacy* with the mysterious North Wing, made her wonder which would be the more horrific right now.

Patrick. Or the not-knowing.

She hedged her bets intuitively. 'Well I, I'd love to stop and catch up Aaron, gosh would love to know what your current *international* business project is, only I do feel, how should I put it, slightly uncomfortable standing in someone's driveway like this.' She deliberately phrased her words ambiguously, to hide her tangential relationship with the house's owners.

'No no Mrs Fewings, I mean Anne. Owners away. Back this evening. Come, come I show you.'

Though this made Patrick's appearance this morning all the more singular, her dilemma was done and she eagerly followed Aaron back to his ladder. Well if the *husband's away:* this was more appetising a prospect than cheap white wine and calamari staring at a creek full of boats.

'Well I got the gig didn't I Anne! I thank Paul for that.'

'Paul got you a job here?'

Suddenly embarrassed by his potential betrayal of confidence in the matter of the day to which he had unwittingly referred, he backtracked and decided that a poor grasp of English might be his momentary saviour. 'No, no, Paul he give me confidence one day. Says I have to knock on doors. All the rich people.'

'Oh I see.'

'And he told me that everything north of the pond was a good starting point. I came up the hill and tried here and they said yes. So yes I thank Paul for giving me the confidence.'

'So your contract is for the whole house?' she asked, deliberately infusing the question with a certain flattery of importance.

'Yes, well first they say that I only do main house, but then they change their mind and say please can do the North Wing too so I renegotiated and here I am.'

'Did it seem strange to you that they told you to add it as a *renegotiated* business plan?'

'Well I think first, they don't have the money. But they only want it done on an haddock basis. I was not sure what fish had to do with it, but it seems that haddock must be getting rarer in the seas, like cod, and you only do it occasionally.'

'*Ad hoc*, Aaron. It's Latin. It well yes it means what you think it does. Haddock, ha ha. I'll remember that for my next dinner party. And they are a bloody whole lot *haddock* these days…'

Aaron smiled nervously, eager to please his curiously unintelligible part-time employer.

'Anyway Aaron, indulge me now. You know how fascinated I am with old properties. I'm very *nosey.*'

'No see?'

'No, nosey. It means you like to see what's behind other people's curtains. See how perfect strangers live. Oh come on Aaron. Tell me. The Palmers - don't they have a daughter?'

'You know Mr and Mrs Palmer?'

'Well not personally really no. It's just that Brenham is such a small place. *Everyone* knows that The Old Vicarage belongs to the Palmers. So this daughter Aaron. You know, you don't have to be coy, I mean shy, about it. But you must actually look *through* the windows when you are cleaning them?'

Aaron shrugged his shoulders in a rather non-committal way.

'So like, are there *knickers* lying all around the floors? Does a messy young lady live there?' Anne felt like a tart as she delivered her words, all oozing with the understated authority of an autocratic mistress-in-waiting.

Aaron, with the barest sense of misgiving through his undoubted loyalty to Paul, whom he rather regarded as the man of the house, as any man should surely be in any English house, unwittingly rose to her carefully crafted bait. 'Knickers Anne? I mean I would never see *your* knickers lying around *your* house now would I?'

Anne effected a pouty-lip fake annoyance at the remark in such a way as to encourage outright flirtation at this point. It was true that she was a bit of a slut, in the strict sense of leaving her underwear all over the place whenever she had to shower quickly and run out of the house, late *again*, for whatever it was. She refused to believe that it was all a tease for the Polish window cleaner as she'd been like this for years. But did she ever run out of the house *knowing* that there were multiple definitions of slut and she was all of them? A vision of Aaron and she with a whole bottle of wine watching boats on the creek together entered her head; the innocent yet coquettish thought not quite becoming a fantasy as the guilt of a returning Paul pushed it back inside of her. Inside of her. She felt a sexiness, a wantonness purr in her thighs, her knees, the back of her neck. Aaron would not dare to think of violating her and yet, she wondered, that if this was his fantasy of this day, she really would not be displeased one iota.

'No not my knickers Aaron. I mean. I am sure you are too much of a gentlemen to stare at my knickers if I ever left them on the floor, by the bed, by the window.'

Aaron was feeling a bit uncomfortable now. There was a girl in Lublin and he regularly thought about modifying his business plan to reduce his year-end profits by flying out to see her. The word *expenses* was disrespectful he knew, but he thought about her often and what he would like to do to her after a four-hour flight from Stansted. His Polish mates had told him time and time again that they had to keep themselves to themselves in England to make it work. Sometimes a party would be held in one of the fruit-picking shacks at a local farm and relationships quickly formed. He was tempted often but he knew that marriage was never far away in his culture and he wasn't ready to settle down. *The girls in the town,* he would say to his mates, *they dress like they are on heat. Where is the harm?* He would be slapped down. *No Aaron. It doesn't work like that. There is a harmony here and we can't break it. The English girls dress like whores. You can have them in London. But out here? Are you kidding? No, Aaron my friend, you fuck one of them and we're all fucked.*

But did this logic extend to an older, finer married lady, a lady like Anne? He had an awful sense that it probably didn't, if you went about it in the right way.

His discomfort, he realised with horror, had spread downwards to about halfway within him physically and he rapidly made a radical business decision to remove the thought of removing her knickers and littering her bedroom floor with them. 'No, no, I...I could not disrespect your property like that.'

Anne's flirtation had ended, which she realised was a good thing. Her brief wildness was done. They were not going to get drunk in The Ship and come back to bushes by the North Wing and perform unspeakably lewd acts upon each other; the whole thing was absurd. Paul would be back later and she felt ashamed with herself. 'So no-one really living there then Aaron?'

'That is just it Anne. I cannot know. All the windows are black. No, not black like dirt; there was a lot of dirt but I clean. There is black...film...like black sheets that cover the inside of each window. I don't ask questions. I need money.'

'What, *all* of them?'

'Well, yes all the ones I clean. They say do not clean dormer windows on the top. Mr Palmer he very strict about that. *Do not go on roof.* Roof would collapse and I will die.'

Anne glanced up to the top of the ladder. It extended a few feet above the parapet, which seemed solid enough. She began to wonder if Mr Palmer would ever consider that this peculiarly unlikely admonition might be shared by

Aaron, and least of all with her. Anne suddenly felt embarrassed to be there. The subject of dirty knickers, hers included, seemed juvenile now and the report of the blacked-out windows disturbed her in some uncertain way. 'Aaron, it was lovely to see you. The best of luck with it all. Great job you have here.'

'You too Anne. Will I see you again?' He thought that came out all wrong. Why did his English do that sometimes when he least wanted it to. 'I mean, sorry, yes Anne, I will see you again, OK?'

Anne sensed that he was struggling but wanted to make light of it. 'Yes we will see each other again.' It sounded equally strange to her and she added by way of glossing over her awkwardness, 'So what time do you finish?' realising with horror, as she said it, that he might think she had not given *up* on him yet.

He looked at his watch and paused. 'Lech we have drink. I meet him at two o'clock. Maybe Tomasz joins. We have food too. So I can go back up ladder again! Lech, he's my new mate. Good speak Polish sometimes. Speak of home.'

'Well yes take it easy on that ladder and,' she really could not resist it, one last tease, oh why not, 'no looking through the dormer windows; you don't want a naked young woman being the last thing you see before you crash through the roof.'

They both laughed and the awkwardness seemed to have vanished again.

Sitting outside the pub, it really was most glorious, she felt. The red sky of earlier seemed impotent now, the sun's rays shimmering on the gently rippling waters of the creek. Sips of cool white wine began to fire her imagination. She tried to think of Paul coming home and what they would do and say to each other. There would be dinner with all three of them in the pub first and he would have to behave himself. Any overt signs of affection, least of all anything remotely physical, would disgust Ellie to such an extent that their meal would quickly become silent.

But there was the lingering anxiety that there might be some awful revelation in the estate papers. It was silly to think this after all these years, but she was on edge at the prospect all the same. It was far easier, as the wine lazily infused within her bloodstream, to wonder at the mystery of The Old Vicarage's blacked-out North Wing windows. Perhaps it was all very innocent. If the wing was barred to them during the original tour of the house because it was not being used, then why would it *not* have blacked-out windows? She repeatedly tried to move her thoughts on to other things, like what Paul would have to tell her about his big deal, but it was no good. What *was* in the North Wing? It was the only question that stirred her slowly numbing thoughts as she returned to the table with her second large glass of wine.

People watching…yes that would do the trick. That would take your mind of anything! The acting public that filed casually past her would provide the backdrop to one of her favourite private games: what was the relationship between people?

The game proved boring at first. Small children ran ahead of their parents, followed by momentary raised voices as they strayed too near to the creek's banks. Easy, too easy. Couples, old, young, no matter: easier yet still. Well this is Brenham after all. Not much unorthodoxy in relationships here is there?

But what was this? This was more interesting. A couple, late fifties, early sixties? A young lady close behind them. Not smiling. No-one talking. Why not? But then the young woman's face lit up and she was pointing, shouting. Had she seen something amazing?

A swan. She was ecstatic about a swan.

The man turned around to the young woman and smiled meekly, touched her elbow with his hand. He then glanced over to Anne and his smile warped into something almost apologetic. His daughter had learning difficulties and she was elated because she had seen a swan.

At that moment Anne had a virulent, uncontrollable desire to run over to them, say it was alright, yes the swan is beautiful and we will all let the world know together, come on let's shriek together.

Perhaps the man detected this, had felt it all his life: the saccharine, manic kindness of strangers and Anne thought his eyes narrowed, just slightly. A plea to the woman drinking alone and watching the world go by perhaps.

This is the way it is, will always be. I perceive your kindness. But the best kindness is that which lets us be the world that walks by you, the same as the other worlds that walk by you this fine and lovely lunchtime. So, thank you for this other kindness. But please let us pass by.

And thus Anne did nothing. She did nothing but she thought something. She thought that we never really know the lives of others. So the Palmers had a daughter. The Palmers had a daughter. The words repeated in her head. So what if the Palmers had a daughter and for some terrible secret or tragedy of the family, she lived there as a recluse in the North Wing? So what and why was it any of her business? It was none of her business. The family with the swan-loving daughter had passed by. Other groups of people strolled past in each direction, but she was oblivious to them now.

Anne knew that it was wrong, but she felt herself walking home by the same way that she had arrived at the pub. She looked at her watch. Two o'clock. She must just have missed Aaron coming the other way, she felt relieved to realise. Lunchtime grog made her squiffy and slightly slutty -

characteristics best left to quiet, intimate picnics with Paul after her embarrassing performance by the ladder earlier. She pretended she hadn't the slightest interest in glancing to her right, to the gates that barred her way to something utterly unknowable.

But something deep and dark within, some silent Sucubus, forced her head to turn and the cedar tree, its hidden ally, pulled her in, past the gate, and looked down upon her.

But it is your business Anne, isn't it.

What gripped her now was a knowing that was a not-knowing, an existential state of obedience to fatalistic forces that rule our lives. To live, to be, the North Wing beckoned. She crossed the gravel drive. She began to climb the ladder. She held within her the vague sense that logically it was all wrong. It was not her ladder. It was not her house. It was not her North Wing against which this ladder lay. If a cedar tree could turn to watch, it did so now.

Sum Succubus.

And still she climbed, past windows blackened like time suspended, the event horizons of gargantuan gravitational forces of the mind within. Her mind, someone else's mind, separated all gossamer-thin from each other, like parallel universes so close to each other and yet undetected by all mankind save witches, black and white. She glided herself like a witch now, unaware of her feet gaining rungs in gentle rhythm. She crested the final summit and floated down to a wall, a wall which was the point of no return. And if there were a hesitation, it was barely perceptible because she was beyond return. And she felt the cedar tree turn back to where it was content to be: sentinel once more to the approaching world, his work now done.

She swam as if a spawning salmon up the shelving roof slates and her goal was there. As a salmon stares down finally into the motionless waters below seeking gravel and new life, she looked down into the dormer window of another new life. Or rather it was an old life.

For she was staring into Ellie's bedroom.

Yes Ellie's bedroom. But it was a 1960s Ellie's bedroom. The wallpaper was a beautifully overbearing patina of hues of pea green, peach and saffron aside others: foils of neo-pre-Raphaelite greys, all twisted together like the sinews of maidens bathing, lying prostrate in silent, sunny streams. The windows were her windows, but the curtains were tangerine, sixties atomic tangerine, suffused with light that came not from the sun but spotlights pointing away from a blackened screen. The bed, this bed, why it was the bed in the photos they had surely seen on the day of their visit. Anne was a time-traveller, a witch with powers untamed, driven by a force that was either good or evil, but irresistible and she levered the window open, effortlessly open. She rotated herself into the aperture until only her legs held the slate outside.

Cheap white wine rose up into her throat. Or rather down as the plumb line pulls. And she retched. Her convulsions pulled her clear, clear from delusion, clear from her floating world of indestructibility and her training state, the gate before the waiting world of witches. She was Anne again, a plain and simple human who was drunk on cheap liquor from a public house. She was very high up on the side of a roof of a house, a house in which she was now half-inside, legs kicking and flailing outside.

And as she kicked her legs to return to the great normality outside, to descend the ladder to a peaceful English garden owned by a normal English couple whom she barely knew, away from the strange, but now frighteningly sinister scene before her, she fell in.

And as she fell, she was in a dreamless dream of utter blackness. The dreamless dream of a person knocked unconscious by a glancing blow to the head upon the side of a child's wooden bed.

Chapter Twenty-One

'Ahh-ne, we're home!' The cats swam around Paul's legs, something that usually annoyed him, but he now realised that he'd missed them. 'Um, Ellie, be a love and feed the cats will you. Eight o'clock; bang on their supper time.' Paul's mild annoyance at not having received the expected grand and gushing home welcoming from Anne, began almost immediately to turn into a slightly mild anxiety. At weekends it was Anne's custom to feed Graham and Eric up to an hour earlier, at seven o'clock, as a *treat*, though he suspected that this was a metaphor for *they're crying for food and they think I don't love them,* but he didn't want to alarm Ellie. Anne had probably fallen asleep somewhere. If it was in their bed, he determined, he might wake her up in a very special way that she liked, with the door firmly closed to wandering cats and children.

'*Anne,*' he ventured in that shouty-whispery voice that achieved neither function. But still there was nothing. The bathroom was empty, so she hadn't fallen asleep surrounded by Far East candles, and the bedroom was not just vacant but exceedingly tidy. She'd made the bed like you find in a hotel, a knack she possessed that amazed him, as he could not even fold back the blanket and sheet without it looking like the hastily exited bed of a fleeing lover, window flung open, murderous husband upon the stairs.

The more of the house he searched the more its stillness weighed upon him, the more her strange and unexpected absence preyed upon him. There was something wrong and it seemed to be both all around and inside of him. There was only the garden left to mollify him; the chance that she was possibly asleep, probably in the summerhouse. He kept his face neutral as he passed Ellie in the kitchen. 'God Dad. They are wolfing it down. Graham's on his second pouch already!'

'Won't be a second Ellie.'

'Where's Anne?'

'Ah, not sure. Let me just check.'

The back French windows were locked before he slid them open; he was now quite sure that she would be nowhere here either, though he felt a sudden wave of nausea at the thought of finding her prone and still body upon the ground, the victim of some terrible deed. The summerhouse was empty as was the rest of the garden. Her teacup from this morning was still on the outside patio table, a further reminder of the terrifying loss to him if there really were something wrong. Before he returned to the French windows, he hesitated and reached for the phone in his pocket. He had a very bad feeling that he was about to leave a voicemail on Anne's phone and he doubted that he could contain the desperation in his voice in front of Ellie and that it should therefore be done in private.

He waited, heart pounding. To hear her voice now, the real live one, not the pre-recorded voice of a ghost, would propel him to the most blissful state imaginable. It rang.

And then it went to voicemail.

Hi, sorry I can't take your call right now….

'Anne, hi, darling, it's me. We're home. Where *are* you? Getting pissed with your secret lover no doubt!' his pathetic attempt to inject whimsy into his desperation failing impossibly, 'Anne. Look I'm really worried. I…there are no missed calls on my phone from you, no texts. Please, *please* call me as *soon* as you get this. I love you darling. I love you and I miss you very much.'

He realised that his words were faltering as he hung up, forcing a wave of self-pity; tears stung his eyes. A few heavy drops of rain began to spring from a foreboding purple sky and he turned his face up to it to splash them away. Unfathomably, he thought of the farm shop carpark.

His face all shiny with rain, he returned to the kitchen and realised that Ellie was covering up for them both now too. 'Where's the minibar when you need it Dad? Oh look, what's this? A maxi-bar, let's see what extortionate items we can purchase this evening,' and she swung the fridge door open. 'Well let me see. A quarter of a bottle of semi-skimmed milk. Yours for five Euros. Or why not really live it up: a third of a bottle of the cheapest French wine from Calais. Only twelve Euros.'

'Yep that one will do for me Ellie. Please add it to the final bill.' He loved her for it. This teenage girl, so recently vulnerable and all alone in a hotel in Dublin, trying to cheer her dad up as she decanted a glass for him. He necked the cold wine down until the chill raced up through the roof of his mouth and hit him hard like a skewer in his head.

I'll take that a million times over. Just please let it be the three of us here tonight.

But why was he capitulating so easily? It was pathetic. 'Ellie, is there a note on the table, on the sideboard, anywhere?' They both started pouring their eyes over kitchen surfaces, the coffee table along in the living room. Nothing.

'Wait Dad. There's something on the floor under the table. Perhaps the cats knocked it off.' Ellie bent down and retrieved it.

'Well?' demanded Paul frantically.

'Oh it's a poem…I think…makes no sense. *For Anne to be the girl she is, needeth the hand of sweet Jesus*. But she's written it over and over. Dunno. Like a weird poem I guess.'

Paul froze. This was the strange stanza that Anne had mumbled down the phone that night in Galway. Now it was no longer mysterious, unsettling even; now it was like slices of broken glass gouging at the darkest recesses of his brain, words ugly-twinned with *Anne-who-is-missing*. Thunder rumbled outside and the purple sky hung like a filthy old jacket about to be washed away, overcome by a brutish aquatic force of destruction.

'Look we don't know what it is Ellie. Perhaps she's had stuff on her mind and went off for a wander somewhere. I…I don't know. I mean how did she sound this morning when you spoke to her – just before we entered the ferry port?'

'Good. She sounded good…I mean…*fine*. She sounded fine. You remember she even joked that we could all have dinner tonight in the pub? But it wasn't a joke. She meant it. She said she was going to *book* it.'

'Well yes that's encouraging. Tell you what, I'll have a drive around. I'll nip over to the pub first to see if the table's still booked. I might have to cancel it.' He realised that his use of the subjunctive was really just desperate optimism. 'But Ellie, look I don't want to sound alarmist, but, just, but please do not leave the house, OK? Only open the door if you know it's me, or Anne. Don't go in the garden—'

'You think I'm going out in *that*?'

'No-one OK, only Anne, me or a policeman, or woman.'

'The *police* Dad?'

As soon as he said it, he regretted it. It was something he'd always said, ever since she was little. If Daddy faints in the street, it's OK to go up to a police officer and ask for help. But now the word *police* took on a sinister meaning, some unspoken brutality of possibilities too appalling to contemplate.

'No, no Ellie. I don't think we need the police,' the word *yet* formed on his lips but he managed to suppress it, 'What I meant was like when you were younger. Only open the front door to me, your mother, or Anne and you remember I said you could include the police, but you had to ask them for ID?'

'Oh, OK. Dad…please don't be long will you?' The fear of being left alone again flooded her insides, 'Just, just don't do anything stupid, OK?'

'It'll be fine darling. Just, stay calm. Call me if you have to. If I'm driving I promise I'll stop and call you right back.'

'OK Dad, just go.'

Paul went to leave and then rushed back to hug her. 'I love you Ellie.'

And not for the first time, Ellie thought ruefully, he was gone.

Paul ran to the car where it was parked in a side road a few yards from the High Street. He ran because it was raining heavily. But he also ran through fear. A menacing, overhanging cloud base, pregnant with collusion, bore down upon him as it belched thunder and lit up the sky with its shocking electric luminescence. As time was of the essence he'd already decided to ditch the visit to the pub. What would they say? *Oh Mr Fewings, did you not know that your wife cancelled the booking?* That was unlikely for whatever reason he could think of right now. Once he hit the accelerator he sped up the hill not really knowing where he was going but it seemed obvious perhaps unconsciously to drive to where there was civilisation, people, and a few near-empty parks with late dog walkers who might fear less the madman who asks: *Have you seen my wife? She may have appeared agitated. If you do see her, she's not dangerous; you can approach her. Tell her everything is going to be OK. You must then, as in you have to, call the police.*

But first the town centre. She likes antique shop windows, even when they are closed. It was a desperate supposition. The pedestrianised market-place allowed drivers access in the evenings but was generally frowned upon. He was in no mood for petty English mores and politeness tonight and turned left from the local ring road into the cobbled street which led to the central square of Brenham. Drunkenness had yet to start, for it was only half past eight, but that peculiarly English preface to the brawling bacchanalia to come was all around.

'Awright mate!' A white-shirted, perfectly groomed, leering youth with his pre-fight back-up crew and stilettoed, spray-tanned future wife, gave him the thumbs up as Paul motored slowly past. The driving precipitation only added to the youth's sense of oneness with the world. Paul nodded his respect. Would he dare to wind his window down and ask him if he'd seen…but he'd stupidly not brought a photo of her with him. He drove quietly on.

As he passed the old town hall, a dozen or so early diners were exiting their cars; middle-aged couples exuding garrulous *bonhomie* as they contemplated their special evening in the Brenham Baltihouse, or perhaps the adjacent Kent Thai Village, jackets raised above their heads to fend off the rain that bore down upon them. He halted to let them pass, uncharacteristically impervious to a mild, barely perceptible look of disdain on one of the men's faces. *We're parking here to bring much-needed custom to the town. What exactly is your business here I wonder?*

'Fuck you,' mouthed Paul straight back at the source of disdain. *Do you want it? Do you want some?* He felt curiously ready for violence, whether it impeded the logistics of his drive or not. It would certainly take the decision of whether to call the police out of his hands.

He swung the car left into Redhouse Lane, where there were several pubs and braked suddenly as a man stumbled straight out of the door of The Mermaid into his path. The man banged his fist on the car bonnet as if to remonstrate and glared at him, his face very slightly familiar. Paul's English reticence was blown, lost. He leapt out of the car and ran around its front to confront the man, his right fist a ball of relentless and bellicose intent.

'Sorry I slammed the front of my car into your fist as you left the pub. You wanna slam your face into this?' Paul reared his fist into the air behind him, ready to strike, to despatch this human to the gutter, for daring to interrupt his mission this evening.

'Paul, no!'

It was Aaron.

'It is Lech. He deserves smash in the face if you have to, but you don't must have to; he is all over your place.' A tirade of Polish invective hurtled from Aaron towards the stumbling Lech, who raised his palms in the universal language of a man with new-found servility to his erstwhile combatant. Paul lowered his fist and nodded at Aaron, partially mollified by the drunken expression of Slavic regret performed so hastily before him.

'Ah Paul, my *friend*,' announced Lech, his arm around Paul's shoulders. 'You must forgive the drunken Polish. We are all friends now. My father's father. His father fights the Germans in the sky right here,' as he pointed to the static sky above, rain cascading down his beery, beaming face.

A car horn sounded from behind and Paul raised his hand momentarily to the driver. 'Hey Lech, we cool. Aaron, we cool too.'

'You no home with your wife Paul? She really miss you.'

'What's that? She misses me? How would you know that?'

The car horn sounded again. This time Paul turned around and again raised his hand but with his middle finger raised. He had drunken Polish for back-up.

'Mrs Fewings, I mean Anne. She stop by my work today. The Old Vicarage. We talk a bit.'

'The Old Vicarage Aaron; what time was this?'

'Just before lunch. I have to go meet Lech for drink. This why he drunk. He never leave the pub all day.'

'Where was she going? Did she say anything? Anything? Just tell me anything?'

'Just small talking Paul. She want to know why I clean North Wing windows.'

'And?'

Another car horn. 'Look mate, I haven't got all day,' he heard vaguely from behind. He would take a black-eye right now, two black-eyes for the slightest morsel from Aaron about Anne. *And her known last sighting.*

'She curious to know who lives in North Wing. She wants me for information. I just tell her the windows are all black. I don't know—'

But Paul was already back in his car and driving. Fast. Too fast for a pedestrianised Brenham. For Paul possessed but a single mission now. He was driving to The Old Vicarage. He had no idea what connected it to Anne's disappearance but nothing could be clearer to him now than that he must arrive there immediately.

It was here again.

The crackling, crawling, dark thing that had consumed him on too many occasions recently, the moment after Ellie's brief disappearance and return, the sense of helplessness in the Galway inn, the thing that lurked and stalked him. It was coming into the open now. He wanted to see it.

To know it. To confront it. He had once wanted the enormity of its shadow to lie all latent and viral, inactivated. But the denouement was nigh. He was upon it. Out in the open he would run at it like he did in his nightmares when a hidden fiend bore down upon him, slashing and gorging, prepared to awaken or die.

It was collecting, condensing within; drips from the viscera of two worlds collided and yet apart. Anne had leaked into the other place and flagelline strings of an alternative universe, its separation gossamer thin, were binding her to them and feeding from the entrails of her blinding innocence. A diaspora of demonic coagulation oozing against the tide of human hope; sunken in an abyss of torture, all set to strike upon those who dare to probe its depths. The hidden forces within the darkened cave, where nothing lurks but the thing that smites all accrued enlightenment and meaning, that reduces the story of a single life to balls of soaking paper, the ink upon it all run once more into the ground. Ferried unto the point of peering into this other world, he could now not return from the vastness of its certainty. Like air sucked all clumsy by a piston of festering rags from a shaft of stagnant water.

The car braked hard. It was beside The Old Vicarage gates. They were closed. Paul revved the engine until it roared and eased the clutch back until it rode and screamed. Screamed words into his ears.

The trifurcation of the innocent upon a bed of lies.

Jesus wept as men walked by.

Paul rammed his car through the gates like a rampant skirmisher's lance through an outlying, impotent vanguard and gained the yards to the house in an instant.

He screeched to a stop and leapt out of the car.

Now he was pounding upon the front door, possessed, not by a demon but by a purpose. Englishness, so long an inertia of self-deprecation and obsequiousness within him, had become a ruthless crusade. A crusade against a hidden cowardly enemy, a covert insurgency that did not care to show its face.

'Anne!' he cried.

But all he could hear was thunder and all he could see was lightning and all he could feel was the driving rain against his cheeks and eyes.

He ran to the window of the living room. There were moving shapes inside but he could not discern their outline behind the sheets of rain that drenched and drove against the window pane. He banged his fists against it so hard he sensed the imminence of glassy shards mingled with severed arteries. Did he see a hesitation of a figure? Was it a figure at all or a trick of the lightning against the soundless, dormant furniture within? He was going to find out. He looked around, for a large object, a stone, anything.

There was a terrific cracking sound behind him as the air around turned into fire. A lightning bolt had hit the Cedar Tree and a smouldering branch was fallen to his feet.

He picked it up. There was blood in this wood. The blood of rightful vengeance and retribution. In this wood was murder. He looked up at the Cedar Tree. 'Thank you Old Tree. I always knew we were in this together.'

He turned and charged at the window.

Chapter Twenty-Two

Anne opened her eyes. But she was dreaming. How funny when that happens, she said to herself in her dream. It's a bit cruel really because you have to find that fine line between *knowing* you're dreaming and having some real fun and *knowing too much* you are dreaming through the fear of the conscious mind getting rather cross and taking over and then the fun is over. It was like the time she was being followed by lions and then she knew it was a dream and she turned and ran at them: 'Yaargghhh!' and for a few lovely seconds she was lying with them and kissing them and …then she was awake. There had been naughty ones too. There had been the one when the policeman had told her off for eating too much cake – her face was covered with cream – and she could not stop eating all the cream cakes. He became increasingly authoritarian and when he said, 'Now look young lady…' she realised that he had the face of an old school teacher and it was all a dream. With so little time and the realisation that dreams were not cheating, she pulled down her knickers and wiped herself with the cream from her face and said, 'Officer, how do you know it's cream?'

How would this dream go, she wondered? Well it's quite a genteel dream. Oh look, I've gone back in time. To the 1960s. Ellie's room in the 1960s. I'm a bit of Bernie, a bit of Bernie in the late 1960s. Oh good show Bernie. I *love* the wallpaper. It's like in the photos but here it's just so, so, well I don't *know*, it's so, goodness me, it's so *lovely*. The wallpaper a beautifully overbearing patina of hues of pea green, peach and saffron aside others: foils of neo-pre-Raphaelite greys, all twisted together like the sinews of maidens bathing, lying prostrate in silent, sunny streams. The curtains all tangerine, sixties atomic tangerine.

Anne floated upwards. Steady girl. Easy. Pretend you don't know. Boring reality will take over and you'll wake up with a nasty hangover or something. Because she could feel it there, trying to pull her back into the real world. A right old headache. Would Paul be there? She missed Paul. Where is he? If he would just enter her dream, oh what fun they would have in sixties Lounsley. She crossed the room wiping her brow. She turned the door knob, excited to stretch her dream to other rooms. There was blood on the door knob. No, no I don't want it to be one of those dreams. It has to be lovely. If it's not to be lovely then I will force the wake-up. You'll lose out, Dream. Dream, be lovely now. Let us work together.

She walked out onto the landing. Ah that's better. All is calm again. She entered the other upstairs bedroom. Oh how quaint. There was paint all around. Not decorators' paint but the paint of artists and lovers – paint that liberated a thousand souls before a decade of austerity. She was awash in a sea of paint and above the canvasses and detritus of love and paint, two beds were perched high in the room; half the remaining ceiling torn from the joists and made into tiny beds with ladders below. Oh that's nice. Oh Bernie, did you do that? Sleepover children. You clever girl. I hope you come into the dream because actually I miss you and would like to ask you why you did it this way.

She glided downstairs to the first floor. Not an eddy of consciousness in sight, not the slightest hint that the killjoy of wakefulness was stalking her.

Oh no I don't like *that* Bernie, she said in her dream, frowning at the double-bed before her. It's the wrong side of the room and its one of those old-fashioned double-beds you read about – how did you find room to sleep beside each other? Perhaps they had sex all the time in those days. What would she do if a young, naked Patrick appeared before her now, all aroused and smiling, flecks of paint in the artist's hair? Would she be naughty? Would she let him paint her inner thighs butter yellow and deep pink, the colours of girls' lipstick on cream bodices? Because you cannot cheat in dreams.

She could not be too greedy now and inspect the bathroom and loo. What if she awoke and missed the *piece de resistance*, the magnificent ground-floor? She descended the stairs. This dream was so real she felt her feet in front of each other. This is the most vivid dream I ever had. Please don't desert me now.

Oh yes, oh yes, oh yes. This, this is how it was. The knocked-through living room. In her dream she loved the newness of it, the smell of polypropylene and psychedelic, moulded foam. It's funny, because in her real world she didn't like newness. But here in her dream, where she could never be judged, she loved it. It was the swinging sixties and those old minis in *Here We Go Round The Mulberry Bush*? Why, new! Biba: retro? Wrong again: new… Jimi Hendrix – influential guitarist? Not so. Ground-breaking, modern, impertinent upstart. *New!*

She danced now around this room, these two rooms all knocked through. It was her room but not her room. They were her walls but not her walls. The flocks of cut vivid

253

velvet on Mylar by Du Pont, she liked that, she might try that, but like the best poems in her dreams she would wake and they would become meaningless and when she went to write them down, just absurd, but not in a creative, abstract way. Just a bit shit.

So now, now it was time really to have some fun. What is outside in 1960s Lounsley? Paul and she had both agreed when they had first met that being able to go back in time, incognito, or better still *invisible,* walking around any town, village or city in almost any decade in history, would be the perfect fantasy. Paul had even conceded that he would swap unlimited indulgencies in a huge harem with walking along Brenham or Lounsley High Streets in the middle of the 19th Century, just for five minutes. Did she have five minutes? Just one minute in 1960s Lounsley before she woke, that would be like a thousand spa treatments and eating chocolate all day and never becoming fat. She entered the hallway. Empty. Well in dreams there are no rules. No shoes. No coats. No rules.

She turned the knob of the grand old front door. It was reassuringly the same look and feel of theirs in the real world and she stepped outside…into another hallway. Oh no that's not fair, Dream. I just wanted one minute of men with sideburns and sports cars and girlfriends with mini-skirts and *She Loves You Yeah Yeah Yeah* and white dog shit and bottles of milk all atop with cream…and you give me this? You can't be serious. Oh how original: a hallway leading to another hallway. Right. *Hold* on dream. You do know who's in charge here? *I'm* in charge. You are my dream. I created you. I will tell you what to do.

She entered the hallway. It led both left and right. Oh so like a dream of choices. But it's my dream so it really doesn't matter which way I turn, does it? She turned right, along a narrow corridor, curiously bare, but this was a dream in her head so why clutter it with anything?

I think I'm going to meet someone, she said to herself in the dream. The next corner I go round, someone I know will be there. But it wasn't a salivating, cream-loving policeman, or a salacious, naked younger Patrick, or the man she missed and loved, her Paul, whom she suddenly wanted to be there.

It was her dead brother.

They would embrace, but very lightly as sudden movements can wake you. They would talk and even if it were for a few dozen seconds it would be enough. He would be alive and she could ask him how he was, how it was on the other side, in that other world. Not the waking world but that further world where she hoped they would one day be together again, but this time forever. I can make this happen, she said to herself in her dream. It is my dream and it is my brother. And my brother is going to be in my dream.

She turned to her left, at the end of the corridor and there was a door. She turned the handle to this door and opening it she stepped into a room. A room she had seen before. But it wasn't her brother before her.

The last people she had expected to see in this room.

Were her parents.

Ellie counted the minutes. She was not at all happy. She was absolutely terrified, not knowing where Anne was and she had seen the same in her dad's eyes. But it was also the first time that she had been alone in the house since she read *that* article. Two disappearances? Was it this house? Things came in threes right? She tried to push the superstition backwards, somewhere behind more practical thoughts. At some point she realised she would have to call the police if her dad did not ring her soon. It had been half an hour since he had left. She decided to make a soda pop to calm herself and strode to the kitchen counter. The torrential rain outside and intermittent thunder and lightning were not helping much either. Another clap of thunder resonated against the French windows behind her.

Interlaced with a scream.

Or was that her nerves playing mind games on her?

And again. But not a scream. An old woman's voice, delivered in a scream.

For Anne to be the girl she is, needeth the hand of sweet Jesus!

She froze. She had no idea what it meant, this screamed message, but she didn't like it one bit. It was about someone called Anne. And an Anne, their Anne, *her* Anne was missing. She needed to tell Dad. She abandoned the filling of the soda stream with the green-coloured, syrupy substance and reached for her phone. A flash of lightning lit up the entire garden through the huge French windows in front of her. She thought she discerned a figure. Could it have been Anne after all, awoken from some hiding place in the garden, which Dad had somehow earlier missed? She pulled on the cord of one of the venetian blinds. Darkness. But then another explosion of lightning, like a Very Light on No-man's land.

It lit up the rabid, snarling face of Mrs Carmichael, pressed up against the window.

It was a hideous, terrible apparition. As if from the screen of the TV when they all guiltily watched a horror film.

But this was not a horror film. This was actually happening. *Please let this not be the third thing.*

Mrs Carmichael's shrieking voice was now pitched as high is it ever could surely be.

'Get out. Get out of the house. Get out of the house right now!'

Ellie stood silent and still, unable to move, aware only of the frightening apparition before her, a silhouette against the blurry, watery moon, and the phone calling her dad by her ear. At least he would tell her what to do.

But he didn't.

Instead he asked her to leave a message. But there was no message to leave and if there was one outside of the realm of mad things, it was no good anyway, as she had lost the power of speech.

Mrs Carmichael banged upon the window, oblivious to the gusting gale around her. 'It is a house of sin. You must leave this house of sin!'

Ellie backed away from the face at the window, not taking her eyes off it for one moment as she edged back further still into the hallway. She inched her rain-proof parker over her shoulders and opened the front door.

If things came in three tonight, it would not be in this House of Sin.

Fran is awoken by a puff of something. Or rather she feels it is the puff of something coming from her bedroom window. She is curious as to what it might be and decides to investigate. She gets out of bed. This she does with some care, for though Mummy and Daddy are in the habit of telling her what a big girl she is now, she is clever enough to realise that if she doesn't slide out of bed carefully, it is quite a distance to drop to the rug by the bed and she doesn't want to get a Poorly on her knee or her foot.

But now she is by the window and stands on the little stool so that she can see the world outside. She'd like to push the windows open wide if she could, the better to see it, but Daddy got a man to put some bits of metal on them so that she can only push the windows open wide enough to poke her nose through.

It is dark, because bedtime was ages ago and the Man-In-The-Moon is staring down at her in that curious way of his. She feels the puff again but it's not really a puff but a big sound, a pumping music that is coming up from the kitchen below by way of the air outside, all mixed up with cigarette smoke that is sweet and heavy.

Mummy and Daddy are having a night-time party and she has not been invited. That's not nice. But she is used to it. The night-time parties are not like her parties. The cake smells sweet but it's all smoky, like the cigarettes that adults smoke. When they have friends around she is sometimes allowed to stay up a bit longer and everyone makes a fuss over her. Sometimes she is really naughty and after Mummy or Daddy have read her her story, she opens the door and sneaks down to the bottom staircase and tries to listen and see what is going on. All the adults drink a lot and they must be really nice drinks because they are all happy. Some of the drinks are orange, like squash, sometimes fizzy too or fizzy yellow. That must be banana. Why isn't she allowed fizzy banana for treats? She wants some now and thinks she'll risk a secret trip to the bottom stairs.

She turns the door knob to her room but the door doesn't open. That's mean. She knows she is too little to attend the night-time parties but she doesn't have to be locked in. What if she needs the toilet? Annoyed, she swivels to see that the potty is in the corner. Now she is angry because Mummy and Daddy know that she stopped using that a long time ago. She is nearly four! She knows it is naughty and she will be told off but she wants Mummy and Daddy's friends to know that she uses the toilet now, not the stupid potty. She decides to work out how to leave the room and peers through the key-hole 'that used to have a key in the Olden Days,' Daddy told her. There is a metal strip of some kind on the other side so she goes to her pencil case and gets a pencil and puts it through the Olden Days key-hole and pushes it upwards. She has to push really, really hard, but the bit of metal shoots upwards on the other side and clatters to the floor and she pushes the button and lifts the latch and she is standing on the landing. What a clever girl she is! She tip-toes down the top stairs and the music gets louder. Now she is in the Loovatorium or whatever Mummy calls it, which is really the Toilet and she makes a point of using it. She doesn't turn on any lights because she realises she is being naughty but it doesn't matter because all the Hide-And-Seeks mean that she really doesn't need any lights. She creeps down the bottom stairs and the music is now humming away in her ears. But there is another sound, all mingled in with the music. It is funny, like Old MacDonald Had A Farm. Is this a party game? The adults have to make the grunting sounds of animals to see who was the winner. Or is it like when the music stops and whoever forgets to stop making the grunting noise last is the loser and their chair is removed?

But the music doesn't stop and neither do the grunting noises.

Is that Mummy's farm voice she can hear now? My goodness she wants to win this game! But she is trying too hard to win the game and Fran doesn't like it one bit. It's your party Mummy so you don't have to win everything; you have to let friends win some things. That's what Mummy told her when she tried to keep the parcel from passing on her birthday. But Mummy's Moo Cow, or was it a Piggy, is becoming silly now and she wants to tell her off. She raises the latch not now caring if they would all stare at her and tell her off, and take her back to bed.

But nobody stares at her. Nobody notices her. They are all busy playing their silly game.

Mummy is on the floor all nude and it was like that time when they were watching the boring telly programme about the Countryside and farmers on the night before they had to take her to the Nursery. A daddy cow was jumping on a mummy cow's back and Daddy, her daddy, ran to the telly and quickly changed the channel to an even more boring programme where a man read his big school news to them.

But it isn't Daddy jumping on Mummy tonight. It is one of Daddy's friends and he must be really good at the game as they were both probably going to win it by the sounds of it. But she wants Mummy and Daddy to win it together, or be really nice to their friends and let someone else win it. At least Daddy is being nice. He is being a much quieter animal, like a sheep trying to pretend to be asleep as a lady lion sniffs all over him, trying to taste whether he would be good enough to eat.

She doesn't like this game anymore and she doesn't think she is big enough to stop it even if she screams. So she closes the door and tiptoes upstairs to the landing. She doesn't know what to do now. She is too scared to go downstairs again but she also feels a little too frightened to go upstairs, back to bed. So she goes into the bathroom. There is a stool in there and if she places it by the washbasin she can reach the taps and splash her face with lovely cold water and sip it from her hands, like Daddy taught her. As she walks over to the stool she trips over something. It is some clothes from the laundry basket that they keep in the big box at the end of the bath. Naughty Mummy! But then she hears a whisper. It is coming from the end of the bath where the laundry normally was and she recognises the voice.

'Francesca!'

She turns and pulls on the piece of string by the doorway which turns the light on, the one Daddy made longer, just for her. When she turns back, it is the boy from next door. His face is sticking up out of the hole that is the top of the laundry box, just as she thought, at the end of the bath. 'Francesca, I mean Fran, it's me. I want to be your friend. Will you come and be my friend and come and play with me?'

Fran stares at him and cannot help but smile. She always wanted an older brother and she sometimes used to have silly, lovely thoughts that the boy next door was her older brother. Perhaps he was. How else had he managed to appear in her bathroom? 'Are you, are you…my brother?' she asks uncertainly. She thinks she can hear the lady-next-door's voice behind the boy, whispering something, something urgent.

'Yes, yes, I am your older brother, Calum…didn't you know?'

'I like that you are my older brother, Calum!' Francesca turns around one last time to look down the stairs and makes up her mind.

'Where can we play?'

'Here, right here in this magic box. Let me show you my magic box,' and the boy beckons her in to where he is crouching. She sits there with him and feels herself all giggly as they are hiding in a magic box and he giggles back at her and makes a shoosh noise with his

260

finger on his lips. He beckons her to the back of the box which is all dark now and she feels the cold metal through her pyjama legs.

'Oh that feels funny!' she cries but he shooshes her again and he sort of leans backwards and suddenly it is like they are on a funny little rollercoaster and they flip upside down and back-to-front and they are still in the box and her brother Calum pushes the lid open and they are in the bathroom again. But, hey! This was the magic: the bathroom has changed. It is different colours and the carpet is thicker and it smells all different. The boy, her older brother, Calum, takes her hand and leads her out of the box and then out through the bathroom door.

The lady from next door is smiling at her. 'You are safe now my little lamb. Away from all the sin. Come, let me make you a nice hot cocoa and then I can tell you and your brother Calum a lovely, lovely bed-time story.' Fran feels safe now. The lady next door is so kind and she is going to love having an older brother. When Mummy and Daddy are doing silly things she will be able to talk to him and feel all safe inside.

Francesca sips the lovely hot cocoa in the magic kitchen, which is like her kitchen and yet unlike her kitchen: she got there by the magic box, the magic box that gave her an older brother. And as the lady tells them both a story as they sit on two comfy chairs in the kitchen, she feels all sleepy and before the lady could tell her what the man with the tinderbox did next, she is asleep.

'Paul, no!'

As Paul charged at the window with the lightning branch, he faltered slightly because he knew that voice. This was the voice that he had been searching for. This was the one voice in all the world that he wanted to hear.

It was the voice of Anne.

She smashed into him sideways and they tumbled to the ground together, wet gravel mashing his left cheek and the lightning branch spiralling away from his clutches redundantly onto the ground beside him. Anne straddled him where he lay, her skirt all ridden up to her waist and her long beautiful hair cascading a small waterfall of droplets onto his upturned face.

'Anne? Anne, is it really you?'

She leant forwards and took both his cheeks in her hands and kissed him gently on his lips. 'Oh my darling. Yes it is I, your Anne. I am here. I have missed you so much. I *love* you so much. But what are you *doing* here? How could you possibly know that I was here?'

'I, I. I just knew. I had to save you…from something. I knew you were here, *somehow*, and I had to save you from something.'

'Paul, I need to tell you something. My parents—'

'No no, Anne. Please don't say anything. Don't say a word.' He looked up but her face was a silhouette and he saw no expression, just felt her panting salty breath in the air, and the coolness of her dripping thighs around him. 'Anne, it cannot really wait you see. I have to tell you now before you…but I really don't know why…you say something you might regret. Something that might make you eternally sad.'

Anne's breath was all around him, her hands still pinning his arms to the wet gravel as if he were a man about to be forced to confess a terrible thing.

'Your parents. They are. They were. You…You were adopted.'

Her breaths slowing now, almost held as he felt her take the impact.

'I'm. I'm so sorry Anne, my darling Anne.'

And then Anne reared her head, pushed her face to the swirling, cascading sky. And laughed.

'I, I don't understand,' ventured Paul.

'Neither do I,' said Anne, her eyes slightly wild, as she eventually returned his gaze. 'Today nothing makes sense any more. What you just told me, I...it doesn't seem quite so insane as it might have done yesterday. It's almost as if...Paul. I love you so much. Come, I need you to meet someone again. Two someones actually.'

It was not the reaction he had expected and yet he was so elated to see her that if she were now completely mad, he doubted that it would make one ounce of difference to his love for her and his wish to grow old with her.

As Anne led Paul through the driving rain to the main door of The Old Vicarage, she realised she didn't remember much about her life before she was about four-years old, or so she estimated. Girls at school would show off and say they remembered when they were two. Anne said *three* in case they thought she was odd, sad, strange, *different*. But privately she, well she really didn't know.

Her earliest memory *might* have been in a car, on a backseat, on a very long journey. She had slept through most of that journey but when she was awake she hadn't minded because her big brother was beside her and he would squeeze her hand and he would give her some more warm cocoa from a bottle and she would nod off again. At some point, though this might have been a dream, the car drove onto a big ship and they sailed somewhere for ages and ages. When next she woke, or maybe she woke from a dream within a dream, she could not really be sure, she was in her house. Her really big house with Mother and Father in the Irish countryside, the land of her birth.

But something had changed in the last half hour. Right now her real first actual memory, the memory that was real, was sitting on Mother's lap and her mother smiling down at her and chanting a sort of nursery rhyme, a very special nursery rhyme, as it was all about her.

For Anne to be the girl she is, needeth the hand of Sweet Jesus.

She was sure that the rhyme was said to her often, as it filled her head. Had she said it in her sleep to herself, in the garden? She was always humming tunes and day-dreaming without really knowing it. She once found herself chanting, 'Sing, if you're glad to be gay, sing if you're happy that way,' in the shopping centre in Canterbury and then ran into the nearest shop, giggling at her apparent public expression of her new-found identity. How else could Mrs Carmichael have picked it up, copied such an early childhood memory?

'For Anne to be the girl she is, needeth the hand of sweet Jesus.'

'What did you say darling?' asked Paul.

'Oh it's my earliest memory is all. Mother used to say it to me over and over again. It's all I can remember really.'

'Narancia. A narancia. An arancia. Arancia,' said Paul.

'What did you say darling?' asked Anne as they stood now in the porchway, the rain no longer driving down on them.

'It was Ellie's homework. She explained to me how *narancia* in Spanish came to be *orange* in English.'

'Clever that girl.'

'But she told me something else really sad; I might as well tell you now, before we go in, as it's well, it might be a bit awkward, if, if certain people are inside.'

'Go on.'

'A little girl went missing from our house in 1969. It, I mean she, was the Palmers' daughter. She was never found. It's so sad.'

'Oh,' said Anne as if a curious thought were materialising inside. 'Narancia. A narancia. An arancia. Arancia.'

'Oh,' said Paul in an instant, 'oh yes, oh yes, I see it now. I hear it now.'

Paul's phone rang. 'Ellie?'

'Da-ad. Where *are* you?'

'I'm at The Old Vicarage. Are you OK Ellie?'

'Yes, I'm fine, just very wet. What are you doing at The Old Vicarage?'

'It's great news Ellie. I found Anne!'

'Oh Dad, that's, that's just brilliant…'

'We'll be home soon so don't go anywhere. Hold on, did you say you were wet? You are at home right?'

'No I'm not Dad. I had to get out.'

'But why? I told you under no circumstances—'

'Dad, I wasn't safe there. Mrs Carmichael went all loony and started screaming at me through the French windows. I was petrified. She kept telling me to get out of the house of sin. And then kept saying weird stuff about "For Anne to be—"'

'Where are you now darling?' It was his turn to cut in. He just needed her in his arms right now.

'I'm near the pond. Shall I walk up the hill to where you are? It is up the hill isn't it from here?'

'No Ellie, you stay by the pond. But right by the main road, under a street light. Be all confident and look like you are on the phone. I'm coming in the car right now. Three minutes max.'

He hung up and turned to Anne. 'Look whatever it is you want to show me, it'll have to wait a few minutes. Ellie left the house. I just need to get her. She's by the pond. Won't be long. Don't go anywhere OK.'

'She's alright?'

'Yes, yes. Mrs Carmichael just spooked her is all. She's been shouting at her your "For Anne to be…" line and telling her to get out of the house of sin. Daft old cow. Love you. Stay there…'

But as Paul ran back out into the rain and to the car, she didn't stay there. Something made her back away from the house, shivering. She continued to back away until she reached the relative shelter of the cedar tree. And suddenly there were thoughts. And memories. And she realised that her earliest memory wasn't sitting on her mother's knee and listening to the strange and yet familiar intonation of *For Anne to be the girl she is, needeth the hand of sweet Jesus*.

It had been:
Fran to be the girl she is, needeth the hand of sweet Jesus.
The car dream was real.
And very slowly but surely, memories before that.
A little girl, awoken from a night-time party.

Paul raced back through the battered gates. Anne was no longer in the porchway. He screeched to a halt, opened the car door and ran to the house, dark thoughts forming once more.

'Paul, here!' Anne yelled from the tree.

'Anne? Thank god you're still here. I thought—'

'Anne!' Ellie cried, as she too ran from the car, but directly to the cedar tree. Anne in turn ran to her and they embraced; they embraced so hard that Anne thought that she could never live without Paul's, this, this, daughter, this Ellie. She was sure that she was, in some sense, her daughter too for they were both crying now, crying outside of the rain, not looking up to the sky to swap rain drops for tears.

Paul joined them and hugged them closer still. It was dark beneath the Cedar Tree but a darkness had lifted from him.

'Ellie, darling,' said Anne, 'I have some news for you. Some really good news.'

Ellie looked up at her and even in the darkness Anne could see the shine of her eyes.

'The little girl that went missing from the house. She's been found. She's alive. And she's safe now.'

'Oh Anne, really? I, I, thank you, thank you, thank you for telling me.'

And with that, they separated and trudged through the now diminishing rain back to the house. It was like the first time, only different.

The door opened and, like before, Bernie and Patrick stood and smiled and went to take their dripping jackets from them. 'How lovely to see you all again,' they said together.

Anne turned to Paul and Ellie.

'Paul, Ellie, please meet Mum and Dad.'

Chapter Twenty-Three

It was a late Saturday afternoon in mid-October and as Paul looked up from his deckchair at the piercing shards of light that lanced through the branches of the Cedar Tree, he wondered if this Indian summer would never end.

The summer itself had passed in a whirlwind. His promotion to Junior Partner didn't just mean considerably more money, though that was very handsome in helping maintain The Old Vicarage to a suitable standard. It meant more time working from home. Yes there were more trips to Dublin, that was to be expected. But the sense of observing a decorum of attempted frugality had vanished. He now submitted his expenses without the mildest attempt at explanation or justification.

Had he really changed? Yes, yes he rather thought that he had. The deeds to The Old Vicarage were now theirs and what with his promotion, how could he not but be seduced into a sense of arrival in life, of accomplished self-determination? But it wasn't that in itself he realised. It was the new man within him that seemed to have materialised at the very moment when he had come to discuss with Anne the practicalities of living in their new home.

She was, needless to say, beyond delight with the new arrangement. Her parents had insisted that Paul, Anne and Ellie move into the place, with the proviso that they themselves be allowed to reside in the North Wing, now a sort of peaceful retirement annexe. But Paul saw it differently. He could see it all from a more detached, dare he think it, a more *interested* angle. It was clear to him, almost from the day of the *revelation*, that there might be complications if the full import of the story were ever to be digested by that pariah of his, the *authorities*.

There were so many considerations.

Did any of them have the stomach for the increasingly elderly Mrs Carmichael to be investigated for complicity in child abduction? The legal papers themselves suggested that Anne's adoptive parents really could not possibly have known of this part of the arrangement. Could it have been that the visiting superior cleric in one of the photos *did* know about the reports of a House of Sin in England; was somehow connected to Mrs Carmichael, and that he had been the diviner of the abduction, arranging with the orphanage, over whose financial hegemony he presided, to be bit-part players in the deception?

Besides, Anne's step-parents were dead. And the dead cannot be interviewed.

No, the only thing of which they could be sure was that Mrs Carmichael was Anglican, a member of the Church of Ireland. That's why she hadn't made the sign of the cross in the garden that evening. Anne had unconsciously understood the connection between Mrs Carmichael and her father's strand of Christianity, without determining it cognitively.

And what of Calum's part? Paul was not convinced that Anne's step-parents even knew that he was not her brother. Had the orphanage coerced the parents, under the guile of the senior cleric's sinister influence, to pretend that she had an older brother, just for a while, so that the story of how she had arrived in Ireland would remain a true memory? Or did the Church have something on

Anne's father, some terrible truth, that meant he had to go along with the ruse?

They would never know, and perhaps it was best that way.

No, for Paul, he had played his cards right. Going to the authorities, the police themselves inevitably, would have meant Mrs Carmichael giving her side of the story. And her description of a House of Sin, even with the most retrospectively historical-liberal interpretation of that terrible night, would have made for awful, lurid national newspaper headlines for the Palmers.

Child Neglect. Child abducted whilst parents…

Whatever the decade, they were appalling words. And they all knew it.

And Paul in particular knew it.

He had gone out for a drink one evening with Patrick, just the two men; it somehow seemed inevitable really that a man-to-man chat was on the cards. Perhaps Patrick knew only too well which of the two actors there gathered was also *Director* of the unfolding drama, the writer of the script. And he was right. In the pub that night, in a quiet dark corner, Paul's emotions had slid from one of almost defiant righteousness to one of uncomfortable pity as Patrick trotted out his explanations of that horrendous night, his attempts to justify in some small way its awful denouement.

'I know it must seem like a cliché now Paul old chap, but in 1969, well it really was the end of an era. What we did was unforgiveable really but most of our friends had children too. We took it in turns to host the parties. We were never *ashamed* of them. It was just a part of the times. We were never hippies as such, but the whole *free love* thing. Well no-one really took it very seriously. We knew it wouldn't last. It was a time of ephemerality and excess, of plastic and paper chairs, and lurid carpets and wallpaper. Were we collectively mimicking the very furniture around us

I wonder? And perhaps that's why we were a bit blasé with the child care arrangements. It was only ever meant to have been a *phase*. At least there was a sense amongst us all that it was thus.'

Paul had chosen, whether involuntarily or otherwise that night he could not say with authority, to remain mostly silent, his new-found role of confessor suiting the occasion in some pertinent way.

And it had worked.

After the night of the grand revelation, in the ensuing days it just *felt* as if nothing official was going to happen and therefore it just *felt* amongst the four adults that Paul would dictate the strands of their future mutual fate. Perhaps Anne, so fractured, but simultaneously elated by the discovery that her blood parents were alive, that she'd even already met them, was astonishingly grateful that Paul would take control, just as he had when she'd received the solicitors letter all those months ago, the thing that had started it all really.

So when he'd sat her down and insisted that the title deeds of The Old Vicarage be transferred to them absolutely, she'd meekly consented. It was still too early within the arrangement for him to be absolutely sure that there might not be a modicum of *pay-back* within Anne's psyche for what essentially had been an abdication of parental responsibility all those years ago; he rather suspected that there was.

Anyway, the *ex gratia* bequeathing of the North Wing to her parents was the obvious thing to do. They had long-renovated and redecorated it to be a replica of the sixties-version of the house in Lounsley and to be slightly corny about it: *they made their bed and they can now lie in it.*

He was still not absolutely sure of the psychology behind the wing's redefinition, its *reconstruction*.

He knew he had to tread carefully around Anne on this. But from the slightly awkward conversations the two of them had had, it seemed that Bernie and Patrick could not bear to carry on living in the house in Lounsley, yet could never bring themselves either to start a new life elsewhere, plagued by the infinitesimally unlikely, yet mathematically possible, sudden return of their missing daughter to her last known sighting. They'd changed their surnames, both to hide their inner torment and shame, but also so that they could live a relatively less-complicated and intrusive life a mile away in Brenham. Far away not to relive the horror on a daily basis, but close enough just to be near it.

And that in turn explained what they had done with the North Wing. It served the purpose of *leaving her things just the way they were*, that pitiful gambit and end-game of grieving parents the world over, but sufficiently tucked away into the shadows of the north garden so that, if they chose, they could ignore it, ignore *her* when it all became too much. For months, years even, they might not visit it at all. Then at other times, like the recent pretence of taking a holiday in Cornwall, they had forced themselves, via that very ruse to the outside world, to remain in the *pretend Lounsley House* for a whole week, a mixture of atonement, grieving, remembering, *being close to her*.

Now that their daughter had miraculously and joyously reappeared into their lives, the North Wing was no longer a house of horror. Conceivably it was penitential to a latent degree, but ultimately they could wallow in it once more, alongside the knowledge of the certainty that the person they had missed, coveted, never stopped loving and adoring, was now living next door to them. And so what if she shared it financially with her husband that they hardly knew, and his daughter who barely registered their existence? If that was penance then it was the least masochistic imaginable. They would redecorate it naturally, in fact were halfway there already, still becoming used to the incredible prices some of the furniture and fittings were attracting on eBay. A sixties retro shop in nearby Whitstable had sent a van round and negotiated hundreds of pounds for a plastic table, Habitat-style chairs and an old music centre. A crafty, and suddenly conversational Ellie, had even bagged herself upon request, a fabulous Ferrari-red Romeo Rega desk for her own private study on the first floor of the main house.

Originally, when they'd put Lounsley on the market, as soon as the new deeds had been transferred to them, Paul had been a little too gung-ho. He'd been amazed at how much the Lounsley house had appreciated – it would almost pay off the mortgage. He'd thought he was being charitable even when he suggested to Anne that they give her parents first refusal on the sale.

'Wouldn't that, let's face it, be almost perfect for them? To have their old house back, no longer afraid of its ghastly memories, their daughter just a mile away from them?'

Anne had dismissed it almost immediately. It's one thing for them to *give us* The Old Vicarage, but to send them packing to Lounsley, to *that* house. Oh Paul, how could you be so cruel, she'd said. And he never mentioned it again.

There had been some awkward moments. As soon as a slightly bemused Lech had finished tanking the main house cellar (*my good friend Paul, we fight on the same side…*), Paul had set about helping Patrick transfer some of the stored objects to the North Wing, including the boxes of old photos. Paul had picked up from the floor the photo of the girl on the wall, *Katie*, and when he realised its significance in the great story of discovery, or rather its potential embarrassment to the Palmers, he furtively tried to hide it. But it had been too late. Patrick had seen him and had clearly made the decision to air his thoughts aloud.

'It's OK Paul. I'll try to explain. When we christened Fran we were torn between Francesca Kathleen and Kathleen Francesca. The reality was that she would then have been called either Fran or Katie. I can't remember the exact reason, I think Francesca was becoming sort of famous-actressy at the time, so we went with that. When…when we realised that Fran was never coming back we started inventing a story to our newer friends in Brenham that we did have a daughter. We couldn't really say that her name was Fran, that would have been unbearable, so we compromised with Katie.'

He'd paused and seemed to look out of a cellar window that wasn't there. Paul had held his silence to let him dwell on his thoughts and Patrick had continued. 'Grief you see …grief does funny things to you. You cling on so desperately to what you can never know. That's the worst thing – the not knowing. But you invent and fantasise versions of reality. Otherwise one simply goes mad.'

'Patrick. I don't think I told you but I saw her, this woman in the photo, in Canterbury a few months ago. It was a bit embarrassing really. I…I don't mean that in an admonitory way…l just thought you should know that the pretend Katie really might not live that far away. I'm not sure if you knew? You know? I mean, actually, do you know this other woman?'

Patrick had shaken his head, before adding, 'Oh, I see, so that explains it. I said to Bernie a few years ago, well it's all very well us having a daughter called Katie, but would it not be a little strange if we didn't have a photo of her on our wall as a grown-up? She'd assented and the next thing I knew I was strolling up and down outside a photographic studio on the outskirts of Canterbury. There's one in Brenham but it was too dangerous; questions might have been asked. Other customers with whom I was acquainted might have thought my behaviour curious. But Canterbury. I know it's only seven miles away but, one is sort of more anonymous in that city don't you think? Anyway, I'd been sort of stalking it for an hour or so until I was sure that the manager or owner or whoever he was, had left for presumably a lunch break, before I entered the shop and realised that a very young lady had been left to look after things. There were examples of the studio's work all around the walls, ghastly things really, like the father of a new-born holding it flat on the palm of one of his hands, or a whole family bedecked in clothes from the Wild West, curiously wearing trainers instead of Cowboy boots.

'But there was one photo that struck my eye. She must have been the same age as I believed that Francesca would have been by now; her eyes and faintest of smiles spoke to me. Yes, I thought. You must be my Katie. My words came naturally enough and I was surprised that I acted the part rather well. I'd feigned mild surprise that the photo was on display and the young lady looked up at it and told me how lovely my daughter looked. She'd somehow and miraculously initiated the deception, her complicity in the matter, and the rest was easy. I told her I needed a copy in a hurry, for a birthday surprise and she seemed so eager to please. She looked up the price, including frame, and the transaction was done, cash of course. It's hung on the wall ever since. Only…' He fell silent.

'It's OK Patrick.' Even holding all the trump cards in the pack since the great revelation, Paul was not minded to tell Patrick about his breaking and entering the house all those months ago. Even with the truth of everything, it would just have seemed an unedifying admission.

'…Only. She never said why. Bernie that is. But after you left, after that first visit, she became very quiet, depressed almost. The next morning I looked at the wall and the photo was gone. I asked her why but I never received a straight answer. I think she said something like, "The way that girl looked at her, her eyes bore through the lie." Whether it was just the photo or not, I can't recall but your visit had interfered with her in some unfathomable way.'

'Yes.'

'Perhaps we can all guess why now, do you think Paul?'

'I think we can Patrick.'

Paul's thoughts now meandered further as the licks of withering light descended upon him through the Cedar Tree's branches.

Thwock!

The croquet ball hit a leg of his sun lounger and snapped him from his thoughts.

'Sorr-yee Dad.'

'It's not played like a game of cricket Ellie, it's meant to be a genteel English pastime.'

Ellie ran over to where he now sat up, stretching for the ball to throw back to her, but her body language indicated that she wanted to make the journey to him anyway.

'Da-ad.'

Oh, she wanted something, he thought, looking nervously past her at the two school friends with whom she was attempting to hit balls through the hoops.

'Mathilda and Bea.'

'Ye-es?'

'Well, um, they like it here, I mean why wouldn't they and I just wondered if…'

'Ye-es?'

'If, well you know it's Half Term next week. And I just wondered.'

Paul tilted his head, mock concern upon his brow. She had him.

'I just wondered if they could stay here for the week?'

'Hmm…well let me see. I mean where would we put them? Do we even have enough space to put beds up?'

At that moment, if Mathilda and Bea had not been witnessing the rare occasion of daughter and father having a serious conversation, she probably would have leapt upon him and smitten him with the palms of her hands. For The Old Vicarage, even without its strange North Wing, the full story of which she had yet to fathom, was really quite enormous and the challenge for two friends staying over was the opposite of what it might have been in the house in Lounsley. There, if she did have friends staying, which was rare, as they all lived in either Hammersmith or Fulham, it was always a matter of putting up an extra bed in the spare room. That ended up being a futile gesture as they all slept together in the same room anyway, feasting on snacks and drinks, as girls of that age are wont to do until the early hours of the next morning. No, in The Old Vicarage the challenge was *not* to be a ridiculously great distance apart. There were so many bedrooms there she had lost count.

'I'll take that as a yes then Dad?'

'You may, my beautiful daughter. No boys though,' he laughed.

It was really too much and she leapt on him anyway and he was glad of it.

As Ellie walked nonchalantly back to her croquet hoops and new-found social standing, Paul returned to his reflections of recent events. Some knots were still there and he wanted to untie them.

There had been only one time in the last several months that there had been anything approaching something as open, as evocatively vulgar as a *meeting* between the four of them. He remembered a rather nervous Patrick asking if they could all convene *at ours* one evening. He recalled the strangeness of the expression, the rawness of everything so recently altered within, as they'd walked around to the new North Wing entrance, an hastily-constructed exterior door to a hallway within.

The Palmers had been hesitant at first but after pouring the attendees all a glass of wine, they presented a sort of *fait accompli*. All the adults had, to that point, agreed to the new divisions of property so calculatingly insisted upon by Paul, but what until that moment Paul and Anne had been less sensitive about, was just how all of it might be explained to friends and family, albeit distant ones. Paul and Anne's social lives were quite limited, so much so that it had become a sort of gallows humour of contention in the Lounsley house. They'd quite forgotten just how gregarious were her parents' lives by contrast. It had been Bernie that now took the lead.

'We need all to agree a plan. It needn't be complicated. One of the great assets of becoming old, and there aren't that many admittedly, is that one can be terribly vague, *mistaken* even about almost anything. But at the simplest level, we probably should all have our stories straight. Agreed?'

There were nods all around.

'The main challenge you see is explaining why it is that the couple that we only just met a few months ago, lovely and charming though they are, are now living in our old house, sorry: the more recent of our old houses, whilst we seem perfectly content—'

'Oh and we are by the way,' interrupted Patrick.

'Thank you for clarifying darling…*perfectly content* to live in the North wing.'

She paused, whether for meaning or as an invitation for a brain-storming session, Anne wasn't entirely sure and a brief silence ensued.

'So I thought,' continued Bernie, 'well it's just great that Paul received his promotion—'

'And we really mean that actually,' interrupted Patrick once more.

'Yes, yes thank you Patrick, it's amazing that we're both on the same wavelength here. As I was *saying*, well with promotion to Partner, that could mean one hell of a difference in circumstance, couldn't it really? Let's say we all met up one day and it came up in conversation. You both said that it was the opportunity you had been waiting for, to upgrade to something bigger.'

'One hell of a promotion, if only,' Paul decided to enter the fray.

'Ah yes I thought of that. But what of the finalisation of probate in Galway? We all know how that ended, not *quite* in the way you perhaps had originally envisaged. But who, actually, *does* know? Just the four of us. And your charming daughter Paul. I suppose we should come on to her in a minute. No what I mean is, what if there really were significant residuals from the estate, some kind of maturation of a policy somewhere even? Which person, which nosiest person in the world, let alone Brenham, would dare to grill a bereaved daughter on the final financial circumstances of her parents' passing? Even the craftiest journalist, working for the greasiest tabloid, would uncover the simple truth that Paul really did visit the solicitors firm in Galway in June. It's on record.

'And let us say that during that interesting chat about the upturn in your fortunes, we happened to laugh and admit to the fact that coincidentally, we really had begun to struggle with the upkeep of the house. One of us would have said for a joke, "To be honest the North Wing alone would do for us now…"'

She paused again, clearly now for effect thought Anne, and well she deserved it for the story was brilliant.

'That's, that's going to work isn't it Bernie, I mean Mum, because—'

'No!' boomed Patrick, so thunderously that they all started. 'Sorry, sorry, I didn't mean to come over like that Anne darling, it's just that, and I know it's going to be difficult, you can never really call us Mum or Dad in public, you do know that, don't you? And therefore, and I have a heavy heart saying this, it's probably best if you call us by our Christian names all the time, otherwise you'll become thoroughly schizophrenic about it all.'

'Thank you, my darling *Patrick*', replied Anne, 'but I am going to buy you a birthday card with *Dad* on it whether you like it or not. You'll just have to throw it in the fire as soon as you get it.'

A very slight degree of mirth had descended upon the table of four and Paul began to relax.

'As I was saying everyone,' continued Anne, 'oh no, before I go on, you've got *me* thinking now…it never occurred to me, but you are OK referring to me as Anne and not Fran? Only I'm not sure I'm going to get away with that, nor do I particularly *feel* like a Fran: lovely name though.'

'My darling Anne,' said Bernie stretching her hands out across the table to grasp those of her daughter, 'you have no idea. What's in a name? You are our flesh and blood and you are in our lives again.' Paul began to choke back tears at this manifest and no longer repressed signalling of familial affection; but then let them well up as he realised that they were all experiencing the same.

'Thank you M*ummy!*' Anne turning to Patrick defiantly as she said it. 'No what I was saying is that your story makes complete sense, because you never stopped loving Brenham, half your friends are here. I mean, where else would you go to downsize *to*? These are your grounds, your trees, your shrubs. You could also say that since the interest rates dropped, your retirement plans and investments were looking decidedly shaky. Blame *Brexit* for goodness sake; Lord knows most of your arty friends would love you for *that* sentiment. And so by selling the house to us, those charming Fewings, who so epitomised the next generation of aspiring, slightly arty, hard-working people, you were, ah that's it, you were not only making your own futures financially secure, you were giving us an opportunity to move on, and hey, in the manner of the chain of these things, yet *another* generation of slightly creative people would be the next to enjoy the house in Lounsley. Perfect.'

'But what of your...erm...*other* daughter, Katie?' chimed in Paul.

'Ah simple,' replied Patrick, 'Family rift! I don't know a single one of our friends who hasn't fallen out with their children at some point. It's actually quite shocking when you come across families who are perfectly integrated and civilised to each other, in my experience. No, no that's the great thing about the English. If anyone were so bold as to ask how she was, an ensuing awkward silence of about ...ooh I don't know…a millisecond, would curtail the line of enquiry in perpetuity. Thank Albion for awkward silences.'

They all laughed and when it receded, for one ensuing moment Anne wondered if just such an awkward silence had now arisen. Bernie's reticent tone when she began her next sentence, turning towards Paul, rather reinforced the thought.

'So Ellie.'

'Look,' began Paul, 'to be perfectly honest I know where you're going to go with this, so let me put you out of your misery. What you have to understand about teenagers…' Paul realised his error almost immediately and froze.

'It's OK Paul,' interjected Bernie, 'Really it's OK. We all have to make adjustments, don't we. Please just speak your mind.'

'No that was insensitive of me, sorry guys, really I am.' He smiled meekly and apologetically at them. 'But yeah, basically, they, how can I put this, they just don't really *care* about any of this sort of stuff. At the same time they are incredibly, just hugely, sensitive to confidentiality, about all sorts of things. There are just certain lines they never cross. I've never understood it really. I'll give you an example, an example of which I'm not very proud at all. As Ellie was growing up I'm not convinced I didn't use the F-word in frustration, or occasionally joy – renewed success at Chelsea was a long time coming, let me tell you - almost every day. And yet in her most confrontational, rebellious moods, where almost anything and everything was exploit-ed to seek gain to her moral compass of defiance to the world, not once did she ever mimic me. I mean, she could have. What could I have said in reply? What hypocrisy. But no, I've never heard her use that word once.

'And that somehow extends to confidences generally. At that age, they just *get* the important stuff. They might not understand all the contrivances, the subtleties. But when I sit down with her and explain all this, I assure you she'll shrug her shoulders, tell me it's fine and there'll be a guaran-teed "Like, whatever," and that'll be it.'

'What a relief,' said Bernie, 'but…does her mother know about any of this?'

'No she doesn't. Before I drove Ellie back to London that following Sunday evening, back when it all happened, I just said to her casually in the car, "Best we keep this to the three of us." She simply nodded and that was the end of it.'

There seemed finally to be a mass exhalation of breath, as if the last *elephant in the room* had been quietly led away into the night. It appeared also to be a cue for Patrick.

'Champers anyone?'

The reliving of the memory made him feel suddenly reassured about everything. Anne was happy, Ellie was seemingly happy – how could you ever know with teenagers and their hidden angsts – and well yes he rather supposed that he now experienced something approaching happiness. He still had to pinch himself, mentally, metaphorically, that this was all his, theirs.

'Paul!'

He looked over to where the voices came from, to the North Wing of The Old Vicarage. The three of them, Anne and her parents, were waving at him cheerfully.

'Darling,' shouted Anne, 'darling, Ma...Bernie and Patrick have invited us over for dinner tonight. Are you OK for eight o'clock you indolent person you...'

'Sounds great, thanks for the invite Patrick and Bernie.'

'Quite alright old chap,' replied Patrick, 'come round earlier, seven-thirty if you like and we'll have a game of snooker.'

'Snooker? How's that then?'

'Well only if you don't mind. The table's yours of course, how presumptuous of me.'

'What, where; are you winding me up old fellow?' Paul shouted.

'You didn't know? The out building, the Old Buttery, the one right at the very back.'

'I didn't have the key. I just thought it was an old storage dump of some kind. And what's with your obsession with the *Old* everything? What next, the *Old Lavatory*?'

'Ha ha. Well I am the *Old Everything* now. Dump? Well Bernie thinks it is. A storage dump for a lovely three-quarter size snooker table. We got it at auction when they closed Brenham Police Station – it's what the off-duty officers would get up to before and after a shift. It's all yours!'

Blimey, a three-quarters-sized snooker table, thought Paul, and all mine; not being full-size, I might even pocket three balls in a row.

'That case Patrick, I'll go have a shower now. See you at seven mate, if that's OK. Beers in the fridge and all that. Are women allowed in there?'

Ridiculously, he thought, but quite spontaneously, they all laughed.

And Paul wondered at that moment, for the first time in his life he realised, whether he was indeed approaching something that could, by the analysis of the most pessimistic observer imaginable, be called happy.

He looked up at his friend the Cedar Tree and cocked his head as if to seek approbation in the matter.

A barely discernible and yet unexpected breeze swept through the whole of the grand tree at that moment and Paul was glad of it.

Epilogue

'She never said *boyfriend*; he's a boy and he's a friend.'

Anne realised that she had to tread carefully. She'd been a father's daughter once and, whilst the mores of acceptable social behaviour had been unusually conservative when she'd been the same age as Ellie was now, she was extraordinarily sensitive to what Paul must be experiencing.

'Well, let's not split hairs,' Paul replied, 'It's more that, well, I know she turns fifteen soon, but she is still fourteen you know. And from what I can gather, this lad is already sixteen.'

'Yes, I know that must seem quite a gap at that age, but actually it's not such a rare thing. And from what I understand, they only want to go for a walk into town and back — *hang out*.'

'Hang. Out. What does that actually mean?'

'Look Paul darling. Let me tell you a tale. A true story as it happens. Not sure if I ever told you.'

Paul didn't like the sound of this one bit and his neck muscles tightened. He thought they'd told each other everything about…everything.

'I was probably only Ellie's age when we went on holiday to Italy, well OK, maybe a year older. It was a village not far from Rome. Dad, he was secretly a bit fascinated with Rome. He could not go there on any sort of official business — that would have been frowned upon by the Church. But you have to understand that the Church Of Ireland, certainly in the West, isn't what you really associate with a Reformed Church, visually I mean. It's what is referred to as *High Church*. That means it reserves largely a lot of the ceremonial aspects of Catholicism. My father would have walked along the aisle, the nave, swinging a thurible, a sort of canister from which emanated a pungent, smoky, incense: almost medieval really. So there were aspects of what some of those outside his congregation, further north, which was more *low church*, might have cynically referred to as *Popery*, to which he was, at a symbolic rather than a Christian-doctrinal level, clandestinely sort of attracted.

'So going on a holiday to Italy was hardly considered by the General Synod to have been a heresy. It was reformation not *refutation*. Anyway there we were in this Italian village in the middle of nowhere. Only it *was* somewhere. There was a campsite nearby and, I could only have been fifteen, maybe sixteen. Mother and Father probably realised that a holiday in the middle of nowhere might be a bit dull for a teenage girl, and one evening we walked the half mile or so to the campsite. I say *campsite* but it was more of a resort really. Swimming pool, games rooms, a restaurant and a bar. When the dining was over they'd push the tables to one side and turn it into a sort of disco. The evenings were so hot that it would all spill out on to the veranda, by the pool. So we joined in that evening. I don't think I'd ever danced before in front of my parents. Even Father must have drunk extra wine that evening as he was throwing some very funny shapes indeed; I don't think I ever saw Mother quite so amused.

'About two evenings later I told them I was going for a walk. "Don't be back too late Anne," they'd both chimed. Naturally my walk took me to the campsite. I had the sense that they must have known this and I still don't know to this day why they allowed it. It felt daring. A much older boy, well he was a man really, a young Italian man with passable English; he made a beeline for me. And that was it really.'

'What do you mean, that was it? What does that mean? Fascinating as your story about a holiday in Italy is, you haven't exactly shared any sort of knowledge about girls of that age and older boys.'

Anne laughed. 'Well there's not much to tell really and that's my whole point. We kissed, needless to say; I wanted that, it felt all adult and I knew that I had to give him something. He had his own car, can you believe it? What would they say in this generation about your teenage daughter going off in cars with strangers in foreign lands? I then met him every evening, naturally. I liked to think it was a holiday romance. He probably didn't give up trying until the last evening before we had to leave. As in, trying to get a bit further than just snogging. But it was never going to happen. I, and this is my point, was quite innocent for my age. I didn't even *think* about sexual things, let alone feel anything, well that I would have understood. No, it was as much to boast to my friends back home when I returned that I'd had a holiday romance as much as anything. Poor bastard, I actually forget his name, honestly I do Paul, I'm not just making that up – he must have waved me off with monk's balls.'

'Monk's balls?'

'Yes, they say that in Ireland. It was the only time I ever heard Mother come anywhere near to uttering a profanity. She must have had a glass of sherry or something, because I remember going back for a visit – must have been in my twenties – and I asked her how life was at home. Were they both happy, et cetera. She hinted that, even after Father had officially retired from Church duty, he had to continue to act in the community with a certain amount of decorum. And that's when she said, "At least he doesn't have monk's balls like the other lot."'

'Oh I see.'

'So Ellie, I know she acts all adult, tries to be all worldly, and in a sense she is much more so than I ever was at that age. But actually in other ways she's not that different to how I was. So yes, you could go all *Victorian Dad* on her and become proscriptive. That would be easy. But I think Ellie would find a way around it all and she would probably be tempted into being even *more* adult than she would otherwise choose to be. So my advice darling is – just let her have a boyfriend, if that's what it is here. Be vigilant, be advisory and all that, yes you are her father, why wouldn't you, but just let her go, just a little bit, one step at a time.'

'Thank you. That's why I love you. You are just so…so lovely and caring. Thank you darling.'

They kissed each other and hugged.

But not for long.

'Oh, speak of the devil,' said Paul. Ellie was walking towards him, where he was sitting beneath the Cedar Tree, a taller teenage boy beside her, looking appropriately sheepish, Paul was glad to note.

'All yours darling,' said Anne as she smiled and turned away, before strolling back to the house.

'Dad, this is my new friend. I just wanted to ask if you were OK us going for a walk into town?'

'Well now. Hello…sorry lad, what's your name?'

'Calum,' the boy answered.

'Calum, pleased to meet you.' Paul shook his hand but something made him start a new sentence as he looked at his daughter. 'Ellie darling, please can you give me a moment alone with Calum?'

Ellie looked at him with suspicion. Did her eyes light up defiantly momentarily? he wondered. But she knew this was not the time to pick a fight and she reluctantly walked away towards the front gates, as if to dare Paul to resist her request.

'Calum. You have a surname?'

'Calum Carmichael, sir.'

Paul flinched. But kept his cool. 'Ooh I do like an alliterative name, Calum Carmichael. And please call me Paul.'

'Not much I can do about my name sir, I mean Paul. It was my father's name and his before him.'

Whether the boy was ignorant of the word *alliteration* or was perturbed by the strange conversation with the father of a girl that he had only just met, Paul could not be sure, but the boy before him seemed noticeably uncomfortable. Good, thought Paul. The way it should be.

'Sorry with all the questions Calum, but your parents: they local? I mean I might know them, you never know. Possible.'

'Well they split up when I was quite young. I've mostly lived with my mum in Brenham but weekends I used to go and stay with my dad where he lives in Canterbury. Still do I suppose quite a lot.'

'Grandparents?'

'Yes, well only three now. Grandma and Grandad, that's my mum's parents. They live just outside Tunbridge Wells so we see them a few times a year. But my nan, that's Dad's mum, she lives on her own. My grandad died a long time ago. I didn't know him.'

'So your nan, Calum, she is of the generation where people would refer to her as Mrs Carmichael, correct?'

'Well yes, I suppose, I never really thought about it like that. She's always just been Nan.'

'You visit your nan much Calum?'

'Yes I try to. She and Dad fell out a long time ago. He doesn't like to talk about it. He, he just told me that I should be free to go and check up on her from time to time, which I do try to do. She's not all *there* these days and I sometimes even wonder if she knows who I am. But she'll make me cocoa in the kitchen so she must know that I'm family.'

Paul felt something lurch inside.

And now Ellie was positively marching toward him, her defiance no longer latent, but manifest.

'Quick last question Calum.'

'Yes?'

'Your Nan, Mrs Carmichael, where does she live?'

'Lounsley sir, I mean Paul. She lives in one of that pair of old Regency townhouses on the main road.'

Paul felt the back of his neck shiver.

'Ellie, you're back!'

'Yes Dad, I'm back.'

'Well enjoy your walk you two won't you. And Calum. If you ever...'

He paused. Ellie glared at him. It was all wrong. It was time to let her go.

'If you ever...find yourself in a spot of bother whilst you're out with my daughter, please call me? Ellie will give you my number. Thanks.'

'Of course I will Paul. I, I will look after...your...Ellie for you.'

And then they walked away from him and through the gates into another world.

Paul looked up at the Cedar Tree.

'Ah, Tree old friend. Another mystery probably solved. Do you know Tree? There's a part of me that wants Ellie to get on really well with this Calum. Because then us parents would have to meet, correct? I mean is that how these things go?'

He paused to learn of the Tree's assent.

'Can you imagine Calum's father, the other Calum, being invited to The Old Vicarage for tea? I wonder how well that would go down with my darlingest Anne?

'But for now Tree, no more dramas. Can I please just go a month without any more dramas.'

The Cedar Tree deflected, it seemed at that very moment, a final, gentle breeze down to him.

Acknowledgements

I owe a debt of gratitude to Christina Hansford who, without the slightest interest in profiteering from the exercise, provided a huge degree of invaluable editorial input to the curious story that was, without notice, presented to her.

Thank you to The Faversham Society, and in particular Clive Foreman, for allowing me private access to historical archives of The Faversham Times in order to determine the generic style of local journalists of the late 1960s.

Cassie Seal: you have no idea how talented you are.

Jacob Reeves-Gale: you gently pushed me online through the kindness of your heart and I salute you for it.

Last but not least, thank you to Anna Speed-Andrews, a rather remarkable woman who, upon being asked for her opinion about a whole range of grammatical considerations, was not only content to provide them, but somehow allowed herself to become my ultimate inspiration.

Printed in Great Britain
by Amazon